How to Wed an Earl

Ivory Lei

CRIMSON
ROMANCE

F+W Media, Inc.

This edition published by
Crimson Romance
an imprint of F+W Media, Inc.
10151 Carver Road, Suite 200
Blue Ash, Ohio 45242
www.crimsonromance.com

ISBN 10: 1-4405-7318-2
ISBN 13: 978-1-4405-7318-7
eISBN 10: 1-4405-7317-4
eISBN 13: 978-1-4405-7317-0

Cover art © istock/com/jcarroll-images, istock.com/illustrart, istock.com/
GoodLifeStudio

Acknowledgments

To my husband, Tom, and my first reader, Laura—thank you. I am also grateful for the support of friends and family whom I've no doubt would love to be mentioned here. So, there.

Sincere gratitude goes out to the Crimson Romance team as well for their editing genius and for taking a chance on Penelope. Finally, a big shout out goes to the gentleman from Connemara and everyone who lived in early nineteenth-century Britain. This book would not have been possible without you.

Prologue

Maitland Hall
Colton, England, 1805

There was nowhere to hide. Penelope Maitland considered her options as her cousin, and world's tallest nine-year-old, David, continued counting. The salon's chairs had those annoying, thin legs, and so did the sideboard. Those were no good. The curtains were too sheer and the table … the *table!*

She crawled under the table just as David finished counting, turned around and headed straight for her.

"You always hide in the most obvious places!" he complained, crouching to meet her eyes beneath the furniture. "How did you ever manage to get away from your nurse?"

"I have my ways." Penelope took David's proffered hand as she squeezed out from under the table. In truth, she never needed to hide from Nurse. The woman liked David more, and she was far too busy prettying herself up to notice Penelope slipping out of the schoolroom. She never needed to hide from anyone. David was the only one who ever sought her out, and he rarely visited.

Talking about Nurse seemed to conjure her up, because she burst into the salon, breathless, her big bosom heaving. "Master David! Thank goodness you found Miss Penelope. I've been looking everywhere for her." She pressed David's grinning face to her breast and glowered at Penelope. "The baron wants to see you."

"Father's home!" she jumped, earning another glare from Nurse. "Where is he? When did he arrive? How long has he been here? Did he receive my letter?"

Nurse smirked. "He's in his study. He's been here since dawn."

But … it was nearly suppertime. He must have forgotten about her. Again. *Still,* she thought as Nurse led her into the study, *Father is home. And she'd missed him.*

That was all that mattered.

"There's my little pet!" Father said, as he looked up from the papers laid out on his desk. He was dark and handsome, like a prince from a fairy tale. But he was grinning at Nurse, so perhaps the greeting wasn't meant for Penelope.

"Father! Did you get my letter? Is that why you're home?"

After dismissing Nurse with a nod, Father reluctantly turned his hazel eyes on her. "Yes, I received your letter." He motioned for her to sit across from him and waited until she was comfortable. "You know, Penelope … 'love' has an 'e' at the end."

"Oh."

"That's right, it also has an 'o' in the middle, not a 'u.'"

He looked disappointed in her. "I'm sorry. I'll do better, Father, if you teach me."

She would not cry. She *wouldn't*. Father didn't like tears, from her or Mama.

Father cleared his throat and shuffled the papers on his desk. "Well, there is a way you can make up for your failings, and your mother thinks it's time you are told. You might be a girl, but you can make a lot of money for us, Penelope." He grinned, looking proud of himself. "You see, three years ago, I gave your hand away in marriage to a future earl."

Marriage? He was surely jesting. She was six! "Can I still live here?"

"You don't have to move out for a while yet." Father laughed. "Not until your future husband comes for you. You see, that saves us a London Season, and your future father-in-law is a very wealthy friend of mine. Your Uncle Hugh might have produced the heir, but it will be *you* who will make the family part of an earldom. It's important to us, and that's why I'm here. This is your duty, Penelope, and even my brother can't complain about that."

She doubted it. Uncle Hugh bossed Father around, and he disapproved of almost everything Father did, especially when it had something to do with the "tumbling ladies" Father saw in London. She tried to imagine marrying for duty like her parents had, being wife to a man who was rarely around and having headaches that prompted daily visits with Dr. Walker. Would her husband tease her about not being good at playing hide and seek then abandon her to Nurse, like David had earlier? And David was one of the *good* boys.

"I don't like boys."

Father looked horrified. "Listen, missy, you will marry the future Earl of Ravenstone and help me make up for failing to produce a boy. You don't want your uncle to be the baron, do you? He's awful. You want to help *me*. I need you to do this."

She nodded. He'd never needed her for anything before. Perhaps if she agreed, he would stay.

He grinned, all charming once more. "Don't worry, Penelope. You'd like *this* boy, because he acts like a girl. He's almost twelve but still can't stomach shooting pheasants with me and his sire."

"Why not?"

He shrugged. "He says chicks need their parents. The boy has strange ideas, just like you."

Just like me, but better. He made Father listen. She should write to this boy and ask him how he achieved this feat. "What's his name?"

"Lucas," Father answered after a long pause. He took a feather from his pocket. "He suggested I give you this, though I'm not certain why he thought you'd want it."

Because he wanted her to know she wasn't alone. She was sure of it. He'd never met her, yet he'd thought of her.

He saved pheasants. She smiled. "I'll marry him, Father."

"Good girl." He reached out and ruffled her curls.

"I'll thank him for the feather."

"Do you know how to spell his name?" Father shook his head and sighed. "We want to make a good impression. Proper girls do not just send missives to strange boys, Penelope. They don't misspell anything when they do. Wait for him to write to you. If he wants to hear from you, he will let you know. You don't want to scare him away by being overeager. Trust me, no one likes that. It's annoying."

Was that why Father was never around? Because she was overeager and annoying?

"Now, send Nurse back in here," Father continued. "She's been naughty not teaching you your letters well enough." He chuckled. "She shall be spanked."

Penelope laughed with him, though she wasn't sure why Father found the thought of spanking Nurse so amusing. She would ask Lucas about it.

She had no doubt he would write to her soon. Maybe he would understand and explain the joke to her. That evening, she placed the pheasant feather on her pillow and began writing to a boy whom Father said was just like her. If Father was right, then she already knew what Lucas would want from her. Letters always took a lot of time and effort, but if she began now, then it wouldn't take long for her to reply once Lucas's letter arrived. She would impress him with her skills.

> *Dear Lucas,*
> *Father likes to spank my nurse ...*

She paused, remembering how disappointed Father was when she'd misspelled "love." She continued writing, concentrating on each word until her eyes grew heavy and the letters blurred together. She needed to read the missive again on the morrow, to make sure there were no mistakes. It had to be perfect, and she didn't have much time.

Because Lucas would write soon. Perhaps his letter was on its way at this very moment. When she was ready for bed, she reached for the feather and held it close to her cheek.

Chapter One

London, 1824

Lucas Arthur Phillip Drake, fourth Earl of Ravenstone, sat across from his friend and grudgingly accepted the truth: The dead in his family had cunning ways of exacting revenge from beyond the grave. Their ghosts haunted the living, demanding justice. Demanding vengeance.

And in this instance, they demanded a wedding.

The earl fell silent after imparting this information to his friend and stared at the fireplace in moody contemplation, resigned to the untenable situation in which he found himself.

"You're looking very grim for an eager bridegroom."

Lucas's gaze snapped back to his friend, the amiable Anthony Milthorpe, Viscount Westville, who sat opposite Lucas at their table near the grand marble fireplace in the opulently styled room of his gentlemen's club while they savored the excellent brandy one expected to be served at Brooks's.

This afternoon, however, he had more than just the communal enjoyment of expensive spirits on his mind. One look at the empty mahogany tables and plush leather chairs confirmed that he'd chosen the best time of day for the meeting. Except for a small group of elegantly attired young gentlemen seated at the other end of the room, it was entirely vacant.

Shifting his gaze back to Westville, Lucas realized his companion was waiting for him to explain why he was so "very grim." He knew he appeared almost sinister compared to his childhood friend. Fair-haired, tall and lean, Anthony was his exact opposite in looks and temperament. Lucas had inherited his Spanish mother's dark coloring and his father's monstrous build.

They did have one thing in common, though, he thought. *Information.* Anthony was the only person outside of Lucas's family who knew about the infuriating terms of his father's will.

He crossed his arms over his broad chest, leaned back in the oversized leather armchair, and sighed before quietly announcing the reason for their meeting and his demeanor. "I'm leaving for the South Lakes tonight to collect the little baggage."

"Good God, man, that's no way to refer to a fiancée!"

Leave it to Anthony to be gallant. What else was Lucas to call a fiancée he had neither proposed to nor even met?

"You're the expert at charming the ladies." Lucas stretched his long legs out in front of him and gave Anthony a mocking glance. "What would you have me call someone I've been promised to since I was a boy, whom I now need to wed if I don't want to lose all the lands that go with my earldom?"

Anthony grinned. "Destiny?"

He let out a low, embittered laugh that rumbled from his chest and shook his shoulders. Then he took a healthy swallow of his brandy, refusing to dignify Anthony's daft suggestion with any reply.

Apparently sensing that Lucas was not in the mood for jests, Anthony cleared his throat and soberly said, "You're not the only one being forced into this marriage, you know."

"I've given her enough time to cry off." Lucas gave an indifferent shrug, then added, "In any case, it hardly matters now. I've only four years left to meet the terms of Father's will, and I see no point in delaying the inevitable any longer."

Especially since a title would be of little use without most of the vast holdings his father had chosen not to entail on Lucas. Everyone who relied on him rightfully expected him to hold on to the properties if he could.

"I still can't believe your father did it," Anthony muttered as he splashed more brandy into both their glasses, draining what was left in the decanter. "He was not an unkind man. It doesn't make any sense."

"It makes perfect sense," Lucas countered. "I have a duty to sire an heir. Considering my mother's reputation, Father knew it would not be easy to find a willing bride to continue our tainted family line." *And he's using me to exact payment from those who abandoned him at his time of need.* "It just irks me to know that Father didn't think I was capable of finding a bride on my own."

"Tainted? Ravenstone, we both know your mother *was not* insane," Anthony grumbled, but his uneasiness at the topic was evident in the way he shifted in his chair.

"No, but even I could not have described Mother as the embodiment of stability," Lucas said bluntly. He had never been the sort to hide from the *ton's* opinion of his beautiful, unpredictable mother.

The late Countess of Ravenstone had been an emotional pendulum; constantly swinging from extremely high spirits to deep melancholy during what she called the "agony and bliss" that was her life. Her restless soul lurked in the darkest depths of Lucas's past, along with the memory of his dead father lying in a pool of blood in the family's hunting lodge.

Lucas shook his head to dismiss the painful thoughts and decided to return to the business at hand. "I didn't come here to discuss my mother. Am I to assume your aunt is still willing to live in Ravenstone with Olivia while I'm away?"

Anthony snorted. "Aunt Lucy has talked of naught else. I almost feel sorry for your little sister, you know." He gave him a mocking look of contrition. "Five minutes with my aunt and her incessant yammering about the latest in her growing collection of ailments will bore little Olivia to tears."

"Boredom will be a nice change for her," Lucas drawled as he straightened in his chair. At least he didn't have to worry about Olivia while he dealt with the unpleasant business of claiming his bride. "With our parents' demise, her upcoming Season, and my impending marriage, my sister already has enough excitement in her life."

He gave his friend a serious look. "Will you be able to escort your aunt and Olivia to Ravenstone tonight?" When Anthony nodded in the affirmative, Lucas continued, "Excellent. I appreciate your help. Surrey is not far away, but I don't like the thought of them travelling without a male escort. If you call in at my townhouse at, say, half past six, you can be back in London before midnight."

At his friend's ready agreement, Lucas finished his drink and put his glass down, intending to leave when Anthony's softly spoken question stopped him.

"Do you even remember the chit's name?"

He had to suppress an impatient sigh. *Why couldn't Anthony leave the subject alone?*

"Yes. Father's will doesn't mention it, but the betrothal contract does. She is Miss Penelope Maitland, the late Baron Maitland's daughter. Maitland was one of Father's cronies." It was the first time he had spoken his betrothed's name, and he said it slowly, testing the feel of the name on his tongue.

"I didn't know Maitland had a daughter. Is she pretty?"

"I have no idea." He stood, suddenly eager to end the conversation. "Maitland died before she was supposed to have her come-out, and the current baron has yet to let her have one."

Taking his cue, Anthony rose from his chair with a solemn expression and shook hands. "I suppose you'll be a married man when you next step foot in London. Let me be the first to congratulate you on your pending nuptials."

Lucas returned the handshake and nodded, his mouth curving into a bleak smile of resignation. Then he strode out of Brooks's without another word to anyone, oblivious to the wary stares the illustrious club members cast as he passed along the way.

Raging echoes from the grave compelled Lucas to wrestle with fate. And one way or the other, he meant to win.

• • •

Accepting defeat, Penelope Rose Maitland gave in and quickly grabbed a piece of piecrust, furtively dropping it onto the flagstone floor. Her border collie's grateful sigh made her grin.

"I saw that, Polly! Don't even try to deny it." Mari's angry accusation was uttered in a dark voice that barely rose above the constant din of raucous laughter and conversation pervading The Mucky Duck's crowded dining hall.

Penelope gave her friend an exasperated look. Sensing that something other than this minor lapse in proper etiquette was behind her friend's dramatic display, Penelope decided to meet it with an equally convincing portrayal of innocent bewilderment.

"You saw what?" she demanded, leaning back in her chair. "Mari, you're the one who wanted me to try your newest apple and blackberry pie recipe."

"That!" Mari shrieked. Her voice rang shrilly, and her delicate nose wrinkled as she pointed at Nelson accusingly. She looked every bit like a duke's granddaughter. A disinherited one, true, but … "I saw *that*. Polly, why do you always have to share your food with that dog?" Frowning, she added, "I made the pie for you, not him."

Penelope flinched. It never occurred to her that rewarding one loyal companion would insult another. "Forgive me. I didn't mean to seem unappreciative of your generosity," she said in genuine contrition before proceeding to explain her actions. "But you know I never eat the crust, and I'm certain Nelson was grateful to taste a bit of your delicious creation."

"So you liked it?"

"Mari, it was the best pie I have ever tasted." She meant it, too, and she had tasted many, many pies.

"Thank you," Mari murmured, visibly flattered. "I shall ask Mama to add the pie to our menu, then. Papa would be pleased."

Mari's parents had bought this popular coaching inn located in the tiny village of Bouth in the South Lakes after they'd married, but Penelope was the one who sampled all the new food here. Nothing was added to the menu unless she had pre-approved it as delicious—not because Penelope was a food connoisseur, but because Mari was too concerned about maintaining her slim figure to try any of her exquisite concoctions.

"Mari, your parents owe it to the world to add the pie to your menu. Certainly it deserves a place in that recipe book you intend to write."

When Mari smiled, Penelope knew both she and Nelson had been forgiven. Gratified, Penelope took another bite of pie.

"I didn't mean to be harsh, Polly. I'm just worried." Mari hesitated before asking, "Do you remember the governess position that Mrs. Bexley offered me?"

Penelope nodded. "She asked me about it. Mrs. Bexley said her daughter needed to be taught by the best, so she would only offer the position to a beautiful woman with impeccable manners."

Mari's gray eyes twinkled with satisfaction. "I turned it down. I told her there are any number of 'beautiful' women with 'impeccable manners' in Bouth." She gave a sly grin. "Then I suggested she ask *you* about it."

"I did wonder why Mrs. Bexley suddenly contacted me to discuss the job."

"You're perfect for it!" Mari declared loyally. "But don't let Nelson beg for food around Mrs. Bexley." She leaned forward, laying her hands on the scarred oak table. "Oh, please say you accepted the offer. It will help solve your stepfamily's dilemma."

Penelope tensed. Her stepfamily's "dilemma" involved creditors demanding her physician stepfather, Dr. Walker, to settle the family's enormous debt with money everybody knew Papa didn't have, or else give up Highfield Manor and deprive his children of the only home they'd ever known.

The extra income would undoubtedly help. Penelope wasn't averse to working for a living if the opportunity arose. Sadly, no opportunity was forthcoming, and she admitted it in a flat, emotionless voice: "Mrs. Bexley didn't offer me employment."

Mari gaped at her. "I don't understand. I specifically told her that I'm not the only one in Bouth who has a claim to both beauty as well as impeccable manners, and you said she came to you to discuss the position."

"She did."

"Then why—"

"Mrs. Bexley asked me about the position," Penelope confirmed, arching a brow before adding dryly, "She asked if I happened to know anyone, other than you, who 'possessed both beauty and impeccable manners.' She was even gracious enough to give me time to think of an acceptable candidate."

Mari shook her head, causing auburn tendrils to sway against her temples. She started to express her outrage but stopped suddenly.

Penelope sat with her back straight and shoulders rigid, hoping no emotion flickered in her eyes. Mari studied her face for a long minute, and Penelope's lips quivered as she valiantly struggled to keep her smile in place.

Evidently concluding that more indignation about Mrs. Bexley's thoughtless act would only emphasize how the harridan obviously thought Penelope wasn't good enough for the post, Mari said softly, "Mrs. Bexley was … clever, indeed, to have sought your help in finding an excellent governess. She correctly assumed that, as Lord Maitland's daughter, you'd have expert judgment about who deserves the position."

Her friend's considerate words sent a fierce streak of relief through Penelope, leaving her strangely giddy. "Exactly," she agreed, nodding her head as a bubble of laughter escaped her. "Why, my father was so confident in my abilities that he never needed to leave London more than twice a year to visit Mama and me in Maitland Hall."

Mari giggled. "Don't forget your uncle and your cousin! The present baron and his son are clearly impressed with your talents." She paused to swipe away tears of mirth. "If they didn't have such faith in your capabilities, their honorable nature and familial affection would oblige them to at least write to you once in a while."

"My noble relatives are *undeniably* in awe of my accomplishments." Penelope laughed at the sheer absurdity of the entire situation while she affectionately stroked Nelson's furry neck.

Her friendship with Mari, she mused, flourished because of their mutual ability and conscious choice to laugh, instead of wallow, at the disadvantages life handed them. In this little village where the idyllic country life was disrupted only by the occasional trespassing sheep or carriage accident, women had to learn to cope if they wanted to survive in a society where entitlement to opportunities depended largely on nothing more than an accident of birth.

If Penelope had been born a boy, she'd have been the valued heir. She would've secured her father's affection, studied at university and inherited properties. Uncle Hugh wouldn't have been able to cast her out of her own home merely weeks after Father died, and she wouldn't be in the situation she was in now: rejected and forsaken.

On the other hand, she would've never known the blessing of having a warm, caring stepfather or experienced the simple joy of finally seeing Mama's smile, of witnessing the twins grow up.

Thinking of the twins reminded Penelope of the actual reason for her visit to the inn that day. Reaching behind her chair, she pulled out a fistful of daisies, amused by the look of dread on Mari's face.

"Colin asked me to give you these." Penelope released a theatrical sigh and handed the bouquet to her friend. "Yet another dozen flowers have sacrificed their lives for your beauty."

"Oh, *joy*. These daisies are lovely ... but you shouldn't encourage your brother, you know." Mari grimaced as she accepted the bouquet and laid it on the table. "I like Colin. I don't want to be the cause of any pain for the boy."

"You're the cause of a lot of pain for most of the young men in Bouth." Penelope shrugged. "Besides, Colin's fifteen—he needs that kind of pain. He also wrote a poem. Would you like me to read it to you?"

"No."

Penelope ignored her. With a grin, she took a crumpled sheet from her pocket and cleared her throat. She had just opened her mouth to utter the first line when Mari interrupted her.

"I wonder how many flowers your earl will slay when he finally claims you," Mari remarked in a teasing voice.

Her grin faded. *Her earl, indeed.* After the Mrs. Bexley debacle, Mari was probably trying to remind Penelope of her own worth. Unfortunately, Mari's tactic failed because these days she rarely thought of her fiancé—the man people referred to as "Raving Ravenstone." There were only four things Penelope knew about her engagement to "her earl":

First, it was their fathers who had agreed on the betrothal, long before both she and the earl were old enough to understand or refuse.

Second, never in the twenty-two years since the betrothal contract was signed had Lord Ravenstone given any indication he would honor the agreement, and she was quite certain he would never do so. Her usefulness as a baron's daughter died with her father. Since status was everything to the nobility, she had long ago ceased to hope the earl would ever acknowledge her existence.

After recovering from her drastic change in social standing, she considered a plain, little thing like her lucky to be exempted from the ordeal of finding a husband, as women were expected to do.

Penelope had turned twenty-five this year, and if it weren't for her "engagement," she would've already been dismissed as the next in line for the title of Village Spinster. Already, she harbored more animals than "Mad Sally," Bouth's reigning Old Maid, who lived in a cottage with her thirteen cats and spent her days demanding children get off her front garden.

Actually, Penelope doubted the earl even remembered their engagement. The way everyone was still inclined to believe her claims was a small miracle. She hoped she could keep the pretense up until the time Lord Ravenstone decided to marry.

It was imperative to keep people certain about her affianced state. Nothing was more important, because the third thing she definitely knew about her betrothal was she had used it to ask the creditors to give Papa a little more time to pay off debts. Papa would be livid if he found out she'd used her engagement as a bargaining tool, but there had been little else the family could have done. Her stepfather had been away on business, and if she hadn't bargained for more time, they would have already lost Highfield Manor.

The fourth thing she knew about her engagement was there would be the devil to pay if Lord Ravenstone ever found out she'd been using his name without his consent or knowledge.

Penelope sighed and dismissed the gloomy thoughts. She refused to allow unresolved issues and forgetful earls to destroy her day. *This rainy, muddy day.*

"Don't worry, I'm not leaving Rusland anytime soon," she reassured Mari. Rusland Valley was where Highfield Manor was located, a five-minute horse ride north of Bouth. "I haven't received any message from Maitland Hall regarding the earl."

"Speaking of Maitland Hall," Mari said in a hushed tone while she looked around to see if anyone was within hearing distance before deciding that it was safe to go on talking, "A gentleman from London checked in here last night, asking about Baron Maitland and directions to your uncle's estate."

Penelope's eyebrows rose and before she could stop herself, she asked in a tone of mild curiosity, "What did the gentleman want with my uncle?" Mari opened her mouth to speak but Penelope held up her hand for silence as she hastily dismissed the news. "Never mind. Whatever my uncle is up to, it has nothing to do with me. I don't care what Uncle Hugh does as long as he leaves me and Mama out of it."

"Aren't you the least bit interested in this visitor?" Mari pouted, clearly disappointed with her lack of enthusiasm for juicy gossip.

"I'll admit it's an unusual occurrence. No one ever goes to Maitland Hall." She considered that for a moment. "Very well, did the gentleman say what the visit was about? And why are you so sure he's a gentleman?" she couldn't help but ask.

"Penelope, I grew up in a coaching inn." Mari crossed her arms over her chest, looking smug. "I *know* when I see nobility. It's a skill an innkeeper's daughter has to learn. This particular gentleman's clothes were of the finest quality. And even if his clothing were shabby, his accent and good manners would've given him away. Why, even his giant of a horse looked positively regal."

Penelope reined in her sudden impatience. "Did the gentleman have a name? And what did he want?" *Why did she care?*

"Papa was the one who checked him in, so I don't know his name. You know how Papa can be about guests' privacy. But I was the one the man asked about Lord Maitland when I brought his breakfast in this morning. He said he had 'personal business' with the baron."

"Well, that certainly counts Mama and me out," Penelope said cheerfully even as a strange combination of relief and disappointment settled on her chest.

She stiffened. *Disappointment?* What was the matter with her? Hadn't she learned long ago not to hope for anything from her aristocratic, pompous relatives or her equally self-important fiancé? Their social class gave them a bloated sense of entitlement, making them consistently disregard anyone whom they deemed to be useless.

She suspiciously eyed the now empty plate before her on the scarred oak table. Perhaps the apple and blackberry pie wasn't so awesome after all. Perhaps the pie had somehow muddled her mind, for the most trifling matters agitated her. She'd heard that sort of thing happened by eating too many sweets.

"It could have something to do with your beloved earl! Oh, Polly, what if your white knight has come at last?" Mari clasped her hands together, her pretty face alight with excitement. "It's so romantic! Just imagine—a chivalrous knight in shining armor, riding his glorious steed to rescue his fair maiden."

"Why would I want to marry a medieval knight?" she scoffed. "You forget those 'heroic' knights were paid to be ambitious murderers, and I'll wager they also carried the scent of the Middle Ages."

Mari's look of dismay made her laugh heartily.

"I'll tell you a secret," she continued, still chuckling, "I can assure you my 'beloved earl' has long since forgotten about me."

She gave Nelson one final pat on the head before rising to leave when a captivatingly deep, curt, male voice addressed her from the staircase behind them.

"I wouldn't be too quick with giving assurances, if I were you, Miss Maitland."

Penelope and Mari whirled in unison toward the staircase where an imposingly huge, well-dressed man loomed.

"And who, pray tell, are *you?*" Penelope demanded, refusing to be cowed by such a haughty individual. She placed her hands on her hips and tapped her foot. "Didn't anyone tell you it's considered ill mannered to eavesdrop on other peoples' conversations?" Somehow, she managed to crane her neck, look the man straight in the eye, and ignore Mari's horrified gasp.

The tall, black-haired beast of a man stalked to her and Mari with a purpose that lent deadly grace to his soundless footsteps. Ill-concealed interest and amusement glittered in his midnight-dark eyes as his bold gaze raked her insolently from the top of her bonneted head to the tips of her well worn half-boots, then travelled back up to meet her eyes.

"Didn't anyone tell *you* it's considered ill mannered to talk about one's fiancé with so little respect?" the arrogant man said in a gentle, chiding tone that, if Penelope hadn't known how deliberately unpleasant she'd just been to him, she would have thought the stranger was actually flirting with her.

She stole a glance at Mari to gauge her reaction. Her friend had always known more about men because unlike her, Mari had a nicely trimmed form and a face of classic beauty.

At the moment, however, Mari seemed unable to do anything but stand there, gawking nervously.

Penelope had a sudden, sinking feeling of foreboding in the pit of her stomach as she dragged her eyes to meet the giant's dark, steady gaze. "Who are you, sir?" she asked again in the barest of whispers.

Please, God, let me be wrong, she silently prayed.

In answer, the immaculately dressed gentleman bowed in one swift, smooth motion, then grabbed her bare hand and brushed his lips against her knuckles.

At the touch of his lips on her skin, Penelope felt a disturbing, unwanted tingling sensation all the way up her arm that made her heart pound while a strange—if late—warning rang inside her head like distant church bells and ... *the man refused to let go of her hand!* She must've tried to tug her hand free from his iron grip at least three times by now.

"I am delighted to finally meet you, Penelope," the stranger murmured in an inappropriately intimate voice, a smile tugging at his lips. "Please allow me to introduce myself. My name is Lucas Arthur Phillip Drake. And I, my dear, am your 'beloved earl.'"

Penelope paled. A ghost from the past had come back to haunt her.

And she was in big trouble.

Chapter Two

She watched the Earl of Ravenstone dwarf the private reception room of The Mucky Duck while he paced the flagstone floor and stopped in front of the cozy fireplace, looking more like a fierce warrior than a self-important peer of the realm, despite the elegant cut of his dark blue coat and buff riding breeches.

He looked so out of place and alone that she had an almost overwhelming impulse to pat his powerful shoulder and tell him everything was going to be all right.

But first, she had to make sure he was real.

Because Penelope *knew* she was hallucinating. This wasn't the first time she'd imagined the earl coming for her, though it had been at least seven years since she'd last daydreamed about him.

She sat on the red velvet settee opposite the hearth, not sure of what to make of the situation. Perhaps, if she blinked, he would disappear.

She blinked. Hard.

He is still here. Either she was feverish or she'd actually stepped into one of those "horrid" novels she and her sister Sarah loved to read. Except she wasn't a miserable, beautiful damsel in distress. *No, indeed.*

She fought to contain a wayward, sympathetic grin, imagining how the earl must have felt seeing her for the first time, standing in the dining hall next to the gorgeous Mari. What a surprise that must have been for him.

A disappointing one, she thought deprecatingly.

When she was with Mari, men generally regarded Penelope in the same manner one regards a side vegetable no one asked for but was always served with the meat nonetheless.

She looked down at her plain, eucalyptus-hued wool gown, inspected her mud-splattered half boots, and felt another urge to giggle inappropriately. *Was I worth waiting twenty-two years for, my lord?* She almost asked him the question as he continued to stare into the flames, his back to her. *I do hope you like your women plain, short, and plump.*

She forced herself to stop fidgeting with the ties of her reticule. Fidgeting was a clear sign that one's nerves were rattled, and she was someone with very strong nerves. It would take more than this man to send her scurrying for a vinaigrette.

When the silence stretched and became awkward, Penelope scrambled for something to say but didn't know exactly how to begin. What did one say to a fiancé who, despite everything she knew about him, was still technically a stranger? A fiancé whose name one had been using to fend off creditors without his permission?

She considered starting the conversation by asking him about his journey, but somehow that didn't seem appropriate. Perhaps a direct approach would be the most effective one as well. She cleared her throat and broke the silence.

"I suppose you're here to ask me to cry off from the betrothal, my lord?" she ventured.

He whirled to her, surprise evident in his sharp, forbidding features that somehow reminded her of the craggy fells surrounding her hometown.

"Why would you think that?"

"Well," Penelope answered, managing to look everywhere but directly at him, "I assumed you plan to marry someone else, and you've come here to demand I break our engagement. I mean, why would you travel all the way from London if not to make certain I cry off?" She directed her gaze to the fire. "It's the only reason I could think of that's important enough for your lordship to honor one such as I with your esteemed presence."

Was that a *bitter* edge in her voice? No, of course not. She was nervous, that's all. She had no cause to be bitter; she was only stating facts. It just so happened the facts were humiliating.

She stole a look at him, and the earl leveled her with a piercing stare for what seemed like several minutes before speaking.

"I have not come here to ask you to break our betrothal," he said in a quiet voice that nevertheless conveyed an iron resolve as he strode toward her with his hands clasped behind his back and continued, "Quite the opposite, actually. I meant to call upon your uncle, but from the conversation out in the hall I gather he isn't responsible for you?"

Penelope shook her head. "I haven't had anything to do with my uncle since my father died." *But you'd know that if you bothered to think of me in the past two decades.*

She gathered up her courage and looked him straight in the eye. Of course, she had to crane her neck all the way up to do so. Did he have to be so tall? He loomed over her, arresting and intimidating and overwhelmingly male.

He probably didn't even realize the effect his low, rumbling voice had on the female population. It was definitely affecting her in a way she found most disturbing. Then the rest of his words sunk in.

He didn't want to break the betrothal?

"If you don't want me to cry off, then what is it you want, my lord?"

His dark eyes flashed with what looked like irritation. "First, I want to know what in the flaming heaven you think you're doing, ensconced in a private salon in a coaching inn with a strange man. Have you no sense of the sort of danger you could put yourself in?"

She opened her mouth to reply, but he silenced her with a wave of his aristocratic hand as he continued to pace in front of her, his back to the fire.

"You came to a coaching inn without an escort of any sort," he bit out. "Not even an Abigail."

Why, the arrogant wretch! He had the nerve to question her actions? He, who'd hardly bothered to send any communication in all the time they'd been engaged. How dared he question her conduct now? He had no right! She couldn't believe she'd actually felt sorry for him a few minutes ago.

If he presumed their engagement authorized him to lecture her, then he'd given her the right to treat him as if he were an imbecile. "If you were paying any attention, my lord, you'd know that I did have an escort. He was eating with me and my friend."

"You had a dog."

"Who is perfectly capable of protecting me better than any lady's maid." She trusted Nelson implicitly. Besides, she couldn't afford a lady's maid. But he didn't need to know that. She reminded herself that she needed this man's cooperation if she wanted to keep fending off the creditors from her family's doorstep.

She sat straighter in the settee and gave him a bright smile. "And I'm confident of my safety now that you are here, my lord. I trust you'll make sure no harm comes to my person."

"Bloody hell."

Her eyes widened at the curse, but she wisely refrained from commenting on his appalling language. "Since you're not here to break the betrothal, I assume you came to do your duty?"

His square jaw seemed to clench. "You assume correctly, Miss Maitland. Is there anyone I should speak to before we get married?"

So he thought he could walk in here and marry her just like that, did he? The earl was obviously a man who was used to getting his own way without any arguments from mere mortals like her.

She suddenly felt a burst of anger over her predicament, and her hand itched to slap the smug look from his lordship's aristocratic face. She clenched her hands to resist the impulse. Her eyes narrowed as an odd sense of betrayal washed over her, heating her blood until it boiled.

She'd been willing to entertain the possibility he'd forgotten her existence, but his very presence in this room proved he'd merely relegated her to the bottom of his list of duties. *The way everyone else did.*

He'd ignored her when she'd wanted him to notice her, and now—when she actually needed him to stay away—he came rushing in. She felt as if the chains of matrimony she'd had dangling around her feet every day for the past two decades had unexpectedly tightened around her neck, strangling her.

It was suddenly all too much. If she were destined to wear chains, then she would make certain the entire world heard them rattling.

"Well!" she glowered at him as she put in, "I would say you should talk to *me* first, don't you think?"

"Your consent was already given when your father, acting as your guardian, signed the betrothal contract," the earl pointed out in that annoyingly calm tone. He arched one raven brow as he added, "I merely wanted to know if there is anyone you would want me to help you break the news of our impending marriage to."

She remained mutinously silent.

"Is there anyone I should speak to before we marry?" he repeated.

"You would know the answer to that if you bothered to send any sort of communication to me in the past two decades!" she shot back, spitting fire.

Standing up, she moved toward him. He was here, he thought he was marrying her, and by God, he had some explaining to do. Very well, she would hear him out. And then she would throw him out.

• • •

Lucas watched a strange look that was a combination of curiosity and determination cross her features as she stood up to join him in the middle of the small room between the fireplace and the settee.

Unbelievably, he actually felt the urge to back away as she advanced on him. His enormous size and reputation were usually enough to warn most people off. No man, let alone a woman, had ever confronted him as this brave, reckless little baggage was doing.

He realized he'd somehow ruffled her feathers at some point since they started talking. Her pretty eyes were suddenly shooting daggers at him. He sighed wearily. He'd been on horseback for several days, deciding it would be faster than his carriage, which had followed him soon after his departure from London. He had no interest in dealing with a shrew who, for some reason, had suddenly found him disagreeable.

A pretty, irritating, alluring, little shrew, Lucas thought as he took in his betrothed's winged brows and guileless hazel eyes that to him seemed strangely reminiscent of the woodlands surrounding this little village. He noted her pert nose, her softly rounded cheeks and proud chin. A chin that was now defiantly lifted even as it quivered with nervousness at his scrutiny.

"Why now?" she whispered, her voice so low he had to lean toward her to hear. "Why have you come here now, after so long? When I thought you'd forgotten about me?"

"I never forgot about you." That at least was true, though he'd be damned if he'd let her know the real reason behind his sudden appearance in her life.

He returned her searching gaze steadily while he wondered where she was trying to lead him with her questions.

A harsh, bitter laugh escaped her. "Don't say you never forgot about me, my lord, because you lie!" She shook her head, her eyes suddenly bright. "We have been engaged for twenty-two years, and in all that time you never once contacted me. If I didn't happen to be here at the same time you are, you wouldn't even know that I don't live with my uncle anymore."

She stepped closer to him, her face alive with pain and accusation. "Twenty-two years and you never once thought to send me a note to ask how I was. You never sent your condolences when my father died."

She proceeded to punctuate her accusations with a poke on his chest. "You never bothered to send your felicitations when my mother married my stepfather, or when I had a new brother and sister. Or ever wished me a happy birthday … " Her eyes widened, as if a thought just occurred to her. "Do you even *know* when my birthday is?"

Lucas opened his mouth to reply, then closed it again, not sure of how to answer her questions. An heir to an earldom was raised to always have his duties and responsibilities as his first priority. He'd never shirked any of his responsibilities. He'd been only sixteen when Father died, but he'd taken over the family's dwindling holdings and made them prosper. He'd taken care of his tenants and made sure they had a livelihood and roofs over their heads. He'd raised little Olivia as best he could …

But he didn't know when Penelope's birthday was. It hadn't occurred to him that Penelope might have wanted letters or to meet him before now.

Then again, *she'd* never sent any to him.

For some reason, that thought rankled. Hadn't it occurred to her that he might have needed to know she no longer lived with her uncle? Or that he might have needed advice on how to raise a little girl when he'd been barely more than a child himself?

How dared she feel outraged at his neglect, when she'd behaved no better! She'd hidden from him all these years like the coward her father was.

He drew himself up. "Do you know when *my* birthday is, Penelope?"

She gasped.

He gave her a cold smile. "I'll admit I haven't acted the way a betrothed person would've normally done all these years, but neither have you." She tried to look away, but he tipped her chin up, forcing her to hold his gaze. "Unlike a normal engaged couple, we both needed to live our lives as fully as we could before taking on the duties that come with a betrothal. Because this isn't a normal betrothal, is it?"

She was silent for so long that he thought she wouldn't answer. He was starting to feel a little disappointed that she lacked the grace to admit her own transgressions when she drew a breath and spoke, her voice ringing with quiet dignity.

"No," she conceded. "This isn't a normal betrothal at all. It was unfair of me to accuse you of abandoning me." She offered a small, conciliatory smile. "And my birthday is in February."

Lucas felt an inappropriate surge of pride at the maturity she displayed. The chit was not only spirited, she was also pragmatic. He liked that. "I'll make a note of it," he murmured, accepting her offer of a truce.

"Why *now?*" she persisted, returning to her original question.

Lucas found himself unwillingly captivated by her tenacity. She wouldn't let the subject drop until she got to the heart of the matter.

He hesitated as he tried to think of a way to tell her the truth without revealing all of it. He had a feeling Penelope would bolt if he told her now about Father's will. He couldn't risk that.

"It's time I marry," he said blithely, stepping closer to the woman whose name had haunted all but the first nine of his thirty-one years. "Since I've given you enough time to cry off, I naturally assumed we're in accord regarding the betrothal."

"Then you assumed *wrong*, my lord!" she shot back, all wounded dignity and female indignation once more. She shook her head in disgust. "Did you actually think I would be so desperate for a husband that I would sit down and meekly wait for some man I've never met to finally deign to marry me?"

Lucas went very still. "Let me see if I understand this correctly," he said tersely. "You are saying you're not going to marry me."

"Precisely," she clarified.

"I don't believe you."

"I don't care!" she burst out, stamping her foot and plunking her hands on her graceful hips. She gave him a good glare, and then she turned toward the door without further warning, obviously intending to leave the room.

Lucas had been so shocked by her breathtaking impertinence that for a moment all he could do was stare at her retreating back. *The outrageous wench!* If she thought she could get rid of him that easily, then she had another think coming.

He caught her arm in a none-too-gentle grip just as she reached the door and whirled her around to face him, holding her as he leaned close. "I was not asking you to care, Miss Maitland. In fact, I wasn't asking you to do anything at all. But I think I have the right to expect you to honor your word."

"Who do you think you are?" she cried, struggling to free her from his grip.

"I *know* who I am, Penelope," he hissed in his most menacing tone. "It's you who seem to have forgotten your identity, so let me remind you. You are Baron Maitland's daughter, and as his daughter, you have a duty to honor your father's wishes. Just as I have a duty to honor *my* father's wishes." He gave her his most imperious look. "I suggest you start acting with the integrity and maturity expected from a lady of your station, instead of behaving like a petulant child."

His words seemed to startle the bravado out of her, for she suddenly looked deflated. *Penelope was finally seeing sense.*

She swallowed visibly and said quietly, "Please let go of my arm, my lord."

So much for seeing sense. "Not so fast, Penelope," he growled, but he loosened his grip on her arm. "Do we have an understanding?"

Her brows met in consternation. "I am sure I am not at all what you wished for or expected in a fiancée."

His eyes narrowed. "We all have our duties to perform, no matter our expectations or wishes."

She brightened immediately. "Ah, then you are in luck!" Her eyes were feverishly bright, making her look like a forest nymph who couldn't wait to grant him a favor. "As it happens, my lord, I am more than willing to set you free from your obligation to me."

"Are you, indeed?"

"For a price," she announced.

"You need money?"

Of course, she needed money. Her plain clothes attested to that fact. She wouldn't have stood there bargaining like a fishwife otherwise. It was a game women had played with him since he'd regained the fortune that came with the earldom. It irked him to know his fiancée turned out to be no better than those women, no better than her father.

She stared at him with wounded pride. "I don't need *your* money."

He looked up at the beamed ceiling, praying for patience. "Then what is it you need?"

"I need your help. If you are willing to help me, I shall release you from your duty to marry me."

"And if I refuse?"

She gave him a smug look. "You won't refuse."

"Bloody hell! What makes you think that?" he snapped. Hadn't he just told her he was here to marry her? The woman seemed to be addled.

"My lord, let us have some honesty here. We both know this betrothal has nothing to do with us, but our fathers, God rest their souls." She went to the window and stared at the raindrops distorting the view of the courtyard. "I know more about you than you think. If you had any interest at all in marrying me, you wouldn't have waited two decades to act on it."

The pain behind her words made Lucas uneasy. He took in her proud countenance, and in spite of his earlier annoyance at her transparent attempts to manipulate him, he couldn't help but be fascinated. He wondered how much it cost her pride to admit to him she knew he didn't want her.

She was wrong, however.

She wasn't a classic beauty to be sure, and he had no doubt men who weren't as observant as he would find her looks passable at best, but he sensed an air of innocence and pride about her that he found … arresting. She bore the same name as that of Odysseus's devoted wife from Homer's famous work, but she had the look of the hero's mistress, the goddess Circe, a forest nymph who drugged men and turned them into beasts.

In fact, she bore an uncanny resemblance to a Romney painting he'd seen of the devious Circe, but the portrait lacked Penelope's look of radiant good health, her air of mischievous humor and calm assurance that captured a man's gaze and held it there.

She turned back to him, her form silhouetted by the light coming in from the window, making her seem ethereal, and his eyes shifted to her generous, plump bow of a mouth. Those soft lips reminded him of sun-ripened peaches. He wondered if they could possibly taste as sweet as they looked even while they curved into a frown of displeasure.

He sucked in a steadying breath as his gaze travelled down her lush breasts and gently curved waist outlined by her simple, practical gown that somehow managed to call attention to her graceful form.

Lucas cursed and tore his gaze from the delightful little baggage who was his fiancée when he realized he was reacting to her physically. He hadn't expected this. Never in all his imaginings during the long journey to this godforsaken place did he think his fiancée would be the most intriguing female he'd set eyes on in a very long time. This was not good. He didn't need this complication.

She is a means to an end, nothing more.

Her father's abandonment had ended his father's life. Lucas's father had become a hollow version of the man he'd been before the loss of his wife and fortune. Penelope's father turning his back on their situation had been the final blow that made Father pull the trigger. Father's will was a testament to how that last betrayal had affected him, for now he was forcing Lucas to make sure Maitland made good on his promise.

Penelope's voice brought him back to the present. "Have you had your fill, my lord? Or would you like to study my nose for a while longer?"

His lips twitched with amusement. "I've had my fill for now, Miss Maitland." He watched as her cheeks flushed a becoming pink. "And you are wrong, you know. I'm not opposed to marrying you. But tell me what it is I can help you with."

Her lips thinned, and her hazel eyes flashed with resentment, and he thought he heard her mutter something under her breath that sounded like "butter the crumpets" before she put her hands on her waist and started tapping her toe.

"It's very gentlemanly of you to spare my feelings, but your actions over the past years speak volumes of how you feel about this whole affair." She gave a sigh of irritation. "All you have to do, my lord, is show up at some functions around the village with me, and pretend that we are actually engaged. And then you can leave."

"But we *are* engaged, Miss Maitland," he reminded her.

"Yes, yes, I know that," she said impatiently. "But certain people need to be reassured of the fact. Now that I think about it, you've chosen the perfect time to grace us with your presence."

"Why?"

She raised clear eyes to his. "My lord?"

"Why do you need to convince people of the legitimacy of our betrothal?"

"It would give me time."

"Time for what?"

"To save face, of course," she muttered after a moment's pause. "The least you could do for the fiancée who stayed faithful all these years is spare her the humiliation of being Anne of Cleves," she added in a desperate tone. "I have to live here after you go. If you leave immediately following our discussion, people will think that, in the manner of Henry VIII, you took one look at me and decided you 'like her not.'"

She could sway even an earl to spend a portion of his valuable time to humor her, and though Lucas wasn't fooled, he was reluctantly impressed. Oh, he could tell she was hiding something from him, but she'd convinced him she was worth the time it would take to find out what it was.

"My lord," she said quietly, "I would be forever grateful if you agree to my terms. That's all I ask of you." She smiled up at him and patted his shoulder in a beseeching manner. "Stay a few days, and I'll repay you in any way I can."

Lucas took hold of her other hand and held it against his chest. "My services won't come cheap."

Her eyes widened. "I don't have a lot of money."

"I don't need your money," he replied, echoing her words from earlier.

"Then what do you want?" she asked, her hands clenching into fists as if to restrain herself from shaking him.

She was a bossy bit of goods, but he was determined to take the lead in this strange bargaining situation.

Lucas pulled her to him and leaned down, smiling against her ear when he heard her gasp of surprise. He was suddenly filled with an overwhelming urge to remind this exasperating woman exactly what her duty was. "I would like you to pay me with a kiss."

And with that, he bent his head to claim her mouth and everything to which he'd been entitled almost from the day she was born. "Should we seal this bargain, Penelope?"

Her gaze dropped to his lips, a mere breath away from hers, as he waited for her to decide. He stood unmoving while she hesitated, then he saw a flash of longing and curiosity in her eyes. A surge of triumph crashed through him when she tilted her head back and rose on tiptoes to meet his mouth.

He reached out and cupped her face in his hand, turning it up to his and savoring the feel of her creamy skin as his thumb stroked her flushed cheek. He inhaled the sweet fragrance of roses and soap wafting off her, beckoning him closer.

He'd intended to give her a brief, gentle touch—a polite greeting between prospective lovers. But the moment she crushed her mouth to his, he was lost. His lips caressed, tasted and molded hers as he claimed her mouth in a seeking kiss of blatant ownership.

His hands moved down her body, exploring her form as he'd been itching to do from the moment he saw her light up the dining hall with her smile. His mouth drank her in, and he reveled in her response to him as she sighed and wrapped her arms around his neck, while he untied her bonnet and shoved it off her head so he could kiss her more thoroughly.

Lucas lifted his mouth from hers to taste the elegant line of her throat, letting his fingers sink into her hair to grab a fistful of the fragrant, reddish brown curls. He heard the pins holding her thick mane fall to the flagstone floor, the sound accompanied by her ragged breathing. She was magnificent. He didn't know why Penelope was letting him touch her so, but he wasn't going to question something that felt this good. He just enjoyed the fact that she was as he trailed kisses up her delicate neck, glorying in the moan that tore from her lips.

He shuddered when he felt her hands glide through his hair. He kissed her proud chin, and she sighed. His mouth curved in a smile as he trailed kisses along her jaw, unable to deny the keen satisfaction he felt at her innocent response to his caresses. She was so responsive, so open, so sweet … With this woman, a man would know exactly where he stood.

"My lord—"

"Lucas," he corrected, his mouth against the tantalizing curve of her ear. He traced it with his tongue, grinning when he heard her gasp. "We are betrothed. You should call me Lucas."

"Lucas," she sighed his name in a beckoning whisper that drove him mad.

He cupped the back of her neck in his hand and drew her mouth closer for another taste. This time he sought to deepen the kiss. His tongue invaded her parted lips, greedily claiming every delicious, silken part.

He growled his approval deep in his throat when she matched his movements. Good God, he could get addicted to her eagerness, her willing response to him. Never had a woman felt so good and soft in his arms. She clung more tightly to him, encouraging him even further. He plundered her generous lips over and over, drinking in the intoxicating taste of her as pure, undiluted lust roared through him.

Then a knock sounded at the door.

Penelope started, tearing her mouth from his.

"Polly?"

He barely heard Penelope's friend calling her through the pounding in his head, but the opportunity it presented was clear.

He could end this and claim Penelope right here. There'd be a witness, and they'd be married by tomorrow at the latest, scruples be damned.

Yes, this was what he should do. He should save his tenants, save his fortune … he lowered his head.

He should kiss her again.

• • •

As Mari's apologetic voice from the other side of the door drifted through the room, Penelope put her hands on Lucas's hard chest to push him away while she drowned in mortification.

Instead of letting her go, his arms tightened even more, forcing her to feel the unyielding evidence of his arousal, which pressed against her through the folds of her gown. The new intimacy made her freeze, her hands still lying on his chest.

His dark eyes glittered as shock and awe played over his stark features.

"Bloody hell," he muttered, his heated gaze roving over her face. Then his grip on her waist tightened as he began to lower his head to hers once more.

"My lord!" Penelope panicked and pushed at his chest again.

"Lucas," he insisted.

"Lucas," she said, watching his onyx eyes smolder as she stood in his embrace. "My friend, Mari, is at the door. I must go see what she wants."

As if on cue, another knock sounded, a louder one.

"What is it, Mari?" Penelope called out, though she couldn't tear her gaze away from Lord Ravenstone. Lucas.

"Ummm, are you and his lordship finished talking? A note arrived from Highfield Manor. Dr. Walker is home."

Penelope's eyes widened at the news. "What does Papa want?"

"I think he's heard about his lordship's presence because he wants you to come home *immediately*."

Dear Lord! That was all it took for her to wriggle out of Lucas's arms, ignore his protest and fling the door wide open, revealing Nelson and Mari on the other side, their eyes full of questions.

Mari gave her a knowing smile. "Where's your bonnet?"

Penelope's hand flew to her unbound hair, which was now hanging down her shoulders and back thanks to Lucas's rapacious fingers. *She probably looked exactly like the newly revealed strumpet that she was.*

Blushing furiously, she followed Mari's amused gaze and saw Lucas once again staring into the fireplace, his back to them.

"Good afternoon, my lord," Mari said in a respectful tone and curtsied.

Lucas looked over his shoulder, inclined his head in a mocking bow and smiled. "Good afternoon Miss Mari, er ... "

"Smythe," Penelope put in helpfully. "Marian Smythe."

Lucas shifted his gaze to her, his smile turning warm and full of promises, sending a shiver down her spine.

"Smythe," he said huskily, without taking his eyes away from Penelope.

Mari loudly cleared her throat, turning everyone's attention to her as she walked into the room and handed a letter to Lucas. "This note is from Penelope's stepfather, my lord. I am to tell you that Dr. Walker respectfully requests your presence at Highfield Manor this evening."

Lucas finally turned away from the fireplace and reached for the note, putting it in his pocket. "Thank you, Miss Smythe. I am looking forward to meeting Penelope's family. Although I regret it means I'll have to do without the excellent meals from this fine establishment tonight."

"Oh, you are too kind, my lord." Mari blushed with pleasure at the compliment to her cooking. "May I be of any further assistance?"

"You can help me with my hair," Penelope answered. "You're much quicker at it than I, and if I don't hurry, Papa will have my hide." She bent down to pick up her bonnet and hairpins from the floor.

"Very well," Mari said with an air of efficiency. "Sit down on the settee and we'll have you ready in no time. I'll just close the door … " She gave Penelope a wry look. "I'd hate for Mama to find you like this. You know she's the biggest gossip in Bouth."

Five minutes later, Penelope had her bonnet back on and was following Mari out the door when Lucas grabbed her shoulder and turned her to face him.

"I'll escort you home."

The notion was so ridiculous she burst out laughing. "Lord Ravenstone, Rusland Valley is but a five-minute horse ride away, I know everyone who lives here, and I have Nelson. I hardly think I'd need an escort."

"Nevertheless, I am providing you with one." He offered his arm to her, forcing her to accept.

She hesitated, but she knew she could hardly refuse without making a scene. "Very well, if you insist." She put her hand on his arm and let him lead her out of the room.

He'd been physically in her life for less than two hours and already he was taking over. He had only to say her name in that dark, possessive way and she fell into his arms.

She'd actually kissed the man! Worse, if Mari hadn't interrupted Penelope probably would have offered all she had to give just to have another taste of being wanted. The minute he'd held her in his arms, she'd reverted to being that naive girl who dreamed of her fiancé, writing letters and wanting him to show her what passion was like. When he held her, she almost believed she really was his cherished betrothed.

But she knew better. He asked her if she knew his birthday. Of course she did. Because of her silly, girlhood dreams and his notoriety, there was little about him she didn't know. She reminded herself that entitled gentlemen only cared about someone if the person were useful to them.

But what possible use could she be to the earl? She had no money or connections to speak of. What did he expect to gain? Men didn't become interested in her unless there was something in it for them.

As they stepped out of the inn, she realized it had stopped raining. It was still muddy, but at least she wouldn't get wet on the short journey home.

"Let me know everything that happens," Mari whispered beside her.

"If I survive it," Penelope whispered back.

There wasn't time to say anything more as Lord Ravenstone held her waist and helped her mount her aging gray gelding. He then mounted the biggest horse she'd ever seen, and as they silently rode off with Nelson trotting behind them, she felt not unlike a convict being led to execution.

It certainly seemed as if her life as she knew it was about to end.

Chapter Three

Lucas ground his teeth in frustration as he watched Penelope ride up the valley with him seated atop her ancient horse.

Lucky horse.

The thought almost made him groan. She had been humiliated after her friend burst into the room. With his plan foiled, he'd had no choice but to stand with his back to them, hiding his erection to avoid making a spectacle of himself. A vision of Penelope bending over to retrieve her bonnet from the floor flashed through his mind, and he had to shake his head to clear it of the tantalizing image.

He'd mishandled their first meeting.

What the devil had come over him? Penelope deserved better than to be forced to engage in outrageous behavior in a damned coaching inn by a lout like him.

She was his fiancée, for Christ's sake, not some tavern whore.

He would do well to remember that fact next time. The clock was ticking, and he couldn't risk scaring her off by acting like some aging lecher.

Lucas sighed as he looked over the place where Penelope grew up, letting the fresh, grass-scented breeze cool his face. He could easily imagine her as a young girl, running through these sun-kissed fields, climbing over the dry stone walls and getting into trouble for feeding scraps from the dinner table to flea-ridden dogs.

Somehow, he couldn't imagine his little forest nymph spending her childhood cooped up indoors like the haughty debutantes he'd seen out in Society.

She had a clever mind and a natural curiosity about the world that would've made her eagerly want to explore it firsthand.

Like the way she'd been naturally curious and eager to explore the rudiments of kissing, twisting him into knots in the process. He felt his breeches tighten uncomfortably as memories of her innocent response to his advances assailed him.

Damn and blast. Maybe he was better off finding another bride. Although Lucas understood his father wanted him to marry Maitland's daughter, his will didn't actually specify Penelope's name.

He could even buy himself another bride—if the gossip about him being "damaged" made it difficult to secure a member of the *ton*, then perhaps some practical merchant's daughter would be willing to marry him for his title. Someone who didn't pose such a threat to his equilibrium or want to get too close.

He knew the dangers that resulted from letting someone too close—the madness of his parents' marriage was proof of that. Lucas had no wish to repeat his father's mistakes. He was still paying for them now, and his father had been dead for fifteen years. A prim, timid Society miss would pose no risk and suit his purposes better.

He wanted a staid marriage with a dutiful wife who'd bear him an heir and let him get on with his life as she went on with hers. No passionate kisses to threaten his self-control. No eager embraces and no tender caresses, no soft, hazel eyes and —

Christ. He raked a hand through his hair and looked at Penelope once more. She glanced at him and smiled, silently reminding him of something vital he'd found out at the inn.

She'd waited for him.

He felt like a bastard for the satisfaction that flowed through his veins at the thought. Her outrage at his late entrance into her life had been real. Only skilled actresses would have been able to fake the pain behind her accusation at his tardiness.

Apparently, she knew nothing of her father's defection. Lucas was certain the current baron knew about it, however. He intended to deal with that man as soon as possible.

He was debating how best to proceed with his plans when she waved her arm in a sweeping gesture toward a charming, two-story Palladian manor of decent proportions with ivy-covered walls. Part of the west wing of the house was used as an apothecary shop, which was now closed for the day.

"Here we are," she remarked.

He dismounted in the front courtyard, which overlooked the open park they'd just ridden through, and held Penelope by the waist to help her off her gray gelding. As they stood facing each other, his hands seemed to develop a will of their own and roamed the lush curve, drawing her nearer to him.

"Thank you for escorting me home, Lucas."

Her eyes shone at the mention of "home," and he automatically bent his head to have another taste of her lips before he remembered where they were and pressed a perfunctory kiss to her forehead instead.

"It was no trouble at all, my dear." He let her go, gave her a gentlemanly bow and mounted his black mare, which was already restlessly pawing the ground. "I'll see you at supper. Tell your stepfather to expect me this evening."

He left her and her dog at the courtyard, his mind working out a stratagem on how to bring about the result he wanted from this affair. He needed more information, and he was likely to get it at the inn.

• • •

Penelope headed straight for the barn after the earl left, with Nelson trailing behind her. The basic principle in caring for animals was the creatures had no concept of late nights, holidays or fiancés suddenly turning up demanding a marriage.

The animals needed her to be there for them—to feed them or groom them—rain or shine, at exactly the same time every day.

Their inflexibility to deviation from the schedule was exactly what she needed right then.

Penelope put on an apron and let the chickens out of the barn so they could scratch the ground while she fed them. She watched as they clucked and flapped their wings at each other, utterly oblivious to the fact her world had just been turned upside down.

Her forgetful fiancé had finally remembered to claim her, and she didn't know how to handle him. He'd agreed to her bargain and asked her for a kiss.

Her first real kiss.

How different a real kiss was from a fantasy one. The kiss hadn't conjured thoughts of flower meadows, puffy clouds and castles. No, her fiancé kissed in an earthy way that dominated and possessed. His seeking mouth robbed her of any thought but kissing him back and joyfully tasting more of the sweet abandonment he offered. The kiss had been thorough, intimate and unforgettable. It made her feel needed as a woman for the first time in her life.

Until he'd come, she'd been content with her lot. She'd learned to accept she wasn't the type of woman who roused a man's passions. She was a puzzle piece that had all the wrong sides, unable to truly fit anywhere: somewhat engaged, somewhat connected to a baron, somewhat a country physician's daughter.

She'd learned to stop dreaming someone would see past her less than pretty exterior and appreciate the woman beneath, and Lucas was reminding her of things she'd once been foolish enough to hope for.

He made her wish for something better when she knew it was impossible. He dangled the dream before her, making her think she could be seen as something other than merely useful. But it wasn't real. To him, she was nothing but a name in a contract.

"You understand exactly how I feel, don't you, boy?" she asked Nelson, who sat next to her, watching the chickens.

Nelson nudged her hand for some bread, which she obligingly gave.

"You were born to be a sheepdog, but you literally couldn't herd a thing to save your life." A sad laugh escaped her. "I was born to be the belle of the ball in London. And look at me now, surrounded by chickens scratching the ground at my feet and a failure of a sheepdog by my side."

Nelson whined.

"Oh, stop that," she admonished, patting the dog's head to lessen the sting of the rebuke. "You have nothing to complain about. I give you a good living here, don't I? Your previous owners would have had none of this whining. It doesn't become you."

She sighed and dusted the remainder of the chicken feed off her apron. "What am I to do now, boy?"

A familiar voice answered. "You could tell me what happened."

Penelope turned and found her little sister, Sarah, approaching the barn with a bright smile on her face, looking like a ray of sunshine in her lemon yellow walking dress against the backdrop of the woods surrounding Highfield Manor.

"So?" Sarah asked when she neared the barn, her brown eyes alight with excitement. "Papa says the earl has arrived! How exciting. It's like one of those novels we read. All we need is a villain so the earl can prove his heroic qualities."

Penelope watched a gust of wind blow Sarah's golden hair free of her bonnet. "This isn't a Minerva Press novel, Sarah. We should approach with caution."

Sarah's brow furrowed. "Did he want to be free of the betrothal?"

"No."

"Perfect!" Sarah clapped her hands. "So we are rich!"

"No," Penelope corrected, crossing her arms over her chest and turning to steer the chickens back to the coop. "We're not rich. He did, however, agree to help us convince the creditors to give us more time."

"Did he ask for a kiss as payment for the favor? That's what happened in *The Prince's Castle*."

"I'm afraid the meeting took place at The Mucky Duck, not a castle."

"So he kissed you!" Sarah chortled. "Oh, my goodness me! That was fast, don't you think?"

Penelope made sure the chickens were safely inside their coop before turning to Sarah. "I do not appreciate being called 'fast,' sister."

Sarah clamped a hand over her mouth. "I'm sorry, Polly, I didn't mean to say you were fast." She started twirling her blonde curls around her finger. "I mean, considering you've been engaged for more than two decades and he has only now got 'round to kissing you, well … that's actually very slow, isn't it?"

Penelope snorted. "Fine, I'll forgive you this time. But you have to carry that bucket of feed back into the barn."

Sarah grimaced. "I don't understand why you insist we keep these chickens." She picked up the bucket and headed for the barn door. "The horses, I understand. They were old and no one else would have them. Especially poor Jingles; he hasn't had a good life at all."

She heard the loud banging of the metal bucket against the barn wall as Sarah continued her diatribe. "And I appreciate how you saved Nelson from going to heaven because he couldn't herd sheep. Even Daisy the cow at least can give us milk now that her wounds have healed. But those chickens are good for nothing!"

Sarah emerged from the barn. "They were way past the egg-laying phase when you took them from Mrs. Gray, and they've become too much like pets to eat now that their feathers have grown back."

Penelope took off her soiled apron and folded it under her arm. "Well, they do help you wake up in the morning."

"All the more reason to get rid of them." Sarah made a face, then she took Penelope's other arm as they started walking back to the house. "Are you ready to face Papa now?"

She took a deep breath and slowly released it. "Of course I am. The chickens merely needed feeding. It's not as if I was hiding from him."

Sarah looked skeptical, so she changed the subject. "Where's Colin?"

"How would I know?" Sarah retorted.

"You're his twin, aren't you?" Penelope arched a brow. "I thought twins had a mystical connection or some such."

Sarah let go of her arm and started walking briskly. "Stop teasing me about that. I've long given up on mentally speaking to Colin." She crossed her arms over her chest. "It's obviously pure rubbish."

"Are you certain? Perhaps we should ask him to think of a number and let you guess it again, only this time we limit the range. How about a number between one and fifty?"

Sarah waved her hand in a dismissive gesture. "Oh, that's easy enough to answer. He'd probably think of how many pairs of his shoes I put marbles in this morning."

"Three," Colin answered, glowering at Sarah as he leaned against the front door of the house, his dark blonde hair swaying just above his shoulders.

"Oh, there you are, Colin. Have you heard about the earl?" Sarah asked. "Polly met him when she went to the inn to give your flowers to Mari."

Colin's green gaze shifted to Penelope. "Yes. That's why I came out here to meet you. Polly, does this mean I can go back to school?"

She winced. "I don't know, Colin … I wouldn't want to importune Lord Ravenstone with requests for that sort of thing yet. I've only just met the man." *You should keep that in mind next time you throw yourself at him.*

She sighed. Grandfather had died two years ago, and that's when the family had learned of his gambling debts. All they had left now was this house, and the creditors were determined to take it, too.

Colin had to quit school, Sarah had no governess, their mother spent most of her time grinding herbs to sell at the apothecary shop, and Papa traveled farther, working longer hours, while Penelope had taken over the household management.

Part of the problem, she knew, was that Papa often worked for no pay, seeing as most of the villagers had so little in terms of financial assets.

It was a miracle some of the servants stayed, even though the family couldn't afford to give them any more than board and lodging. If her family didn't possess such a good sense of humor, they would be in complete despair.

"Speaking of Papa," Penelope pressed on, "why hasn't he summoned me yet? I thought he wanted to talk to me, and I've been home for two hours."

Colin shrugged. "He was very tired when he came back from visiting a patient, so he fell asleep as soon as he sent that note to the inn."

Something in the way he spoke made her eye him suspiciously as he stepped aside to let them into the house. "What did you do, Colin?"

"I don't know what you mean."

"Yes, you do." She stared at him. "Did you put something in Papa's tea?"

"Don't worry about it, Polly." He grinned. "He won't wake up until just before supper."

Sarah guffawed, then covered her mouth with her hand and kept silent as she passed Colin in the foyer.

Penelope eyed her younger brother with mock severity before smiling reluctantly. She really couldn't handle an interview with Papa at that moment. "Thank you, Colin. I do appreciate it."

He winked at her. "I thought you might."

"Well, I'm going to go change for supper," Sarah piped up, heading for the stairs. "What's appropriate wear for receiving an earl, Polly?"

"Just wear what you'd normally wear for supper. I talked to Lord Ravenstone in this gown and he didn't seem to mind." *He seemed to like it, in fact,* Penelope added silently, remembering how Lucas's large hands had explored her this afternoon. She fought down another blush. She had to stop thinking about that.

Colin headed up the stairs as well. "We all better get ready for supper. Since Mama's taken over the kitchen and is busy ordering Cook about, I've no doubt Papa won't be happy when he wakes up. And I don't want to be the first one he sees when he does."

Penelope was about to follow her siblings when she realized she had to warn Lucas of what to say in front of her stepfather at supper. Or, rather, what *not* to say. Their bargain had to remain a secret, since Papa didn't know about her arrangement with the creditors.

"You go on ahead," she said, heading for the library. "I need to write down a few notes about the cow's state of health. If I don't do it now, I'm likely to forget all about it."

She closed the library door and proceeded to compose her secret letter to the earl. The last time she'd penned a secret note to him, she'd been eighteen and heartbroken, forced to accept that he, too, had forsaken her. This time, she vowed, she'd be in control of her destiny. She felt no emotion as she continued to write.

Chapter Four

Lucas entered Highfield Manor, his eyes drawn to the beautifully curved, cantilever stone staircase supported and framed by three long, delicate pillars, which dominated the foyer, while handing his cloak and top hat to the elderly maidservant who'd materialized at his side.

The maidservant nervously took his cloak and hat, turned and tripped over the edge of the worn rug covering most of the stone floor of the wide, dimly lit hall.

Lucas grabbed the woman's arm to keep her from falling.

"Are you well?" he asked the old woman.

"Yes'r, m'lord earl," the woman chimed with nervous enthusiasm. "Thank ye, kindly. I was jest … jest wantin' to show ye into the drawin' room."

"I would certainly appreciate that, madam. Please, lead on."

"This way, m'lord earl!" the woman shrieked.

Lucas resisted the urge to grimace. The poorly trained servant confirmed what he'd learned about the Walkers this afternoon after he'd received the ridiculous note his fiancée had sent to him. The chit had actually suggested a few lines of dialogue for him to consider as preparation for supper with her stepfamily, along with the warning that under no circumstances was he to mention their bargain to her stepfather.

The maidservant opened a door, and Lucas went through it when he was motioned to do so. He'd scarcely taken a step inside the room when the door was firmly shut behind him. The drawing room was long rather than wide in dimension, with two sitting areas, one by the hearth and another at the opposite end of the room by a big window that looked out over the manor's gardens. Lucas paused behind a column, a few steps from the sitting area by the window where the Walker family was too engrossed in their discussion to notice him.

"I have yet to talk to Polly about this," a man Lucas assumed was Dr. Walker said in a low voice.

A blonde woman Lucas recognized as Penelope's mother, Lady Eleanor Maitland, gave an indelicate snort. "What is there to talk about? We've always known he would claim her one day. You knew that when we married."

"Not like this … I didn't know he would just walk in here and take my little girl—"

"Papa, Polly's twenty-five," a boy of about fifteen pointed out. "She's hardly a little girl. She's not even a *young* girl anymore."

"*Shut up*, Colin," Penelope and a blonde young woman sitting beside Colin chorused.

"And you," Dr. Walker raked a hand through his graying light hair and rounded on the boy called Colin, "I don't know if it was you or Sarah who drugged my tea this afternoon, but when I find out—"

"It was Sarah," Colin readily answered, pointing an accusing finger at the young lady beside him.

"It was *not!*" Sarah denied hotly.

"My lord!" Lady Maitland cried, an uneasy smile fixed on her lips as she stood up, turning everyone's attention. "It's such a pleasure to see you again, after so many years. Please forgive our failure to welcome you formally to Highfield Manor. Gertie was supposed to announce your arrival."

"Lady Maitland," he murmured, bowing in front of the older woman.

"I am Mrs. Eleanor Walker now, my lord," Penelope's mother informed him with an affectionate smile. She proceeded to introduce the rest of the Walkers to him.

Lucas felt oddly bereft when Penelope ignored him even as he sat next to her on the sofa.

Dr. Walker broke the expectant silence that had begun to fill the room.

"I suppose you heard our family meeting, my lord," he grumbled. "I apologize. You weren't supposed to witness it."

He noticed Dr. Walker neither apologized nor tried to deny what the family meeting implied, only that Lucas wasn't supposed to have seen it.

Now he knew where Penelope's straightforward manner came from. "Please call me Lucas. Or Ravenstone, if you prefer. I don't see any need to be so formal, now that we're going to be family soon."

Very soon, if Lucas had anything to say about it. He'd been guilt-stricken about his behavior that afternoon, but since then he'd gleaned some information about the Walkers, the most interesting of which was that they were in dire straits, indeed.

Which meant they needed *him*.

The knowledge went a long way in banishing his remorse. A man in Lucas's position had to do what needed to be done, and he couldn't afford weakening with feelings like guilt.

He offered a tight-lipped smile to everyone as the uncomfortable silence stretched in the room. The ladies fidgeted with their skirts, Colin appeared impatient, and Dr. Walker was looking at him suspiciously. It seemed Lucas would have to work to get on the Walker family's good side.

Very well, if that's what he needed to do, then by thunder, he would do it.

He was convinced of the rightness of marrying Penelope. After all, he was only doing what was best for everyone. He'd overreacted to their shared moments of passion, failing to realize its advantages. For what was better than having a wife who also had the ability to make his blood run hot with lust by doing nothing more than sit silently beside him, making him itch to uncover every inch of the luscious female curves under that prim blue gown?

Good God, even sitting here in front of her damned family, he already craved another taste of her sweet mouth. And another, and another …

You just want to bed her.

Lucas stiffened at the insidious thought. He couldn't deny it. It was how heirs were made, after all.

He wondered how anyone could prefer an angelic blonde to the exotic nymph beside him. He'd certainly never experienced this burning hunger with a simple kiss. He'd merely had one little taste of her and already had the undeniable need to claim her as his. Her effect on him would have been troubling if he didn't know she wanted him, too. He was certain of it. Penelope was too innocent to feign her eager responses to his touch.

He stole a glance at his betrothed, and possessiveness surged through him. She belonged to *him*, even if she didn't realize it yet. Even if her own father didn't realize it. If he had to, he'd prove it to her over and over, until she was convinced. He realized his hands had clenched into fists and he forced himself to relax.

"Lucas," Dr. Walker began, the man's brown eyes regarding him quizzically. "I believe you are here to make your intentions known."

He grabbed Penelope's hand, making her jump. "Yes, sir. I'm here to marry my fiancée."

Dr. Walker rounded on him. "And you could not even be bothered to ask me for her hand?"

"Her father already gave me her hand," he pointed out, ignoring Penelope's warning squeeze.

"I may not have sired her," Dr. Walker was shaking with fury, "but *I* brought her into this world. *I* raised her, and *I* have been more of a father to her than Lord Maitland ever was!"

"Calm down, Robert," Eleanor admonished. "His lordship is not leaving you out of the equation. That is the reason he is here." She faced Lucas with a gentle smile. "I was sorry to hear of your parents' demise, my lord. I was acquainted with your mother. You must miss Vivian very much."

His hold on Penelope's hand tightened. "My mother died in childbirth two years before my father did."

Eleanor winced. "I know, but as with your father's death, I found out about it long after the fact. Maitland rarely came home and when he did, he never told me any news from London." Eleanor looked at him with sad eyes. "I'm sorry I wasn't there for you when your parents passed."

Hell, she looked like she was about to cry. "It was a long time ago, madam."

"Of course." Eleanor gave a suspicious sniff. "Excuse me. I will go check on supper." She left the room with her head bowed.

Penelope finally joined the conversation. "How is Lady Olivia?"

She knew about Olivia? She seemed to know a lot more about him than he did of her. "My sister is preparing for her first Season, and she's excited to meet you." He gave a faint smile, relieved to be talking about something other than his mother.

"And when will that meeting be?" Dr. Walker asked, eyeing their entwined hands.

"As soon as possible. I procured a special license before leaving London, and I have brought it with me in the event that Penelope agrees to marry me."

"She hasn't agreed?" Colin asked, his eyes curious.

Everyone looked at Penelope, their expressions all asking the same question.

Lucas saw the dangerous spark in Penelope's hazel eyes, and he acted swiftly to prevent her from causing any sort of mischief. "She told me she deserves to be courted properly, and I completely agree," he said, reciting one of the lines of dialogue Penelope had suggested in her note. "That means we'll also have some time to get to know each other a little better before we marry."

"Well, it would certainly be nice for you to get to know us, son," Dr. Walker intoned. "But we already know all there is to know about you."

Dr. Walker grinned when he gave a start. "You didn't know that, did you? Our Polly has researched you as thoroughly as she does our medical cases. Of course, that was years ago, when we all believed you were going to come for her." Dr. Walker scowled. "You are very late, Ravenstone."

Lucas felt an odd sense of loss when Penelope let go of his hand.

"Really, Papa," she said. "That comment is hardly appropriate for polite conversation."

He claimed Penelope's hand again, knowing it would be advantageous to show a united front. Besides, he liked holding her hand. But he owed her stepfather an explanation. He gave it now without hesitation. "I apologize for not coming here sooner," he said sincerely. "If I had known I would be welcome here, I would have come years before."

"Years before?" Dr. Walker echoed. "Don't you mean before you became known as Raving Ravenstone?"

"Papa!" Penelope burst out. "That is enough. I would not have you or anyone refer to his lordship by that horrible name. I'll have you remember he's our guest here."

At that moment, Eleanor reentered the room. "Supper is ready," she announced with a smile. "Ravenstone, why don't you escort Penelope?"

"I would be honored, Mrs. Walker," he murmured as he helped Penelope to her feet. He waited for everyone to begin entering the dining room before moving. "Your stepfather does not seem to be fond of me," he whispered to her.

"He's a good man," she whispered back. "He's just been working really hard the past couple of years, and he's always tired."

She glared at him. "Besides, he didn't say anything untrue. You did take much too long to come for me."

"I know, my dear," he admitted. "But I am here now, and I pity any fool who would try to take you from me."

Her eyes narrowed suspiciously. "Is that supposed to be a romantic vow or a threat?"

He chuckled. "Take it whichever way you wish, sweetheart."

If her family thought it was odd that Penelope entered the dining room frowning while his shoulders shook with mirth, they seemed to have finally found their manners and did not comment upon it. If things progressed as smoothly as they had tonight, his inheritance and the future of the Ravenstone family line would be secured.

• • •

Supper with the Walkers had been less awkward than Lucas anticipated, due in no small part to Penelope's remarkable conversational skills. She listened attentively to those who spoke to her, then gave witty replies, which consisted of a combination of intelligence, subtlety and frankness.

The Walkers, for their part, apparently had expected Lucas to come for Penelope, and now that he was here, seemed willing to forgive and forget the length of time it took him to do so. Even Dr. Walker seemed to bend enough to offer a desultory comment or two to the dinner conversation.

When the ladies and Colin departed to let the gentlemen have their port in the dimly lit library, however, the uncomfortable silence returned.

Lucas took a sip from his glass, looking around the room for an inspiration to break Dr. Walker's reticence. His gaze took in the shelves filled with books lining the moss green walls, then wandered to the faded rug and the equally faded rose-colored furniture that he and the doctor sat on opposite the hearth. He noticed the shiny suit of armor standing at the end of one of the bookshelves.

"A family heirloom?" he asked, tipping his head toward the coat of mail.

Dr. Walker followed his gaze and sighed. "No," he answered. "That came with this house, which my father won in a game of cards." He gave Lucas a direct look. "I apologize if I seem less than honored to have you in our house, my lord, but I cannot pretend this situation is normal."

He nodded, accepting the apology. He had little choice but to accept it. "I understand."

"I've tried to take care of my family as best I could, but I have no doubt you've already surmised we are in a somewhat difficult situation at the moment." Dr. Walker paused to take a healthy swallow of his port. "I will not deny it. My father was a gambler. It was his occupation, don't you know. His winning streak paid for my education and provided us with this house. As a rule, however, a winning streak is called that because it is supposed to end. You've seen our house. I am afraid repaying my father's gaming debts when he died meant I could not provide a dowry for my daughters, nor keep my son in school."

Penelope's stepfather put his glass down and looked at his hands, held palm up in front of him, like a man who knew he was defeated but was valiantly refusing to give up fighting.

"I would work all day and all night if I could, to bring my family out of this mess. But I know in the end we would still be in debt. I am stuck in this situation." The doctor sighed. "I work, and I work hard, answering summons across the county. Meanwhile, my children are growing up. I am deprived of seeing the smiles and tears that constitute their lives. I will continue to be deprived, if I want a better life than this for them."

Dr. Walker rose to pour more port from the decanter. "I've no doubt you have your opinions about the way I have provided for Penelope, my lord, but I assure you she has been educated and raised as befits her status. Do not judge us by the current condition of our dwelling."

"Dr. Walker," he replied, putting his glass down on the low table in front of the settee. "Let me make one thing clear to you. I did not come here expecting Penelope to have a large dowry, and I do not need her to have one. My family has had its share of financial difficulties, and I understand the consequences of such a situation. All I ask is to be given the respect due me as your stepdaughter's fiancé, and we shall get along nicely."

The man looked surprised and then distinctly suspicious. "I thought you'd forgotten about my Polly. I don't know what game you are playing, Ravenstone, but if you hurt my stepdaughter in any way, you will deal with me."

He narrowed his own eyes with impatience. "I've come here to marry Penelope, and I intend to do exactly that."

Dr. Walker stared into his glass. "I confess I've become quite worried about her," he whispered after a moment. "The men in the village are too ignorant to recognize her wonderful qualities." He gave Lucas a speculative look. "Her defense of you in the drawing room encourages me. If you're here to do your duty, my lord, I won't stand in your way. Polly needs a husband. She deserves to have her own family. She can't go on living this way for long."

"She doesn't seem to agree with you, sir, but I'll change her mind if you'll let me."

The other man turned, glass still in hand, and started to extend his other hand. "Well, that settles that then, don't you think?"

"Not entirely," he said, rising to his feet as well. "There are some things I would like to know, sir, if you would be so kind as to answer my questions."

Dr. Walker's gray brows rose in astonishment, but he nodded and dropped his frame on the faded green wingback chair adjacent to the settee.

Lucas watched the doctor sit down and get comfortable before walking to the hearth to stoke the fire, which had nearly died down. "I would like for you to tell me what you know of the current Baron Maitland," he said in a no-nonsense voice as he concentrated on prodding the fire with a poker. "Why has he not provided for Penelope and her mother? One would think Penelope's father left some provision for them in his will."

"None whatsoever, my lord." Dr. Walker sighed. "I know Edmund Maitland was your father's friend, but the truth is he rarely visited Eleanor and his daughter while he was alive. He spent his days in London and died in a carriage accident with his mistress when Penelope was ten. We started calling her Polly after I married her mother, to make the transition to her new life easier."

His hand stilled in the act of putting the poker away. "And the current baron? Is he in residence at the moment?"

"I think he is," Dr. Walker replied. "He's been known to ignore the London Season and stay in the country sometimes. Are you planning a visit?"

"I doubt there is any need to visit the baron," he said with cool satisfaction. "I'm content to let sleeping dogs lie for a little bit longer. He will hear of the wedding soon enough."

"Then why were you so concerned about the baron?"

He turned to face Dr. Walker. "Because I believe Penelope's father, with the current baron's help, deliberately hid my fiancée from me when my family's fortunes took a downward turn." He knew his smile was cold. "It will be interesting to see Maitland's reaction when he finds out I've married his niece, after all."

"Well, this news comes as no surprise. I daresay Polly's father was a coward for trying to weasel out of the betrothal contract.

Then again, he lived his life trying to weasel out of a lot of things, don't you know, including being a husband and father."

Lucas inclined his head in a respectful gesture. "From what I have learned since coming here, I owe you a great debt of gratitude, Dr. Walker. You have raised Penelope and treated her as your own."

Dr. Walker grinned. "With all due respect, Ravenstone, I believe your debt of gratitude is a mite premature. Polly hasn't agreed to marry you yet."

"She will," he promised.

Chapter Five

Penelope sat in the library, watching Ravenstone eat the last of the scones Gertie had brought in along with the tea.

She'd eaten a fair bit of the scones herself, but with the plate empty, she lost her only excuse to delay giving Lucas the invitation Papa had ordered her to extend before her stepfather left this morning on his rounds. Whatever Lucas and her stepfather talked about in this room last night, it had obviously swayed Papa to the earl's side.

There was nothing for it but to forge ahead. It would be better to get it over with, before they left for their walk in the village green. Yet Penelope found herself delaying once more. "Were the scones to your liking, my lord?"

Ravenstone leaned back on the settee, his eyes as dark as dueling pistols, glinting in the light from the window as he watched her with what looked like amusement. "They were very fine, nymph."

"*Nymph?*"

"Mmmm," he said thoughtfully. "You remind me of a forest nymph, my dear. I thought it the first time I met you. Even more so today, actually. Your ice blue gown calls to mind a clear sky on a winter morning in the woods."

It irritated her that he called her "nymph" and "my dear," as if he assumed their relationship had developed to a level where he could casually use affectionate nicknames. The thrill she got from the way he called her those endearments irritated her even more.

She clasped her hands in her lap and studied him, noting his elegant coffee-brown coat and trousers that hugged his powerful build as he lounged on her settee. He looked exactly as she had imagined he would all those years ago. Tall and proud, with features as fierce as his warrior ancestors. Everything about him screamed strength, power and control. She couldn't see how people ever thought of him as "Raving Ravenstone."

Surely, the epithet had more to do with his mother than Lucas himself. Penelope could only imagine what it had been like for him, raised by a mother famous for her extreme mood swings. How had it felt when she locked herself in her room for days, attacked by her frequent bouts of melancholia?

What had it been like to have a heartbroken widower of a father suddenly taken from him in a hunting accident, leaving a boy in charge of a dwindling estate and a two-year-old girl?

No wonder Ravenstone held onto his control with ruthless discipline. Many of the things that happened in his life had been beyond his control, including their betrothal.

Her smile was sad when she replied to his comment. "I am no nymph, my lord. I'm merely an ordinary woman trying to make the best of things that have been handed to me." She took a deep breath and slowly released it. "Which brings me to the reason I invited you here before we go for our walk in the village green."

Penelope raised her head to meet his midnight eyes. "I am to tell you that Papa would be delighted if you were to stay with us here in Highfield Manor for the duration of your visit. We are, after all, engaged. I am sure you will find your accommodations here much more comfortable than The Mucky Duck."

The look of smug satisfaction on his face made her add her own conditions. "You are, however, to keep in mind that we have a set budget for things such as food, candles and firewood. I doubt Papa thought about that when he invited you to stay with us." It was difficult to keep a straight face when his dark brows met in dismay. "We will, of course, need to ration our resources—eat smaller meals, use fewer candles and such—to make certain the entire household gets to have those necessities."

"You are enjoying this, are you not?"

She sat just a little bit straighter on the settee. "What do you mean, my lord?"

He made a gesture that encompassed the whole house. "Being in charge. Do not worry, nymph, I will make a contribution toward my lodging."

"You don't have to do that, sir."

"And you don't have to call me 'sir,'" he stated in a voice typically reserved for announcing royal edicts. "I am only six years older than you are, and yesterday you called me Lucas. Considering the kiss we shared, I think we are past titular ceremony, don't you?"

She tried to hide the blush his words brought by brushing imaginary lint from her skirts. "If you insist."

"I do."

"Very well, then." Heavens, she didn't know how much longer she could talk without addressing him as anything at all.

It was disconcerting how he seemed so at ease discussing their kiss, as if the topic were on the same level as the weather. For him, kissing must be so commonplace that it was nothing more significant than the state of atmospheric humidity. An attractive, titled gentleman would have no shortage of women volunteering to kiss him.

She frowned. Her lack of experience and his obvious amusement was making her edgy.

Still, for the next few days, this enigmatic man would be courting her. His blatant masculinity made her feel very feminine; she might as well enjoy it. She just had to remember to keep her heart in check, because she had no intention of letting him break it again.

"Are you ready to leave?" she asked. "It's good to be visible at this time of day, when the village is at its busiest."

"Why do you want to be on display?"

"I told you, it's best if people saw us together. When we break the betrothal, they'll assume it's because our personalities didn't suit, not because we hated each other on sight."

"And once they see us together, your stepfather's creditors would be more amenable to extending the loan repayment schedule," he stated flatly.

Penelope started. Astonished, she caught his predatory look. "What did you say?" she croaked.

"You heard me," Lucas drawled, openly relishing her chagrin. "Did you honestly think you'd be able to hide your little secret for long? That I wouldn't figure it out?"

She squirmed beneath his intense gaze. "I planned to tell you about it."

"When?"

"After the loan's been repaid," she confessed.

Lucas chuckled at her admission of guilt, but he refused to relent. "How long have you been using my name to delay the repayment process?"

"Not very long."

"Define 'very.'"

"Six months," she bit out, deciding there was no reason to dissemble further. "If it makes you feel any better, my lord," she continued when she noted the earl's self-satisfied look, "using your name wasn't my first choice. I originally planned to claim I was engaged to a bold, virile, honorable shipping magnate whom I would marry upon his return from the high seas."

Lucas frowned.

She gave him a dazzling smile. "However, to my unbearable consternation, I remembered I was already betrothed to *you*. I, therefore, had no alternative but to adapt my story to the known history of my life." She shrugged. "It would have been more exciting to be the pretend fiancée of an adventurous shipping magnate, but I suppose one can't have everything."

"You do realize I could sue you for this," he warned.

"You do realize I had little choice in the matter," Penelope shot back. "I never meant for your lordship to be inconvenienced by my scheme. How was I to know you'd come galloping to Bouth?"

"I'm pleased to find you didn't mean to cause any inconvenience," he replied with sarcasm. "But the deed is done, and my name has been bandied about without my consent. Thus, I'm afraid I have to insist we modify our bargain's terms."

"What did you have in mind?"

His smile was thoroughly wolfish. "In return for participating in your scheme, you will agree to let me court you, and you will seriously contemplate accepting my suit."

Penelope blinked. "That's it?"

Something akin to pride lit his eyes. "Yes, nymph, that's it," he confirmed, his voice gentle, light. Caressing.

She stood up abruptly. "Well, that settles it then. If you would kindly wait here, I'll go upstairs to fetch my pelisse, and we can leave for our walk."

It was time to put on a show for people. A show—nothing more—but she vowed it would be the best one this village had ever seen.

• • •

Penelope was not oblivious to the looks the gentry were giving her and Lucas as they promenaded through the village green that afternoon. Everyone smiled at her, as always, but their gazes would skitter to the earl and then dart away.

For heaven's sake, she knew he had a reputation, but it was silly for people to act as if they expected him to explode into a fit of temper without any provocation.

It had been much better this morning, when they were going through the shops, buying supplies for Highfield Manor. The merchants did not care who bought their wares as long as they had enough blunt to pay for their purchases, and they were very happy to entertain the business of someone who looked like he could buy the entire shop.

Lucas's presence did make it harder to bargain, however. Mr. Wilkes, the butcher, had taken one look at the earl and gave her full price for the meat order. "Well, if that doesn't butter the crumpets," she muttered to Lucas as they left the butcher's. "Your presence is making the merchants less flexible with their prices. The meat cost me a third less the last time I visited here."

A corner of the earl's hard mouth curved into a half smile. "My apologies, nymph. Had I known you had a reputation for bargaining in these parts, I would have dressed in my jarvey attire."

She looked up at him with a hopeful expression. "Do you really have simpler clothes?" She paused. "Oh, I see. You find this funny. Well, laugh away, but don't blame me when we run out of candles before the week is through because your presence made the tallow more expensive."

"Since I seem to be the reason for driving the prices up," he murmured as he nodded his head to acknowledge a villager who crossed their path on the pavement, "it is only fair I shoulder the fee for the supplies purchased while I lodge with your family."

She gaped at him, overwhelmed by the generosity he was showing to an unwanted fiancée's stepfamily. "We are not destitute, my lord. I assure you, I manage our accounts very well. I would not have agreed to invite you to stay with us if I could not find a way to afford it."

The look of amused indulgence disappeared from his eyes. "Call me Lucas."

"Lucas," she said softly, noting that the muscles in his arm relaxed under her hand. "I do not want to cause you any more trouble than I already have." *And I won't let you bribe me into marrying you*, she added silently.

"It's no trouble." He stopped walking and turned her to face him. "I have neglected my duty to you for two decades. Let me make up for it by making it easier on you and your family while I stay with you."

"But—"

"Penelope," he said in a quiet but firm tone as they started walking again. "If you do not let me pay for these purchases, I will make the orders myself and have the bills sent to me."

"Well, if you plan to be that way about it—"

"I do."

"Suit yourself." She looked around the village square before grinning up at him as an idea took hold. "I just remembered there were some other things we needed to get at the grocer's."

He laughed, startling passersby and drawing attention to them. "You are not going to make me regret my offer, nymph."

"Hah!" she challenged. "We'll just have to see about that."

She had to admit that as great as it was to be in charge of the household, it was nice to have someone share the burden of the responsibility. It was if a great weight had been lifted off her shoulders. It had been a long time since she was able to walk into a shop without worrying about how much deeper in debt they would be by the time she walked out of there.

She enjoyed showing him around the village, pointing out the places she and Mari played as children and the tarn where the twins learned to fish. She thought he would find their childhood haunts too rustic, but he even pointed out a spot in the tarn where he thought the twins might have caught bigger fish. He was being very accommodating, and he deserved more than the wary stares the villagers had been giving him since they started their promenade.

Another neighbor passed them by in the village green without pausing to talk, and Penelope had had enough. "Mr. and Mrs. Neville, how nice to see you this fine afternoon!" she called out just as the elderly couple edged away.

Mrs. Neville halted in her tracks and faced Penelope with a nervous smile. "Good afternoon, Miss Maitland. I almost didn't see you there. How is your family?" The orange plumes in the lady's bonnet wobbled as she gave her husband a pointed look. "Orson, weren't you telling me how we needed to go home to make sure everything is in readiness for your cousin's visit?"

Mr. Neville looked confused. "My cousin isn't visiting until next month." He turned to Penelope. "You must tell Dr. Walker the tonic he prescribed for my cough worked wonders. And who is this fine young man with you, Miss Maitland?"

She gave her neighbor a grateful smile and handled the introductions. She'd always liked the henpecked Mr. Neville more than his wife. Lucas and Penelope promised to be at the county fair later in the week, and as the older couple walked away, she noticed Mrs. Neville whispering to her husband while giving the earl a furtive glance. One quick look at Lucas and she knew he saw it, too.

"Mrs. Neville is a rumormonger," she stated. "Now that she has seen us, it will only be a matter of time before the creditors are reassured. They might even decide to extend the time they've given us to pay yet again."

Lucas's features could have been carved in stone. "I would wager it's not the only gossip she is spreading," he muttered under his breath.

"Well, it would help if you smiled at people once in a while," she suggested.

Lucas turned to her so suddenly she would have surely been knocked over had he not reached out to steady her.

She saw the frown on his face and mimicked it. "See? Would anyone want to be introduced to me if I were looking at them like this?" She frowned harder.

"Are you teasing me, nymph?"

She nodded. "You have to relax a little. For heaven's sake, you are in the Lake District. One would think that would be enough to put a smile on your face."

Humor glinted in his dark eyes. "I have never 'wandered lonely as a cloud.'"

The reference to Wordsworth gave her pause. A walk in the Lakes had famously inspired that poem. Penelope had known Lucas was well read, but until that moment, she would never have thought he was the kind of man to quote romantic poetry.

"Ah," she said softly, "Therein lies the difference between us. For 'my heart with pleasure fills, and dances with the daffodils.'"

He chuckled. "What would fill my heart with pleasure is a respectful wife."

She had to laugh at that one. "You're getting impatient, aren't you? Why don't you escort me home so I can arrange to have your bedchamber readied? You should be able to move in first thing tomorrow."

"Will you be waiting in the bedchamber to welcome me?"

Her eyes widened at his boldness, unsure of what to say. Should she reprimand him? He probably wanted her to do so. Was that why he said it? Would that be flirting?

His gaze dropped to her lips for a few seconds before he looked away after shaking his head, as if to clear it.

Flustered, Penelope retreated behind the veil of humor. "You've made me wait for you for two decades, Lucas. I don't think you're in any position to demand where I do the waiting."

He chuckled. "Very well, nymph, let me take you home."

They walked in companionable silence, greeting villagers who passed them by. Neither of them commented on the subtle change in their relationship as Lucas possessively held her hand, caressing her palm with his gloved finger.

When they reached Highfield Manor, he kissed her hand lingeringly before striding away. She silently watched him leave, pressing the hand he'd kissed to her cheek.

Chapter Six

Penelope faced her family's creditors three days after Lucas moved into Highfield Manor. She had been at the barn feeding Nelson and the chickens when Gertie appeared to tell her the news.

"They want to see ye, miss," Gertie said, wringing her apron. "I put them in the library, since Lord Ravenstone now uses yer father's study for his business during the day." Gertie leaned closer. "I hope ye don't mind, Miss Penelope, but I gave them some of the jam tartlets Miss Mari brought over for ye to taste this morning."

The first thing she felt was outrage that the creditors were enjoying Mari's jam tartlets before she'd had a chance to do so herself, and then panic set in. "What did they look like, Gertie?"

The question clearly perplexed the maidservant. Her wrinkled face scrunched up until Penelope could barely see her eyes. "They looked same as always. Both of them wearing fancy clothes. Mr. Stickford is still fat, and Mr. Henson still has brown hair—"

"I meant," she interrupted, careful not to tread on the clucking hens around her feet as she took her own apron off and started walking to the house. "Did they look happy or serious or—"

"Oh," Gertie's face cleared as she followed Penelope back to the house. "Well, as to that … they looked impatient."

Penelope halted in her tracks. "Impatient?"

"Aye," Gertie averred. "I was jest tryin' to delay them, so they could talk to the lord earl himself, what with his lordship out somewhere with Master Colin, but they di'n't appreciate my story about the gourd that grew into a rude and amusing shape."

Penelope almost laughed. "Oh, Gertie. You're a treasure."

"Aye, I'm a treasure all right. But I doubt anyone other than yerself would hire a clumsy old lady like me. If we lose this house, I've nowhere to go, miss. I don't have any family or nothin'."

"We are not going to lose Highfield Manor," she declared as they reached the house, although her usually strong nerves were, indeed, rattled by the creditors' appearance. "How do I look?"

Gertie scrutinized her features for a long minute. "Same as always, I would say. Still short, with brown hair and—"

"Never mind," she said, reaching for the library door. "Wish me luck."

"Oh, I do, Miss Penelope. I do."

Mr. Stickford and Mr. Henson rose from the settee as she walked into the library.

"Good afternoon, gentlemen," she said with as much poise as she could muster. "I trust you enjoyed the jam tartlets? My good friend made those especially for me."

"Miss Maitland," Mr. Stickford murmured. "You seem to be doing well."

"Does that surprise you?" she asked while she took a seat on the wingback chair by the fire. Mr. Stickford was not so bad, really; it was Mr. Henson who made her nervous.

"To be truthful, it does," Mr. Stickford replied as he sat back down on the settee with Mr. Henson.

"What Mr. Stickford is trying to say, Miss Maitland, is that we've heard Raving Ravenstone is in the village." Mr. Henson gave her a direct stare. "Surely you know your fiancé has a, shall we say, unsavory reputation?"

She stiffened. "No one is to call my fiancé that horrid name in my presence. Is that understood, Mr. Henson?"

Mr. Henson's brows rose, making him look like a startled rat. "We are only trying to make sure our bargain is still in place. Now that the earl is here, we are assuming your family no longer needs an extension."

Her stomach reeled with dread. "What do you mean?"

"I mean, Miss Maitland, we have been extremely patient thus far, and our patience is at an end."

"Well, this is unexpected."

"No doubt," Mr. Henson agreed. "But then so is the fact that we are dealing with you instead of your stepfather or your fiancé. Surely this is a man's business, and I've had enough of your delaying payment." Mr. Henson sneered at her. "Does Lord Ravenstone even know about the dire situation your family is in?"

She bristled. "Of course he does. He's my fiancé."

"Then why isn't he here to talk to us?"

"He isn't here," she replied, her voice crisp as a dawn breeze, "because this is a matter for my family to settle. Since my stepfather and mother are away, I am acting in their stead." She crossed her arms over her chest. "I'm afraid you're going to have to deal with me, whether you like it or not, Mr. Henson."

Mr. Henson gave her a look of distaste. "Such atrocious manners. No wonder your uncle threw you out of Maitland Hall."

She let that insult pass. "Is there any way we could talk of an extension? I promise you we'll be able to come up with the money."

Mr. Henson's greedy eyes gleamed. "There is one way I can give you an extension." He gave her a scathing look. "There's nothing you can offer I would want, but your pretty little sister might be able to sway me."

"You will stay away from my sister, Mr. Henson."

Mr. Henson blinked. "I fail to see why you are being so missish. My proposal is no different from the Smithfield bargain you have with Ravenstone." The sly smile on his gaunt features transformed his face from that of a startled rat to a disgusting lizard. "It's definitely a far better deal than what your little Sarah will have if you don't pay up. She'll end up selling her services on the streets before the year ends."

"Get out," Penelope said quietly. She had known Mr. Henson was reprehensible but until now, she didn't actually think he was a monster. She recalled that Mr. Henson was rumored to have exotic appetites, and it had landed him on the dueling field more than once. Since he was alive and well, sitting in her library, she could only assume he'd gotten away with his sins. How could Grandfather have stomached dealing with this man?

"Out?" Mr. Henson was incredulous. "This is to be my house soon. There is no way your family can make the payment on time."

"Your house?" she asked. "Aren't you forgetting Mr. Stickford?"

"He owed me money, and I've agreed to take his share of the profits from your grandfather's loan as payment."

Penelope stood. "It is not your house yet, Mr. Henson. Now, leave. You can come back when you feel more polite."

Mr. Henson slapped his hat on his head. "I'm leaving. But I will be back in two days, and I expect payment then." He walked out of the room. Mr. Stickford gave her a helpless look before silently following.

As soon as the door closed behind them, she collapsed on the wingback chair. Her mind reeled as she tried to come up with solutions and delaying tactics, but none seemed to be forthcoming.

Her little scheme hadn't worked. She had let everyone down, and they were on the verge of being homeless. Her family, Gertie and the rest of the servants, Nelson and the animals in the barn—all of them trusted her, and she had failed them.

Her gaze fell on the suit of armor adorning a corner in the library.

She had to find Lucas.

• • •

A shot rang out through the valley, agitating the birds pecking peacefully on the ground.

"Nice shot, Ravenstone!" Colin remarked with an admiring smile.

Lucas lowered his pistol. "I aim to please," he quipped. "It's your turn. Remember what I told you: use the bump at the end of the barrel as a guide to the target."

At Colin's nod, he continued with his instructions. "Now, lift the pistol until the target is sitting on top of the bump."

As the lad lifted the pistol, he added, "Slow and steady, Colin. I don't want you accidentally blowing your head off." He watched Colin adjust his aim. Lucas had been tutoring Penelope's brother in the library for most of the three days since he moved into Highfield Manor. Today, however, the lad seemed as frustrated as Lucas was of being indoors, so he decided to take Colin outside for some target practice.

"It's really kind of you to teach me how to shoot. When the boys in the village find out, maybe they'll let me join their hunting parties."

He glanced at the boy. "It was nothing. You're the man of the house while your father is at work, so you have to know how to protect your women."

"I would much rather spend time outside the house," Colin muttered. "Polly and Sarah are good fun, but all my friends are at school." He shrugged. "Someday, I'll be able to go back."

Lucas had been only a year older than Colin when Father had killed himself and he'd had to stop going to school to take over the estate. It had taken a few years before he was able to go to university. He realized Colin must be as lonely as Lucas had been at that age, with tons of responsibility and no one to talk to. Colin needed to learn to be a man, and no one was there to show him how.

In the beginning, Lucas thought of tutoring the boy as merely a way to pass the time while he rusticated in the country, but it had soon become clear his future brother-in-law had a sharp mind.

It was a shame Colin had to quit school, Lucas thought as he began reloading his pistol.

Once he and Penelope were married, he'd make certain the boy got the proper education he deserved. He told himself it was only practical to make sure his future wife's family was educated decently. They were to be associated with his family, after all. It was, therefore, imperative they have a status of living that was beyond reproach. But it was impossible to remain unmoved when every day Lucas saw how the family pulled together to make ends meet.

He'd never seen such a united group, and they welcomed him into their fold as if it were his due. It had been a long time since he had belonged to any sort of group—he'd felt comfortable and safe in his solitary ways.

But the eccentric Walkers would have none of his self-imposed isolation. They knocked on his door. They asked him for advice. They politely ordered him about. They made him feel accepted, as though he had nothing to prove to them.

If only he could feel accepted by his fiancée.

He scowled. He'd been the perfect gentleman for the last few days, trying to convince Penelope to trust him, and he'd never been more frustrated in his entire life. He'd dared to do nothing more than hold her hand in public, and she'd avoided him in private. As a result, he had developed an unhealthy fixation with those hands of hers.

He obsessed about how perfectly they fit in his and the softness of her creamy skin. He'd seen the gentle way those hands healed her clients' ungrateful cattle, and he'd grown hot and hard as a rock each time he saw those hands stroking her patients. She had such pretty hands.

Lucas wanted those hands on him.

He dreamed about having his mouth on those elegant fingers, licking and sucking them until she moaned. He ached to kiss that adorable little scar on the back of her left hand, the one she got when a neighbor's nervous cat scratched her. To have her delicate little fist wrapped around his—

He groaned and looked out over the sleepy rolling hills of Highfield Manor and the bordering woodlands beyond. The woman was driving him mad! Just like the goddess Circe, whom she resembled, his fiancée had turned him into a beast. If he didn't take caution, she'd have him begging for her touch like her slobbering, besotted border collie.

Another shot rang out, interrupting his thoughts.

"I missed!" Colin groaned.

Lucas shifted his gaze to the target. "That's common for beginners. Here, try again." He handed over his pistol.

Colin looked at him curiously before taking it. "Can I ask you something, Ravenstone?"

"As long as the question doesn't involve where babies come from," he replied, half-serious.

"What will you do if Polly decides not to marry you?"

Damn. He thought Colin wanted to ask him something about shooting. "She *will* marry me."

"But what if she—"

"She'll marry me," he repeated in a firmer tone. Then he gave Colin an amused look. "You don't seem to hold a lot of faith in my abilities."

"It's not that. Well, you must have noticed Polly's not like most women," Colin remarked, checking his pistol. Then he looked straight at Lucas. "Why do you want to marry her?"

Wasn't the answer obvious? "She's my fiancée."

"Yes, but you didn't ask for her. Surely there are other women you can marry. Prettier ones. Ones who are not so bossy. Or eccentric. Or poor." The last bit was said in a low voice that, nevertheless, hinted of wounded dignity.

"Or have insolent little brothers," he added to the list. "I've made my decision to marry your sister. So it doesn't matter what other women are like, does it?"

"I s'pose," Colin shrugged, finally turning to face the target.

He let out a breath, glad the questioning was over. He could hardly say he was marrying Penelope because he needed a wife to retain his estates and fulfill Father's need for vengeance as stated by the terms of his will. And the thought of her marrying someone other than him twisted Lucas's stomach into knots.

He had to change tactics. Perhaps he should stop playing the gentleman and just compromise her. Slake his thirst. She would have no choice but to marry him then. That would end his stupid obsession with her. He wouldn't be spending endless nights pacing outside her bedchamber, torturing himself with images of her in bed, sleeping. He would finally be able to go back to his orderly life.

But the nymph would be his. Permanently. He smiled at the thought. It would serve the scheming little chit right.

Perhaps, once they were married, Penelope would learn to care for him with the same devotion she showed her family and the animals she cared for. The thought of her worriedly nursing him back to health with kisses and caresses made his blood sing.

A shout from somewhere in the direction of the manor made both him and Colin whirl toward the sound. And there, standing in the middle of the open field with the sunlight caressing her lovely, indignant features, was the object of his obsession.

"What is going on out here?" Penelope demanded as she strode toward them.

Colin backed up, tripping on the picnic basket Cook had insisted they bring with them. "Ravenstone was teaching me how to shoot, so I can protect you while Papa's away on his rounds with patients," he answered when she reached them.

She bristled. "You never needed to shoot before, and you don't need to now!" She snatched the pistol from her brother's hand, ignoring Colin's protests.

Lucas was suddenly paralyzed with fear. Penelope was holding a loaded pistol, clearly with no idea how to handle it. He'd seen young men injured, and worse, from such a stupid act.

"Polly," Colin cajoled, holding his hands up. "I can assure you Ravenstone is knowledgeable with firearms—"

She whirled on Lucas like an enraged woodland fairy, her faded ivory and sage gown swirling around her. "You should have known better than to give my brother a dangerous weapon!" She brandished the pistol in his direction.

Good God, she looked amazing when riled. Her hazel eyes shone bright in the midday sun, and her cheeks were flushed pink. Her pretty breasts heaved with each angry breath that passed through her parted lips. Would she be as fiery in his bed? He was certain she would be.

"I can't believe you'd do this, Colin!" Penelope choked out, hysterical. "When I think of how I felt hearing those shots, and then *seeing* you with a pistol—" She waved the weapon again.

Another shot rang through the valley. This time it was accompanied by an astonished howl of pain. His.

"Oh my God," Penelope whispered.

"You shot him!" Colin cried.

"Oh my God ... " Penelope repeated.

Lucas held his left arm, aware that he was more shocked than hurt. The little idiot had *shot* him!

Penelope laid the pistol carefully on the ground then slowly approached as he continued to clutch his arm, his bewilderment slowly giving in to simmering rage.

She swallowed. "Lucas? Let me look at your arm." She reached for him but stopped when he let her see his thunderous expression.

"If you are wise, Penelope," he warned, "you will run as fast as you can and avoid me for the next fifty years."

She seemed to register the threat in his voice. "Don't be silly, Lucas. Let me have a look at your arm." She walked toward him again.

"Ummm, Polly ... maybe you should heed his lordship's advice," Colin croaked.

"Lucas will never hurt me."

She seemed so certain of her opinion, and only she knew why. In the mood he was in, he was likely to throttle her if she came any nearer.

"You shot me," he said quietly.

"Yes, but I didn't mean to. I swear it. I'm sorry, Lucas." She gave him a helpless look. "I wanted to talk to you about something, and I shouldn't have got all riled up. Please stop glaring at me."

"You *shot* me!" he roared.

"I know. I'm really sorry," she said in a soothing tone.

Oddly enough, her gentle voice started to work on him like a balm. Then the absurdity of the situation hit him.

"You're *sorry*?" he sputtered. "You don't *apologize* after you've shot someone." He advanced on her. "People apologize after they've spilled someone's drink, or stepped on someone's toes." He took a deep breath, trying to regain control. It didn't work. "*You don't apologize after you've shot someone!*"

He felt the blood seep through his sleeve and fingers. His wound clearly needed attention.

Penelope was apparently of the same opinion. "Let me have a look at your arm, Lucas. Please, darling."

He shot his gaze to Colin, who stood there frozen. "Go and take the pistols back to the house, lad. Your sister and I have some matters to discuss."

The boy nodded and seized on the excuse to get out of there.

When Colin had disappeared, his fiancée approached him carefully. "You have to take your coat off. I need to see how badly you're hurt."

He couldn't resist growling at her, but he obliged.

She let out an anguished cry. He looked down and saw his white shirtsleeve soaked with blood.

"It's only a flesh wound. The bullet barely grazed me. Don't swoon," he warned darkly.

She grew indignant. "I *never* swoon. I've seen bloodier wounds, believe me." She reached into her reticule for her medicines then added, "You have to take off your waistcoat and shirt."

"You'll have to help me," he replied, pulling on his cravat.

There was a picnic basket and a folded blanket on the ground. Penelope spread the blanket out, asked him to sit on it, and took a healing salve from her reticule before turning back to face him.

Lucas stared back at her expectantly, his hand still gripping his arm to staunch the blood.

"We'll need a tourniquet for that wound," she announced, looking around her for something that would be appropriate to use, and grimaced.

She would have to use her petticoat. It was the only thing clean and absorbent enough to do the job, and they both knew it. He watched her closely, waiting to see what she would do.

She didn't hesitate about her actions; she just turned her back on him and lifted her skirts, tearing strips off her petticoat.

He could hardly believe *this* was happening. The nymph was out in the woods with him, nursing him back to health. His well-being seemed to be the only thing she was focused on. All thoughts of whatever had brought her out here in the first place had been forgotten.

How many hours had he fantasized about this? To have those beautiful, healing hands on him? Lucas would gladly shoot his other arm himself. And she'd called him *darling*. Did she even realize that?

Penelope unbuttoned his waistcoat, and he groaned.

"Is it aching?"

Oh, yes, it's aching. Only "it" wasn't his wound. He squirmed, trying to hide his erection. She would surely kill him before this was finished.

"It's fine," he said tightly.

She tossed his waistcoat on the ground and started working on his shirt. Lucas gritted his teeth and clutched his wound tighter to keep from reaching for her.

She finished unbuttoning his shirt. "You have to let go of your arm so I can take the shirt off."

He obeyed with surprising speed; he even managed to grin. Getting shot was his greatest move yet. He should have known blood was the way to Penelope's heart.

• • •

Penelope couldn't believe he was acquiescing to her ministrations so readily. *What was he up to now?* She shoved his shirt off his shoulders and tossed it on the ground by his waistcoat. And she very nearly swooned at the sight of his bare chest. She'd never seen such a splendidly male torso. It was an expanse of hard muscle smattered with soft, springy hairs. She licked her suddenly dry lips. She had to keep her mind on her task.

She examined the wound on his upper left arm. It wasn't deep, but it needed to be cleaned and dressed. When she touched his wound, the muscles in his arm leapt and he let out a low hiss.

She stopped immediately. "Am I hurting you?"

"No," he rasped. "Go on and tend to me, Penelope."

Something in the way he spoke made her look at him sharply. What she saw took her breath away.

His eyes were blazing, and there was a dark hunger in his features that made him look like a starving beast, ready to devour her whole.

She cleared her throat and returned to cleaning his wound. *Why did he have to have this effect on her?* It wasn't fair. She was on the verge of losing her home, and all he had to do was give her one of his hot gazes and she came running.

It was this obsession with him that got her into this mess in the first place.

When she was satisfied that his wound was clean, she gently rubbed her healing salve on it, then she wrapped a strip of her torn petticoat around it.

"How's that?" she asked.

He looked at his arm and flexed it. "Excellent. You did a wonderful job."

She couldn't suppress a nervous chuckle. "Well, I can hardly leave you to bleed to death after I stupidly shot you." She met his midnight gaze, letting him see her sincerity. "I really am sorry for that. I don't know what came over me. One minute I was desperate to talk to you, but when I saw Colin holding that pistol, all I could think of was to get it away from him."

"I will never let anything hurt your little brother," he said quietly.

"I know. But we heal people, Lucas. It's what we do. I suppose that's why I overreacted to seeing my brother with a weapon that can hurt someone. I'm sorry."

She began apologizing again, but he put his index finger on her lips, silencing her.

He slid his finger from her lips and softly traced her cheek then cupped her chin, forcing her to keep her gaze on his.

"I'll forgive you," he murmured, "on one condition." He ran his thumb over her lower lip.

The touch made her shudder with anticipation. "What condition?" she whispered.

His eyes gleamed wickedly. "I'll forgive you only if you'll have lunch with me."

She stared at her fiancé, took in the invitation in his eyes and considered the basket of food on the ground. With the failure of her little creditor scheme, she might not have another chance to be with him again.

She nodded in agreement.

Chapter Seven

She sat on the blanket beside Lucas, sipping some wine while her mind reeled from the shock of the day's events. She put the wineglass down and buried her face in her hands to stop the world from spinning. She'd always tried to do the right thing by people, and now she seemed to be making mistakes left and right. Her family could lose their home because of her ruse. And she had very nearly killed an earl.

"Would you like to tell me about it?"

The question shook her out of her daze. Lucas appeared so calm sitting beside her, casually eating bread and cheese. Who would have thought he would look even more powerful when bared from the waist up?

She watched his mouth as he chewed, fascinated by how masculine he was, how he would be in control of any situation thrust upon him. It was evident even with the way he ate—there was purpose in his every bite, no action was wasted.

"We lost, Lucas," she finally made herself say. "Mr. Henson visited today and demanded his money. He'll be back in a few days to take over Highfield Manor."

"I thought you said our engagement would convince him to give your family an extension."

She gave a shaky laugh. "I thought so, too. It didn't work." She let out an anguished moan. "I don't know why I thought I could convince him. I failed, like I failed at convincing my uncle to let us stay at Maitland Hall when Father died."

"Calm yourself. You're getting overwrought."

"*Overwrought?*" she burst out. "I am more than overwrought, my lord. I'm one second away from losing my breakfast!"

He reached out and his large hand took hold of hers. His strength had a comforting effect. "Tell me what happened at the meeting with Henson."

She told him everything. He appeared calm until she got to the part about Henson's suggestion of using Sarah as a bargaining tool.

"The bastard!" he growled. He let go of her hand and started to get up. "I'll kill him."

"No!" She grabbed his fingers and pulled him back down. "You are not going to kill anyone. Really, is that the male answer to everything?"

One raven brow rose in challenge. "You think he doesn't deserve it for attempting to blackmail you into whoring out a child?"

She clung to him. His comment made an idea take root in her mind. It was going to be risky, but at this point, they had nothing to lose. If she were very careful in the execution of her plan, it might even work. It was so simple; Penelope didn't know why she hadn't thought of it before.

She grinned. "Of course he deserves it! Lucas, you're a genius."

He tucked an errant lock behind her ear. "I know." He got up. "So, where does this Henson live? I'm going to teach him a lesson about taking advantage of distraught women."

She got up, too. "You are not going anywhere near him. He's dangerous."

"You cannot stop me, nymph." He took a step toward the house.

She held his arm again before he could progress further. "Listen to me, Lucas. I know for a fact Mr. Henson has killed at least two men on the dueling field. Will you stop being angry for one minute and think, instead of acting like—"

His eyes turned as chilly as midnight. "Like Raving Ravenstone?"

She grabbed his other arm and shook him. "You will never call yourself that horrible name again, do you hear me?"

His lips twitched and his eyes gleamed with wry amusement. "You are one bossy bit of goods, did you know that?"

Without warning, he pulled her into his arms and covered her mouth with his. The kiss was soft, almost reverent in its tenderness, and Penelope gave herself up to the sweet shock of it as she had done the last time.

Lucas seemed to sense her willingness, for he growled his approval as he lifted his mouth to trail hot kisses down her sensitive neck. "I think you would make an excellent countess, sweetheart." He leaned over and pressed a kiss to her throat. "It would be an honor to be married to you."

She swallowed. "You seem awfully sure I'll marry you," she said shakily.

He touched his tongue to her beating pulse, making her jump. Then he straightened and looked straight into her eyes while his large hands cupped her face.

"Enough of these games," he said in a husky tone. "Will you marry me, Penelope?"

"I don't think we've had enough time to—"

She let out a strangled gasp when he suddenly tugged her down to the blanket and pulled her onto his lap.

"It looks like you need more convincing," he whispered, his hot breath wafting over her, sending a quivering sensation down her belly. Then he claimed her mouth with his, and she drifted her hands up his bare chest to link around his neck, offering herself up to him.

She dimly felt him unbuttoning her gown with a tenderness that was at odds with the wild hunger of his kisses. She'd been waiting to have him kiss her again and she was glad, *eager*, to let him do what he wanted with her, to feel the heady pleasure he gave her.

When he plunged his tongue deep in her mouth, she moaned with delight and held him tighter, loving the feel of his warm, naked skin beneath her hands. She started to move her hands over his broad shoulders, and he lifted his mouth from hers to kiss the area just below her chin.

"Yes. Touch me, my sweet nymph. Let me feel your hands on me," he rasped against her throat.

For once, the nickname he'd given her sounded apt, for Penelope felt rather like a wicked nymph enticing this warrior to share her world in the woods.

She wanted Lucas to be in her world. *She always had.*

Penelope let her hands skim down his back, his taut muscles leaping in reaction to her touch. She was so enthralled with the feel of his naked skin that she barely noticed him shoving her gown down to her waist. Then he pressed open-mouthed kisses down her neck and collarbone, and she stiffened at the new intimacy his caresses demanded.

"Lucas, are you sure … ?"

"Yes," he muttered. "Bloody hell, yes." His eyes were glittering with need. "I've wanted to do this since I first met you." He sucked her breast through her chemise, dampening the sheer fabric, tonguing her nipple as he caressed the other one with his hand, fondling her flesh beneath the thin covering.

Penelope clutched his dark head, not knowing whether she was pulling him to her or pushing him away. All she knew was that Lucas was touching her in ways she never thought a man would want to. Especially not this handsome man who had finally walked into her life, turning it upside down, awakening a dormant part of her she hadn't realized was there until he coaxed it to life with his heated touch and demanding kisses.

He tugged her chemise down, exposing her breasts to his dark, hungry gaze. She squirmed on his lap in embarrassment, then stopped immediately when she heard him groan.

"Don't stop," he murmured hotly against the slope of her breast. He positioned her to sit fully on top of the hard bulge in his trousers, urging her to move as he sucked her breast so hard she cried out with the sheer pleasure of it.

"Do you like that, nymph?" he rasped against her skin.

"Oh, yes ... " she whispered.

"Should I do it again?" he asked, his tongue laving the sensitive tip of her breast, sending a delicious shiver up her spine.

"Please, Lucas ... " She pressed herself against him.

A choked laugh escaped him. "Anything to please you, sweetheart." Then he sucked at her breast again, making her moan.

Her hands gripped his shoulders, and she started to rub herself against his hard thighs shamelessly, straddling him, trying to ease the ache building up inside her that seemed to be concentrated on the damp area between her legs. She cradled his dark head as he released her erect nipple, and his mouth proceeded to suck at her other breast while he caressed the one his mouth just left with his hand, rolling her sensitized flesh between his fingers.

She was lost in the sea of desire that Lucas seemed determined to drown them in as his mouth tugged at her breast and his hands gripped her waist, urging her to keep rubbing against his aroused manhood.

"Yes, nymph. Like that ... God, that feels so good," he whispered against her breast.

Penelope sighed and closed her eyes to savor the feeling. *Good? It felt wonderful! So wonderful.* She held onto him, her head thrown back, giving him access so he could kiss his way up her throat and jaw then lick his way back down to devour her aching breasts once more.

She moaned deep in her throat when she felt him grip her hips more firmly, urging her to move faster. Pure instinct drove her now. She rubbed herself on him harder, faster, against the place she most wanted him as her heart thundered and she raced blindly, frantically, toward whatever it was he offered that she knew was just beyond her reach until ... he stopped.

"Lucas?" she whispered, lost.

He groaned as he kissed her mouth again. Hungrily, fiercely, deeply. He tore his mouth from hers and grabbed her hands, kissing each of her fingers. Then he lifted his head.

"Penelope," he said, his voice filled with regret. "We have to stop. Otherwise you won't have any choice but to marry me."

She opened her eyes and saw him before her, his eyes raking her naked breasts, exposed to him in the harsh midday sun.

Penelope squirmed, barely noticing his hiss as she slid off him, kneeled and turned her back to him as she started adjusting her chemise and gown. She had behaved like some doxy, and he surely would think her no better than one now that she'd proven herself to be a wanton.

She flinched when she felt his hands on her shoulders, then she felt him fastening the buttons of her gown at her back. The kiss he pressed on the nape of her neck did much to soothe her wounded feelings.

When he finished with her buttons, he pulled her between his thighs, wrapping his arms around her from behind, his chin rubbing the top of her head as they sat on the blanket, the gentle breeze ruffling her hair.

He kissed her temple. It was a gentle, tender caress. "You were wonderful, sweetheart," he said in a deep, reassuring voice. "There's no shame in what we did. It's only natural—it's obvious we desire one another."

Reassured, she snuggled in his arms. "Why did you stop? You didn't have to," she asked in a small voice.

His arms tightened around her. "Believe me, stopping was the hardest thing I've ever done," he said hoarsely. Then he sighed against her hair. "Our betrothal was not of our choosing, Penelope, but if we're to marry, I want it to be our decision. I will not ruin you to force you into marrying me."

• • •

Lucas realized he meant the words. He might have considered ruining her to force her hand merely an hour ago, but now he wanted more from her. He wanted her to marry him because she *wanted* to marry him.

He cursed himself for being a fool. But no matter how contrary it was to his own goal, he could not bring himself to force marriage on the sweet creature in his arms. Life had already forced too many things on her.

Penelope turned in his arms, facing him as she kneeled between his legs. "Thank you," she said simply.

Then she kissed him tenderly, sweetly. He responded instinctively, driving his tongue into her soft mouth until he felt his control slipping away again, prompting him to lift his mouth from hers. He couldn't take much more of this. It took all of his control to keep from laying her down on the blanket and taking her right there, in front of God and country.

"Penelope," he groaned, gripping her shoulders to keep her at arm's length. "You have no idea what you do to me, do you?"

Her smile was as bright as the sun framing her lovely form. "I think I have some idea."

She kissed his cheek, turned around again and snuggled against him, and all he could do was hold her against his chest. He wondered how long he could hold her before he snapped. But she felt so good in his arms, he couldn't bring himself to let her go. God, but she made him daft. What would it take to make this woman trust him?

Chapter Eight

Hugh Maitland sat in his study reading contracts of sale when he heard the door open.

"Ah, son, you're back early," he said to the well-dressed, tall, young man who had entered the study. "How was your trip from London? Have a seat." He gestured to one of the two red velvet chairs in front of his desk.

David Maitland's lean build, brown hair and hazel eyes marked him as the next Baron Maitland. Hugh was certain his son would do justice to the title, unlike Hugh's brother, Edmund. In all of David's twenty-eight years, Hugh had never had any reason to worry that his son would ever tarnish the Maitland name. But he had sent David to London for the Season, and the fact that he had returned home with the Season barely beginning was not a good sign.

David took a seat across from him, his features grim. "I have terrible news, Father. Ravenstone has found Penelope. All of London is talking about it. I thought it prudent to come here and tell you personally."

Hugh carefully set the contracts of sale aside. "So he has come. Edmund warned me of this. I would say that with Walker's current financial state, the idiot would welcome the devil himself if it would save that house of his.

"We cannot let your cousin wed that man. He is dangerous. I am quite certain he is bent on revenge."

"I doubt there is anything we can do about it." David sighed. "He is already in Bouth."

"He is out to get me," Hugh whispered. "He couldn't take it out on Edmund, and now I'm his target."

David stilled. "I thought we had not sent communication to Penelope all these years to protect her, not you."

"Do not be an idiot, son," Hugh muttered, shaking his head. "I couldn't care less what happens to the chit. This is about the Maitland name. The Ravenstone line is tainted. His father killed himself, you know."

David gaped at him. "Ravenstone's father died in a hunting accident. Everyone knows that. But I have heard rumors that Ravenstone himself is responsible."

Hugh shook his head again. "Leonard Drake died because Edmund backed out of the betrothal. Leonard killed himself, and now Ravenstone wants revenge. He will destroy us."

David stood up. "I have to warn Penelope."

Hugh slammed his fist on his desk. "It is you who should be warned, son. This is only the beginning. Ravenstone will make sure I end up a pauper, just like his father was when he killed himself."

"What about Penelope?"

"Devil take Penelope!" Hugh roared. "Her father started this mess! If Edmund had not agreed to the betrothal in the first place, we would not even be having this conversation."

"You care more about what Ravenstone will do to you than the damage he will do to an innocent young woman's life?" David's voice was so low that Hugh had to strain to hear him. "You didn't cast Penelope and Aunt Eleanor out to protect them, did you? You wanted to hide Penelope to protect your inheritance."

"This is the way of the world, son. One day, all of this will be yours. It is your duty to protect it."

David stood. "It is my duty to protect my kin, as it is yours, being the head of the family. It is high time I do so. I am going to visit her."

Hugh stood as well. "You stay away from her, son! You have to protect your inheritance! Don't you dare leave!"

David walked out of the study without a backward glance.

Hugh reined in his temper and went to the small table where the brandy decanter was laid and poured a glass.

Ravenstone was here. If Hugh didn't do something, it was only a matter of time before everything he'd worked for was taken away from him. Though Hugh had not been lucky enough to be the firstborn, he had always been the one to make sure the Maitland fortune was secure. He cursed his brother's soul to perdition for this new complication in his life.

All Hugh had ever wanted was to reestablish the Maitland name. He'd convinced Edmund to back out of the betrothal contract, which would have linked the family name to a tainted and impoverished line. Edmund never did think before acting. He did not deserve the barony.

It was Hugh who had always deserved the title. He'd been responsible for making sure his reckless brother did not squander away the family fortune. He'd worked hard to make sure his son had no taint of a scandal and had only the best education. He'd sent David to London to find the best of brides and to let the past finally rest.

His arthritic fingers trembled as they held onto the brandy glass. Ravenstone would not take away what he'd worked so hard for all his life. It was too bad the problems Edmund had brought to the family did not die with him, but Hugh was not afraid of Ravenstone.

He sipped his brandy as he thought of his next move.

• • •

"Are you sure this is going to work?"

Penelope sighed. "For the eleventh time, Colin, all I can say is that it *has* to work." She eyed the jam tartlets laid out on the low table in the library. "I wouldn't normally engage in such extreme practices, but this isn't a normal situation. Can you check with Gertie whether Mr. Henson has arrived yet?"

"I am sure Gertie will announce Mr. Henson's arrival." He looked anxiously from his seat beside her on the settee toward the door. "We should have thought of this before, really. If this works, then we wouldn't need Ravenstone anymore."

"We never needed Ravenstone to get us out of this mess." Penelope sighed again. "Don't tell him that, though. He likes to think he came here to save us."

Colin's gaze shifted to her. "You like him, don't you?"

God help her, she did. Who could not like a man with Lucas's integrity and sense of duty? He was helpfully advising Papa to get out of the financial hole he'd been living in for the past couple of years. With Lucas's advice on investments, Colin might yet have an inheritance. Her fiancé was what the nobility should be and almost never were: honorable, steady and dependable.

Any other man wouldn't have bothered to honor a betrothal contract in which both signatories were already dead, but here he was. Whatever else happened between them after this debacle, she had to remember to thank him for all the help he'd given to a family who, mere days ago, were complete strangers to him.

How lucky she was to have known someone like Lucas in her life. If only he wasn't here just to fulfill his duty. "Yes," she said, "he is a good man."

"So when are you marrying him?"

She was saved from having to form a reply when Gertie opened the door with a foreboding expression. "Mr. Henson is here to see you, Miss Penelope."

"Thank you, Gertie, please show him in." She turned to her brother. "You better leave. I shall tell you how it went later."

"I'll be right outside," he reminded her before walking out of the library.

Mr. Henson entered a few minutes after Colin left, his face as grim as the gray coat and trousers that hugged his thin form. He sat down without bothering to greet her and immediately scoffed down a jam tartlet.

"I trust," he said, while munching on the confection, "that you have come up with the money?"

She watched him swallow and waited until he'd grabbed another from the tray in front of him before speaking. "No, sir, but I have asked you to call on us hoping we can agree on some sort of bargain."

Mr. Henson emitted a sharp crack of laughter. "There's no chance of that, my dear. Unless you have reconsidered making your sister's services available to me, we have nothing to talk about."

"I will never let Sarah near a monster like you."

Mr. Henson paused in the act of grabbing yet another tartlet. "Such spirit. I must say, Miss Maitland, I have never before considered your charms to be palatable. I prefer my partners to be young, but your courage and determination is something I would like to breed into my future children. I am hopeful your sister has inherited those same traits."

He made a move to come closer to her, and Penelope held out a hand to stop him in his tracks. "I wouldn't do that if I were you, Mr. Henson."

"Why not? You want to save this house, don't you?" He licked his lips and walked slowly toward the settee where she was seated.

She looked at him steadily. "How are you feeling, Mr. Henson? Did you like those jam tartlets?"

Mr. Henson looked confused. "What do you mean, how am I feeling?" He glanced at the tray, and then back at her as an expression of horrified comprehension took over his gaunt features. "You murderous wench! You poisoned me, didn't you?" He sank on the chair and started breathing heavily.

She stood up and towered over him. "Some of the medicines my family makes can be poisonous if administered in large doses. I have the antidote to the poison you just ingested. But you have to take it within ten minutes or it will be too late." She held up a vial in one hand and a contract in the other. "Are you willing to bargain with me now, Mr. Henson?"

"You will pay for this," he choked out.

"Perhaps," she allowed. "But you will sign this contract if you want to live long enough to ensure that I pay for my actions. I will not give you the antidote otherwise. Besides, you'll find the terms are fair for everyone concerned. We pay you back in monthly installments and you get your money back within two years." She shook the antidote. "This is in your best interest, Mr. Henson. I suggest you act on it."

Penelope shoved the contract in front of him and he hastily signed it. Once she was certain everything was in good order, she walked to her stepfather's desk and shoved the contract in the drawer. "Thank you for your cooperation."

"The antidote," Mr. Henson rasped. "You said you would give me the antidote."

She turned back to him. "What, this?" She held up the vial again. "This is just lemonade. I did not poison you. You may leave now."

"You bitch!" he roared as he angrily strode to her.

"Take one more step toward my fiancée, and I will make sure you regret it." The chill in Lucas's voice from the doorway stopped Mr. Henson in his tracks. She watched Lucas walk into the library with deceptive calm. "Penelope might not have the stomach to hurt anyone, but I will have no trouble beating you to a bloody pulp if you dare to treat my future countess with such disrespect again."

The blood drained from the creditor's face as he looked up at Lucas. "Lord Ravenstone, I didn't believe you were actually here. Who would have thought an earl would really want to marry a—"

"If you are not out of here in two minutes," Lucas said in a clipped voice, "I will throw you out."

"Yes, my lord." Mr. Henson threw an anxious glance at Penelope and then clapped his hat on his head and started for the door.

Lucas turned to her, his dark eyes glinting with the sunlight coming in from the window. "Remind me never to refuse bargaining with you, nymph."

She felt her blush. Really, all the man had to do was look at her to make her tremble with awareness. It was irritating. "I was desperate, Lucas."

"And effective," he murmured.

She hesitated, clasping her hands behind her back as she walked to the settee. "Now that the trouble with Mr. Henson is solved, there is no reason for you to stay."

"I believe the notion makes you sad, nymph."

Penelope looked at him, memorizing his features. She answered him honestly. "It does. I shall miss you, Lucas. I feel lucky to have finally met you, my lord."

He barked with laughter and snatched her to him. "Do not fret so, little one. I am staying here. I told you I came here to marry you, and that's what I mean to do."

"What?" She put her hands on his chest. "Besides, didn't you hear what Henson said? He is still a threat to your safety."

He tipped her chin up and looked into her eyes. "I will not leave you to face him alone."

She tried to see affection in the dark pools of his eyes, but they merely glinted from the sunlight streaming through the window.

As he lowered his mouth to hers, it occurred to Penelope that she was becoming used to him claiming kisses, and though she knew it was dangerous to keep letting him do this, she let it happen anyway.

Because this was temporary. Duty was all well and good, but she wanted none of it in her own marriage. Her parents had married for duty, and it was a disaster; she could not force that on this man. Lucas was not hers to keep, but for a little while, she wanted to know what it would be like to be his as she had dreamed all those years ago. Penelope wanted this memory to keep, to reminisce about in the lonely years ahead.

So she closed her eyes and savored how good it felt to be in his powerful arms once more, and, as she met his kiss with all the passion and gratitude she felt, she let the dream begin.

Chapter Nine

"You are planning to have an affair with him."

After stating her conclusion, Mari continued stirring the beef stew she was cooking in The Mucky Duck's kitchen.

Penelope watched Mari's trim back and tried to peel the potato her friend had handed her five minutes ago. As far as Mari's opinion went, she thought it best to debate that choice of words.

"I am not planning an affair, exactly." She peeled another strip. It was not as easy as Mari made it look.

Mari sprinkled a dash of freshly ground pepper on the stew and gave it another stir. "What would you call it, then?"

Penelope concentrated on the potato. "A courtship."

Mari whirled with the ladle in her hand, pointing it accusingly. "A courtship that won't lead to marriage! The last I checked, that is called an affair."

The heat from the stove in the steamy kitchen felt suffocating. How could spending time in this place be Mari's idea of fun? The pungent aroma of the beef stew filled the room, and she longed to open the small window for some relief. Her hair clung to her sweaty temples as she struggled with the vegetable. Penelope was uncomfortable and miserable, and she didn't really want to argue semantics any longer. It was already all she could do to try to ignore the tiny voice in her mind telling her that what she was planning was wrong.

Lucas said this attraction between them was natural. But while she was still thrilled he'd admitted he was attracted to her, she was unable squelch the feeling that she shouldn't let him touch her so. Especially when she had no plans of marrying him.

How many other women had Lucas touched the way he did her? Well, it hardly mattered. He probably wouldn't tell her anyway, and she wasn't entirely certain she wanted to know. Because no matter the answer, it wouldn't change the fact that she wanted him. Desperately.

Now that the trouble with Mr. Henson was over, there was no reason for Lucas to stay, despite his assurances that he was determined to marry her. Unless she gave him a reason. If that was a sin, then she would just have to pray for forgiveness later. She simply couldn't bear the thought of Lucas leaving yet.

She resumed her efforts with the potato. "Call it whichever term you prefer. You will not change my mind." She lost patience with the task and yanked hard, narrowly missing nicking her fingers.

Mari finally noticed her struggles and took over. "You must peel with the knife pointed away from you," she advised. "That way, the knife's sharp edge will be pointing away from your fingers."

Penelope squelched a spurt of annoyance as she watched her friend peel away effortlessly at the dratted potato. There wasn't a single stain on Mari's apron, which was supposed to protect her pink day-gown. How could Penelope have a prayer of seducing Lucas when she couldn't even keep her gown tidy while doing nothing more significant than preparing tuber?

She scowled at her friend's pristine profile. "How can you enjoy doing this sort of thing? You know perfectly well one of the staff can take over this task."

Mari proceeded to cut the potato into perfect, small cubes. "I am an innkeeper's daughter. It comes with the territory." She stopped chopping for the moment. "I will not let you change the subject. You do not want to risk your reputation with this scheme, Polly. Mama says a woman's reputation is more important than her virtue."

Penelope shrugged. "Your mother says a lot of things. It is all well and good for someone like you—who has a reason to protect her reputation—to be worried about it. Everyone knows you have the pick of the entire male population in this county."

Mari grunted. "Oh, I have the pick of the lot, all right. I can choose between Martin who is a drunkard, a womanizer like Richard, or a wife-beater like Hamilton. Oh, and let's not forget the sweet but humorless Melvin." She gave her a pointed look. "Thanks, but I'd rather have my recipe book published than be a wife to any of those men."

Penelope contemplated the stew beginning to boil on the stove. "Oh, but you are a spinster *by choice*. Whereas, we both know I've always been doomed to be like Mad Sally. Even my father knew it. Why else would he have felt compelled to force a betrothal between two children?"

"What? That is not true! Mad Sally's world revolves around her cats," Mari pointed out. "Everyone likes you, and you have not been entirely without suitors. Remember Ethan Banks?"

She gave her friend a disgusted look. "Everyone likes me because I'm useful to them. I make sure their cattle are healthy, and I take in any unwanted ones." Her mouth quirked in a humorless smile. "And Ethan Banks told me he wanted to save my bloodlines from the clutches of Raving Ravenstone, then quickly moved on to courting you after he found out I have no dowry to speak of."

"He did? I don't remember him courting me."

She rolled her eyes as she got up to open the window. The room had become unbearably stuffy. "He sent you a couple bouquets of flowers, but you didn't notice them because that was the week of Mr. Farlam's daughter's ball, and the whole inn was filled with flowers from her beaux."

Mari had the grace to look chagrined. "All I remember from that ball is how your cousin told me that my sort had no business being friendly with a baron's daughter."

"Well, I don't understand what David's problem was. Your father owns half of Bouth. And doesn't David know your aunt is married to a knight?" She wisely refrained from mentioning Mari's father had also been disinherited by a duke for marrying a barmaid.

Mari waved a dismissing hand. "In case you didn't realize, Polly, your cousin's middle name should be Haughty, not Henry. I hope someone teaches him a lesson in humility one day." She cocked her head to the side. "But we were talking about you and your dangerous plan to ruin yourself. Let me warn you, your cousin would not approve either."

"I do not particularly care what David thinks. He was nice to me when we were children, but apparently being raised by Uncle Hugh has made him as big a snob as his father." She turned back as the breeze from the window cooled her nape. "I do not intend to grow old without knowing what passion is, and Lucas is the only man I've ever wanted to experience it with."

"Then why not marry him?" Mari burst out. "You're engaged to him, and he said himself he came here to marry you."

She gave her friend a sad smile. "I don't want to trap him into a marriage based only on a misplaced sense of duty."

"Misplaced?" Mari stood up with such force that the stool nearly turned over. She threw the diced potatoes into the simmering stew with a flourish. "The man is beholden to you. He owes you a marriage!"

"Precisely my point," she stated calmly. "He's living his life trying to make up for all the things his father failed to do, such as secure the family fortune and make sure Lady Olivia was raised properly." She bit her lip to stop it from trembling. "He deserves a wife who is more than just another item on his list of duties."

A look of sad comprehension swept over Mari's lovely features. "You're in love with him, aren't you?"

Her eyes widened in affront. Of course she wasn't in love with him! She didn't have to be in love to want to indulge in a passionate adventure before she became too old to do anything but annoy people by pretending to be deaf. Luckily, she was saved from having to answer when Nelson's incessant barking at the inn's courtyard drifted through the open window and caught Mari's attention. "What on earth?"

She was out of the room before Mari could finish the sentence, grateful for the breeze that came with opening the door. Nelson rarely barked. Something had clearly distressed him.

She burst out of the inn to find Nelson harassing a burly carter who held a cane. A quick look at the donkey next to him confirmed that he had used it on the poor animal. If Penelope had time to think, she probably would have used a more polite tone and words. As it was, however, she let fly with the first words that came to mind.

"You bastard! How dare you?" she demanded.

The man pivoted with an irritated expression. "Listen, missy, I have no time to deal with yer meddlin'. I've to get to Ulverston today, and this stupid beast won't go."

Nelson barked again and the man yelled at him, too. "Shut up, or I'll make ye!"

When the man raised his cane to hit Nelson, she saw red. She flew toward the man and grabbed the stick with both hands.

"Look here, wench—"

Penelope yanked hard. "Do not use your cane!" She didn't even manage to loosen it from the man's grip.

The man wrested the cane out of Penelope's grip. "Ye fat, meddlin' wench!" he yelled. "Ye stay out of me business, or I'll use this on ye and make ye squeal like a little piglet!"

"Can't you see your animal is tired?" Penelope put herself between the carter and his donkey. "You won't make him go any farther by beating him up."

"I can do whatever I want with me own, and that there beast is me own—now get out of the way!" He waved the cane in her direction.

Fear raced down her spine. If the man had no qualms about beating animals, then he'd feel no remorse in beating her. Nevertheless, she couldn't let this go on.

Like most beasts of burden, this donkey had probably served his master with all his strength and ability. And as was the case with many beasts, no one cared when those they served betrayed the creatures' trust and loyalty. Unlike the donkey, however, Penelope could do something about it.

"That's true, you can do whatever you want with your own," she conceded, then hit the man's hard head with her palm when he tried to force her out of the way. "But so can I," she pointed out. "This hand is *my own*, and if you don't step back, I'll hit you again with it."

Nelson barked again, taking the man's attention away from her. The carter took Nelson by the scruff and shook him.

She could only watch helplessly as the man continued to shake Nelson. "Release him, sir!"

"Your dog or my donkey, wench?"

She barely heard Lucas's calm voice over Nelson's cries, but his meaning was clear. "How about your apology or your life?"

The man whirled to see who had spoken, and at the sight of Lucas's dangerously imposing figure, the carter dropped Nelson without further argument.

"Good decision," Lucas drawled, stepping forward. He looked down at the smaller man. "Now, apologize to my fiancée. I do not tolerate insults to her."

The man swallowed loudly. "I humbly apologize, miss, for any insult." The man did not even look at her while apologizing. His eyes never left Lucas's face.

Lucas returned the man's gaze steadily. "Are you well, Penelope?"

"Yes," the word was barely a whisper. She cleared her throat and tried again. "Yes, I'm quite all right."

"Then suppose you tell me what in the *living hell* you think you were doing!"

The words were so unexpected that for several seconds she merely stared at him. "What *I* was doing?" she flared, walking toward Lucas. "I was trying to protect my dog and that man's donkey." She frowned at the carter. "You are not going to Ulverston with that donkey today. You will kill him if you do."

"But I have to be in Ulverston for the shipment."

Penelope dismissed the man's protests with a wave of her hand. "The inn will provide you with alternative transport." She felt Lucas's dagger gaze on her. "But I must have your word that you won't hurt any horse the inn provides. I'm responsible for their health, you know."

"Yes, miss."

"Go on then. Tell the inn staff Lord Ravenstone will foot the bill. I'll make sure your donkey is in top health when you return from Ulverston."

The blood left the man's face. "Lord *Ravenstone?*"

"Yes, the very same." *Why do people always listen to* him *and not* her? She gave an impatient sigh as she glared at the carter. "Now kindly do as I have bid. And, sir?"

The man looked questioningly at her. She gave him a small smile before issuing a warning. "If you keep abusing your donkey that way, you won't have him for very much longer. He is quite old. I assume you can't afford to buy another?"

The carter blustered but shook his head.

She nodded. "I gathered as much. He's still got a few good years of service left, but he won't see 1825 if you keep treating him the way you did just now." She crossed her arms over her chest. "And, despite what you think, there is a law against the cruel treatment of animals. If I see you abusing him again, I will take you to court over it."

The man looked dazed. For that matter, so did Lucas. Penelope ignored both of them as she called one of the stable lads to take the donkey to the stables. They discussed the type of food the poor creature was to have, then she promised to send a salve that would help the donkey get over his fatigue. She was asking the boy how his family was doing when she felt a viselike grip on her arm.

"We need to talk," Lucas muttered.

She turned and smiled at him.

He scowled back.

She sighed before relenting. Nelson seemed fine, and it was time to pay the piper. "By all means, my lord. I believe the inn's private dining parlor is free."

• • •

As she watched Lucas pace the flagstone floor, Penelope remembered their first meeting. Had it really only been days ago? It seemed like another lifetime when he'd kissed her for the first time in this room and declared his intention to marry her. Today, she was debating how to convince him to stay long enough for an affair.

Marriage, in her opinion, was meant to be a union of two people who loved each other with liberty—content and satisfied with their spouse's character—as they grew old together. If she could believe Lucas was truly as persuaded of her merit as she was of his, she wouldn't hesitate to marry him. As it was, though, she had to content herself with a brief glimpse of life with Lucas. She wasn't ambitious enough to covet an advantageous marriage founded on nothing more than duty and obligation. She waited for Lucas to give her an opening to discuss their situation.

"Why did you come here alone, Penelope?" he asked, his voice firm and forceful. "I thought I told you not to go anywhere without an escort."

That was hardly the opening she'd hoped for. "I was visiting Mari. And I did have Nelson with me."

He waved a hand to dismiss her words. "I have told you before that Nelson isn't an appropriate escort." He raked his hand through his hair in a distracted manner. "Christ, if the innkeeper had not summoned me, you could have been hurt. Or worse."

She frowned. "I'm quite all right, as you can see. I can take care of myself."

He whirled and fixed his glittering eyes on her. "What possessed you to challenge that man?"

"He was abusing his donkey."

He cursed under his breath. "That was none of your business."

Her chin lifted an inch. "I wasn't going to just stand there and ignore what was happening. This is exactly the reason Martin's Act was passed two years ago. Colonel Martin saw this kind of behavior toward animals must stop."

"Colonel Richard Martin is an eccentric who is a laughing stock in London Town," he said through gritted teeth. "He once fought a duel over a dog. And he brought in an ass to be a witness in a court hearing."

"Good for him!" she huffed. "If I were male, I could have challenged that man for hurting Nelson."

Lucas rubbed the bridge of his nose. "You are not challenging anyone, Penelope, and that is the end of it." He sighed wearily and considered her for a few minutes. "Why do you care so much about these animals?"

The question struck her to the heart. "If I don't, who will?" She got up and moved to the window to stare at the courtyard. "I know how it feels to work for a place in the world, to be forsaken by those you trusted to take care of you." Penelope turned back to him. "I can't change my situation, but I can do something about theirs."

"Do you really think those beasts are smart enough to process all those emotions?"

She gave a small, pain-filled smile. "You don't have to be smart to know when something hurts."

Lucas walked over to her. "Penelope—"

Whatever he was about to say was interrupted by Mari's voice from the other side of the door just before she burst into the room, giving first Penelope, and then Lucas the once over.

She scowled at Mari. "His lordship and I are in the middle of a conversation."

Mari gave her a speaking look. "I need to talk to his lordship now, before it is too late." She paused. "In private."

"Butter the crumpets!" Penelope stomped her foot. "Whatever you are going to say to Lucas, you can say in front of me."

Mari gave her a bright smile. "I would love to, but your mother has sent for you. She and Sarah need help at the apothecary."

Hah! A likely story. "I suppose Mama sent a note with this message?"

"No," Mari said, shaking her head. "But she has sent Gertie to accompany you and Nelson back to Highfield Manor. She likes to talk; you wouldn't want to keep her waiting."

Penelope had been outmaneuvered. She had no choice but to leave, immediately.

"Fine, I'm going." She gave Mari a warning look. "But don't tell him anything I wouldn't."

• • •

Lucas waited for the door to close behind Penelope before giving her friend his full attention. "You are making a habit of interrupting when I'm in the middle of a conversation with my fiancée, Miss Smythe."

The woman had the grace to blush at his blatant rebuke. "I apologize, my lord. But I couldn't risk having Polly act on something I think is ill conceived before I had a chance to stop it."

Lucas gestured to the sofa Penelope had vacated. "Have a seat, Miss Smythe." He waited for her to get comfortable before he went on, "Now, what is my betrothed about to do?"

"She wants to have an affair with you."

Of all the things Miss Smythe could have said, this was the least he had expected. She could have claimed the sky was falling or she had the power to fly into the heavens and Lucas would not have been more shocked.

Penelope wants to have an affair with me.

After he'd regained control, Lucas realized he should have expected his nymph to try something like this. Penelope wanted him, but she wouldn't marry him.

The thought angered him.

He felt as frustrated as a debutante who couldn't get a confirmed bachelor to come up to scratch. Penelope was like a wild mare that had to be convinced, repeatedly, to trust him.

"Why are you telling me this?" he asked. "Surely you are not concerned about my virtue?"

Miss Smythe snorted. "Hardly that, my lord." She looked away, heaving a great sigh. "Penelope loves you. She wouldn't contemplate something this risky otherwise."

To his enormous disgust, his first reaction was pure joy. He shook the feeling off as ridiculous. It wasn't joy he felt, but satisfaction. Things would be easier if Penelope loved him.

"What makes you think Penelope is in love with me?"

"She has *always* been in love with you," Miss Smythe burst out, twisting her handkerchief into knots. "She used to write letters to you, did you know that? She was lonely with her father always gone and her mother depressed." Miss Smythe sighed again. "Some girls write diaries, she wrote to *you*. You've been her confidante for as long as she could write until she turned eighteen and realized you would never come for her."

Lucas's jaw dropped in astonishment. "I didn't know. She never sent me any correspondence."

"She never meant to. She waited for you to either contact her or come for her. Until you did, the letters became her way of staving off the loneliness."

He straightened. "I see."

Miss Smythe glared at him. "At first I thought it was wonderful that you've finally arrived." She shook her head, her hands gripping her handkerchief tighter. "But now she wants to have an affair with you. It's not fair. Penelope deserves a proper marriage. You owe it to her."

"I could not agree more."

"I'll have your word, my lord, that you won't take advantage of my friend. If your intentions are—"

"Honorable?" he provided. "Yes, they are. I came here to marry Penelope, and I intend to do so." He registered the wariness in Miss Smythe's expression. "I believe we both have the same goal here, Miss Smythe."

"In all honesty, my lord, I'm not certain I can trust you."

His jaw tightened. "If you cannot trust me, then trust your friend. She is bound to me by a contract, and she knows it. She has as much obligation to me as I do to her."

"You are right, of course," Miss Smythe admitted.

"It is obvious to me, however," he continued, "that Penelope still needs some convincing. I trust you won't interfere with my goal?"

Miss Smythe stood up. "If your goal is to marry Penelope, then you have my full support, my lord."

"All will be well, Miss Smythe," Lucas assured Penelope's friend. He told the woman to send the carter's bills to him, and then he left for Highfield Manor.

So Penelope planned to seduce him into having an affair, did she? Lucas's lips set into a grim line. She innocently thought to play bedtime games with him, and she approached her goal with the same recklessness she approached everything, from firing a pistol to attacking a man because of a donkey. Luckily, Lucas had absolutely no gentlemanly scruples when it came to getting what he wanted. It was time the nymph learned an important lesson.

And after she learned that lesson, she would be securely in his clutches.

Chapter Ten

Where does she think she's going? Lucas wondered, quietly following Penelope down the dark hallway.

It was the middle of the night and his fiancée was sneaking around like a burglar. If he hadn't been right outside her bedchamber, torturing himself yet again with the fantasy of seeing her sleeping, he wouldn't have heard the wood creak as she carefully opened the door and sneaked out into the hallway.

She was dressed all in black except for her cloak, which was trimmed in gold. When Penelope descended the servants' staircase, Lucas strode back to his room and grabbed his greatcoat, then he went down the cantilever staircase the family used, stopping midway to wait for her to appear in the main hall. *It was a good thing he was still fully dressed,* he thought, when Penelope appeared from the east wing and rushed outside.

She lit a lantern, but the moon was bright, and its light was enough illumination to see the surroundings quite well. She would have seen him if she'd thought to turn around, but the nymph seemed too intent on her clandestine mission to be careful.

The exasperating little idiot. She was entirely too sure of her safety. He had to restrain a powerful urge to march up to her and give her a lecture right there and then on the perils awaiting a well-bred lady tramping out of the house in the dead of night.

Penelope entered the barn, closing the door behind her. Lucas silently opened the barn door a crack to see inside. And there, sitting on an upturned barrel petting a sleeping Nelson, was a familiar face: David Maitland.

"Good evening, cousin. Thank you for agreeing to meet me here." Maitland peered around Penelope's shoulder. "I trust you didn't tell anyone I'm here?"

Penelope approached the young man, shoving the hood of her cloak off her head as she did so. "David," Lucas heard the smile in her voice. "It's nice of you to visit." She looked around the barn. "No one else is with you?"

"Father doesn't know I'm here. I have been staying at the inn, which is why I asked you not to tell anyone of my presence. Have you talked to Ravenstone?"

"Yes, he is staying at Highfield Manor." She began tapping her toe. "David, I am glad to see you have grown up well. And that you still like to play hide and seek."

Maitland grinned and stood up, taking Penelope's hands in his. "You haven't changed much, Penelope. Once again, you've chosen to hide in the most obvious place, and I have found you with little effort." His grin faded as his attractive face took on a serious look. "I've come to warn you, cousin. Stay away from Raving Ravenstone. He is dangerous."

Lucas felt a chill in his gut. He watched Penelope yank her hands from Maitland's grip. "Do not call my fiancé by that dreadful name, David," she warned.

"Confound it," Maitland muttered. "What tale has he spun around you? There are things about him you do not know. You are not safe with him."

Her voice was as final as death. "He wouldn't harm a pheasant. There is nothing about him I don't know."

"Penelope, Uncle Edmund is the reason Ravenstone's father is dead."

Lucas stilled. Penelope was about to discover the truth about him, and there was nothing he could do to stop it. He lost the ability to breathe.

"Don't be ridiculous," he heard her say. "Lucas's father died in a hunting accident."

"That's what I thought, too," Maitland gripped Penelope's shoulders. "There are even rumors Ravenstone himself killed his father. Considering his mother's unstable disposition, no one would be surprised if Lucas Drake did kill his father."

"Rubbish," Penelope struggled ineffectually to free herself from Maitland's grip. "One would only have to look at Ravenstone to know that's nothing but gossip spread by someone who is jealous of him and his achievements."

"Ravenstone's father killed himself after Uncle Edmund's visit."

"*What?*"

"It's true," Maitland said with an emphatic nod. "Uncle Edmund wanted out of the betrothal contract, and Ravenstone's father killed himself after Uncle told him the news."

Lucas felt as if something died within him as he waited for her reaction. A keening sense of loss and regret reverberated from the coldest, darkest part of his soul.

"Well," Penelope finally said. "That certainly explains his comment about coming here sooner if he'd known he would be welcome."

Maitland shook her. "Did you *listen* to me, cousin? You don't know all there is to know about that man, and you would do well to stay away from him."

Penelope laid her hand on top of one of Maitland's. "I heard you, David, but you're wrong. I understand Ravenstone well. I assure you he isn't dangerous. Not to me."

Penelope's cousin let go of her as if she'd burned him. "He's here for revenge, I tell you! I believe he is out to seduce you and leave you ruined."

First Miss Smythe and now Maitland. What was it with these people thinking Lucas intended anything other than having Penelope at the altar as soon as possible?

"Rubbish," she said once more. "If he wanted to ruin me, he'd have done it by now. He's here to marry me, David."

"I have already tried to explain that is not the case, but you won't listen." Maitland grabbed Penelope's arm. "This is for your own good, cousin."

Penelope tried to twist free. "What are you doing?"

"I am taking you away from here. Your stepfather obviously does not know the danger Ravenstone presents. Do not fret, cousin, everything will be fine."

"David, please—"

Lucas opened the barn door and stepped in. "Good evening, Maitland," he said in a bored drawl, watching the other man's face pale. "Fancy seeing you here."

• • •

Penelope whirled to see Lucas standing by the barn door. His eyes had narrowed to slits, and his aristocratic features held a forbidding expression. She had no idea how to convince David that Lucas posed no threat when he stood there looking downright menacing.

"Lucas!" she said brightly. "How nice of you to join us." She took advantage of David's momentary shock to set herself free from his grasp and walk toward her betrothed. "I see that you've met my cousin before."

Lucas kept his attention on David. "Yes, we have met. Your cousin attended Oxford with me."

David finally seemed to shake off his stupor. "Exactly what are you planning, Ravenstone? If you have a problem with the Maitlands, you come to me. Penelope knows nothing about whatever you think my family has done to yours."

Lucas shoved away from the barn door. "I believe you're the one who owes me an explanation, Maitland, as you're the one who was about to spirit off my fiancée."

"I will not let you ruin Penelope."

"No one is spiriting me off, and no one is trying to ruin me," she assured the men. *Gracious, they are discussing me as if I were not right here in front of them. It's insulting.*

David inclined his head and leaned on a wooden column. "Is that true, Ravenstone?"

Lucas shrugged. "You heard the lady."

"Then why you are living here with her stepfamily, and there haven't been any announcements in the papers of an impending marriage?"

"That's my fault," she admitted. "I have yet to agree to marry Lucas."

"You have yet to *agree?*" David rounded on her. "So that is the reason for the delay. Penelope, the man is living in your house. You'd better marry him as soon as possible or you will be—"

"Ruined," she provided. "Yes, I know. But, David, there's no reason to worry. Lucas and I are only taking the time to get to know each other before making such an irrevocable step."

"You have obviously taken leave of your senses!" David roared. He turned back to Lucas. "I'm giving you one week to marry Penelope. If you haven't done so by then, I swear I will hunt you down and make you walk down that aisle." He marched toward her fiancé. "You will not ruin my cousin, even if I have to put a pistol to your head to ensure it."

At the mention of a pistol, Lucas threw his head and shouted with laughter. "I am more than willing to walk down that aisle, as long as you don't let Penelope hold the pistol."

Now that comment was uncalled for! Why did he bring up the shooting incident now? For that matter, why were they discussing their nuptials in a barn in the dead of night? "If you men are through discussing my future without consulting me," she said with all the dignity she could muster, "I am going back to the manor."

David made for the door. "I'll return to the inn." He sent Lucas a speaking look. "I will be back in a week's time to see how things are progressing around here."

"See that you do," Lucas taunted.

There was a long, awkward silence after David left. Finally, Penelope straightened and made for the door. "Well, I am going to bed."

"You have some explaining to do, Penelope," Lucas said quietly.

"How much of it did you hear?"

"Not much," he replied. "Snippets."

"Snippets of everything, most probably," she muttered. "Why do you always sneak up on people like that? Were you spying on me?"

He ignored that question. "Your time is running out, nymph. You'll soon have to decide whether or not you want to marry me."

Lucas held the barn door for her, and she stepped out onto the night. There were faint sounds of crickets, and the balmy breeze cooled her face. They walked together in silence under the stars for a few minutes, lost in their own thoughts.

"I apologize for David's actions," she finally said. "He doesn't realize we have an understanding."

"Do we have an understanding?" Lucas asked, his voice harsh. "You've made me dangle from your fingertips for days. You were on the verge of losing your house, and still you did not give me the answer I seek." He put out his hands to halt her. "Does the notion of being married to *Raving* Ravenstone scare you so?"

She stopped walking. "Stop calling yourself that! Anyone who takes the time to observe you will see that you are a man possessed of ironclad self-control."

"Why do you know so much about me, nymph?"

The question flustered her. She scrambled for a way to answer him without revealing how naive she had been of the ways of the world. "It's as Papa told you that first night. You were a hobby of mine for a good few years, Lucas. I was trained to be a good wife, and good wives know all about their husbands."

It seemed so long ago now when she'd written him letters, hoping against hope he would someday come for her. She knew now it wasn't his fault that it took him so long to fetch her. Just as it wasn't his fault she was in love with him.

Penelope let out a resigned sigh. It was the truth, and she was honest enough to admit it. In fact, she was almost convinced her scheme to use his name to fend off creditors was probably her way of trying to get through to him one last time, for it was impossible to deny her message: *See me. Notice me. Remember me.* Why else did the thought of never seeing him again scare her so?

She'd always loved him, she'd just been angry with him for a time. Her feelings had only grown stronger now that she'd met Lucas the man—flesh and blood. She'd felt a connection with him almost from the moment they'd met. It had grown stronger with each moment they'd spent together. Surly, autocratic, generous Lucas understood her as no other person could.

He accepted and appreciated her for what she was. He never tried to change her to fit into the mold of Society's idea of the perfect lady. *He wanted to marry her.* The knowledge made Penelope's heart sing even as her stomach lurched with dread. He wanted to marry her, and his determination terrified her to the core. Because no matter how much he appreciated her, he didn't *love* her. His only reason for wanting to marry her was to honor his father's word. She had no right to chain him to her and keep him from finding someone he could love in the future. If she did, he'd end up tumbling ladies like her father.

But she didn't know if she had enough strength to refuse Lucas, to do the right thing and set him free. Penelope thought of what her future would be after he left Highfield Manor: empty. The twins would someday find partners and get married. And she would still be here, old and alone. Always alone, surrounded by bleating and clucking unwanted animals who, like her, didn't belong anywhere. It would be almost funny, really, if it didn't hurt so much. She felt like weeping.

What a pickle she'd put herself in.

"People began calling me Raving Ravenstone after my father died," Lucas admitted, snapping her out of her thoughts. "I was sixteen, and I was angry then. Angry at the world, at my situation."

He held her hand, torturing her as his thumb caressed her palm. "One of the boys at school accused me of killing my father, and I beat him half to death. That's when it started. People recalled my mother's unstable disposition, and the epithet stuck, probably because of my size. I've always been a hulking brute."

Lucas gathered her into his arms as if he needed to reassure himself that she'd still welcome his touch. And despite all the turmoil she was in, her heart cried out for him. She lay her hand against his stubbled cheek, looked into the dark depths of his eyes and whispered, "I'm sorry."

For a moment, she thought she saw a flicker of emotion in his eyes before he quickly extinguished it and turned away from her.

"Sorry for what?" Lucas retorted. "It's not your fault people are idiots."

She waited for him to turn back to her. When he finally did, she put her hand on his arm to stay him. "I'm sorry for all the mean things they said about your parents. They had no right to do that."

He sighed. "Just as I had no right to expect you to wait for me for all these years. Forgive me, Penelope. If I had known you were waiting for me, I'd have come sooner."

His simple words meant more to her than she could ever say. She ducked her head and blinked back tears for the little girl whose dreams had been shattered by reality.

She released his arm and started walking back to the manor. "It doesn't matter anymore. One of the things Papa taught us is we should accept that life will not always be kind, and we should always focus on moving on."

"And have you moved on, Penelope? Have you forgiven me?" Lucas asked softly as he opened the manor's back door, letting her precede him.

"I have, now." And she did. She hadn't realized until tonight how much she'd needed to hear him acknowledge the pain she'd felt at his supposed abandonment.

She turned back to check if he was following her up the stairs. Something about sneaking around the darkened manor late at night with a man she was dangerously attracted to made her feel like she was being ... naughty.

She continued talking to distract herself from the effect Lucas's nearness had on her senses. "Papa says reality is what we make of it. Many people are so stuck living in their past or dreaming about their future, they forget the present is the only time we really have any control over. It's what we do in the present that decides our future, and it's the present that will become our past."

"So you're saying we shouldn't learn from our past or look forward to the future?" he whispered, so close behind her she could feel his warm breath caressing her nape.

"Of course not," she whispered back. "Only that we shouldn't be living anywhere but in the present." She certainly didn't want to think of the future right then. She didn't want to think of when he would be nothing more than a distant memory.

They cleared the top of the stairs. When they reached her bedchamber, she put her hand on the door and turned to face him. He was standing so close, the tips of their boots touched. Perhaps she should invite him in. She was not ready to let him go yet.

No, she decided. This was her stepfather's house. There would be more appropriate places to start their affair.

"Good night, Lucas," she whispered. "Thank you for looking out for me." She smiled up at him, turned, and carefully opened the door.

Shock made her stop in her tracks when Lucas put his hand on the doorframe and followed her inside before closing the door with a soft click.

"Do you realize what you are doing?" she whispered furiously, watching him as she tried to calm her rattled nerves and keep her voice low at the same time.

The grin he gave her looked downright wolfish. "I'm living in the present," he replied in a husky tone as he closed the distance between them. "And presently, I am alone with the most desirable woman I have ever known." He cupped her cheek in his large hand. "Based on our past encounters, I have no doubt this one will affect both our futures."

Oh, God, if he only knew ... her lips parted as she closed her eyes and released a tremulous breath while heat seeped through her veins.

"Lucas, you promised not to ruin me," she reminded him as she felt him remove her cloak, letting it fall into a pool of gold-trimmed velvet around her feet.

"I know." He tipped her chin up, silently urging her to meet his heated gaze. "Do you trust me, Penelope?"

She opened her eyes and saw his solemn face. "Yes, Lucas, I trust you." It was herself she couldn't trust around him.

"You're not afraid of me at all, are you?"

"No," she replied sincerely. Then she smiled and added, "I mean, what can you possibly do? Kiss me to death?"

He chuckled. "Watch it, nymph, or I just might do that."

"Hah! I'd like to see you try."

His gaze dropped to her lips. "Would you now?" he rasped as his mouth claimed hers in a fiercely tender kiss that was unlike any of the kisses they'd shared before.

Lucas worshipped her mouth, his tongue plunging in to savor her, and sweetness poured through her veins as he shook the pins out of her hair, tumbling the entire silky mass around them.

Her hands linked behind his neck, and without breaking the kiss, he swept her into his arms and carried her to the frilly bed, laying her gently in the middle of it as he followed her down. Only then did Lucas lift his mouth from hers.

"Penelope," he whispered. "Open your eyes."

Her lashes fluttered before she stared straight at him. He groaned when her hands cupped his face, and he turned his head to plant a kiss into her palm.

"I won't ruin you," he vowed, as he removed his coat and tossed it to the side of the bed.

"You won't ruin me," she said to reassure him, before pulling him down to her.

He stopped a mere an inch from her lips and met her gaze. "Unless you want me to?" he asked, half serious.

Penelope smiled. "Kiss me, Lucas."

Lucas kissed her. Hungrily, deeply, with a savage urgency he'd never shown before. She moaned in pleasure as his hands roamed freely over her, claiming her breasts, while he parted her legs with his knee and settled himself between her thighs.

Penelope gave herself over to the demanding urgency of his kisses as the familiar heat rose in her. He said he wouldn't ruin her, but she was beyond caring as she felt his hands slip underneath her back to work on the fastenings of her gown. She clung to him as he yanked her loosened gown off her shoulders, then past her breasts.

She jumped when his hands cupped her breasts through the thin fabric of her chemise, filling his palms with her soft flesh, kneading them until her eyes clenched shut and she was mindlessly writhing beneath him.

"You like that, sweetheart?"

She sighed. "*Yes!*"

A laughing groan escaped him as he continued fondling her breast. "So sweet, so honest … "

Lucas bent his head and worked the ties of her chemise loose with his teeth, making her gasp and open her eyes as he dragged her chemise down, freeing her breasts, watching as her nipples tightened into proud, erect buds beneath his hungry gaze.

"Beautiful," he whispered reverently as he lowered his head and licked her nipple.

He paused when she couldn't stop the tears shimmering in her eyes. "What is it? Am I hurting you?"

She shook her head and gave a sad, little smile. "You don't have to pretend with me, Lucas," she said, hoping her voice held none of the pain she felt. She touched his arm, carefully avoiding his wound. "I know what I am. I realize that people find me—"

"Lovely? Tempting? Desirable?"

"No," she whispered.

He held her gaze. "Are you sure?" he asked, his voice rough as his thumbs rubbed her nipples. "Because if you're sure, then tell me why you drive me mad with lust just by holding your hand." He placed a soft kiss on her cheek. "Tell me why I've spent sleepless nights imagining you beneath me, like this."

"Lucas … "

"Tell me why I ache to kiss and touch every part of you." He rubbed his rigid arousal against the juncture between her thighs, and she moaned with pleasure. "You know I'm telling the truth, Penelope," he growled. "You can feel how much I want you." He pushed himself against her, his hips pinning her to the bed.

He meant it. Penelope felt it in the urgency of his movements, of the raw hunger of his kiss when he covered her mouth with his, driving his tongue into her mouth again and again as his hips ground against hers. She felt it as he tore his mouth from hers to devour her breasts, and she kissed his dark hair, his temples, any part of him she could reach as she matched his movements and arched up against him, wanting more … needing more …

He suddenly tore his mouth from her breast and stared down at her face. His eyes blazed with desire and his features were taut with need, his breath thick and ragged, making him seem like some great, predatory beast as he lifted off her to lie at her side.

Was that it? Penelope protested the loss with a whimper of disappointment that turned into a shocked gasp as he lifted her skirts and his hand cupped the damp place between her legs. She clamped her thighs together, unable to question the instinct even as he groaned in frustration.

"Don't close against me, sweetheart," he choked out. "Let me feel you ... I only want to feel you."

Responding to the need in his voice, she forced her legs to relax, and he rewarded her with a blatantly carnal kiss while he found the slit in her drawers and slipped his hand inside. She felt him press his palm against the moist curls between her thighs, rubbing her in a manner that made her squirm and arch against his hand.

He kissed her temple when she released a moan of pleasure and she buried her face in his neck, whimpering with need while he continued the delicious movement of his hand.

"Oh, God! Lucas, that's very—"

"Oh yes, it is. Very," he rasped. His voice washed over her like liquid fire as his thumb found a sensitive nub of flesh and he rubbed the spot, teasing it until she writhed and pressed herself against his thumb. She wanted to scream. She wanted him never to stop. She wanted more.

"Please, Lucas!" she begged him. For what, she didn't know.

"Yes, sweetheart." He groaned. "Take it. I'll give it to you, I promise."

He lowered his head to suck at her breasts once more and slid a finger inside her, stroking her in a way that drove her mad as she felt the fire build up in her.

"Yes," he growled as he slid another finger inside her and quickened his strokes. "Reach for it, nymph. Let it happen ... "

The thrusts of his fingers grew firmer, more demanding, pulling at her and beckoning her, sending the flames higher and higher until a sudden explosion of pleasure made her cry out his name. He held her as she quivered and shattered beneath him, arching against his hand as waves of pleasure swept through her.

Lucas's knowing hand gently guided her back from oblivion. He held her as she regained her bearings, stroking her gently and brushing kisses against her cheeks, her temples.

She dropped her hands from around his neck. "That was … "

"Good?" he whispered.

"Amazing. Exquisite. Wonderful."

She looked up at him to see his reaction. What she saw filled her with guilt. His eyes were clenched shut, and the same stark hunger darkened his features as he held himself above her.

"Ummm … is there anything I can do to make you … " She bit her lip as she tried to think of how to say it. Then she spoke again. "I mean, can I … can I do anything?" She made a vague gesture that encompassed the whole of him.

A strained laugh escaped him. "You can't know how I've waited to hear you say that, sweetheart, but it wouldn't be wise. I can only take so much, and if I don't get out of this bed soon I *will* ruin you, no matter what I promised." His eyes blazed at her. "And the servants will be up soon."

"Oh!" She sat up, panicked.

"I better get out of here while I still can." He brushed a kiss against her temple. "Good night, Penelope."

"Good night."

She sighed, suddenly wishing that he wasn't so honorable as she watched him slowly open the door and slip into the darkened hallway, closing the door behind him with a soft click.

Chapter Eleven

"Polly? It's Papa. Can I come in?"

Penelope's eyes snapped open. She blinked against the harsh light as she tried to regain her senses.

"Polly? Are you awake?"

"Ungh. Yes, Papa. Come in."

She watched from her bed as her stepfather came in bearing a tray of food. The comforting smell of freshly made toast and eggs wafted through the room, and she closed her eyes, savoring it.

"You missed breakfast. I thought you might be hungry."

She opened her eyes, sat up and gave a languid smile. "Thanks, Papa."

Papa set the food tray on her writing table, turned and froze. *Froze?*

"What's wrong?"

"Is there anything you want to tell me, Polly?" He approached the bed. "Anything you think I should know about?"

She frowned in confusion. "I don't think so."

Her stepfather scowled back. "I see."

He tossed her dressing gown to the bed and averted his gaze as she put it on. "As I recall, you and the earl said you needed time to get to know each other before deciding to get married. Have you decided yet?"

She opened her mouth to speak, but Papa waylaid her with a wave of his hand. "You shouldn't play games with a man's life, Penelope. I taught you better than that."

"What do you mean?"

"The earl has estates to run, tenants who depend on him and a sister who needs him. Yet you keep him here for an entire week to wait for you to make a decision." He shook his head. "I thought it was a sound idea. It would help us get to know your future husband better."

He put his hands on his hips. "But to be honest, I didn't think you'd keep him dangling this long. There's not much more to find out from spending time with a man for a week that you can't learn in three days."

She watched Papa sit by her writing desk as shame poured through her. Lucas's words after she'd accidentally shot him drifted through her mind: *Enough of these games.*

She buried her face in her hands. "I'm scared, Papa. I've been avoiding making a decision because—"

"I believe you've already made a decision. I've seen you interact with him, and I believe it is a sound match. He's a good man."

"I know he is, Papa, but ... " She faced her stepfather, letting him see her turmoil. "I've seen what an arranged marriage can be like. Mama married my father out of duty, and she wasn't happy because she loved *you*. What would've happened to us if you'd been married when my father died and Uncle Hugh cast us out?"

"I never would've married anyone other than your mother," Papa said quietly. "And if your mother hadn't married Edmund Maitland, you wouldn't be here."

"Well, when you put it that way ... "

"Stop worrying about what happened or what could have happened in the past, Polly. You can do naught about it anymore."

He walked over to put his hand on her shoulder. "What matters is the present," he reminded her. "Either marry the earl or release him from the betrothal. But make the decision, child, because if you wait too long, you will lose your chance. Then it will no longer be your decision to make." His gray brows rose. "The earl can't stay here forever."

What else could she say? She'd convinced herself she deserved to have him for a while longer after waiting for him all those years, but Papa was right. She was being a coward, and she could not keep delaying her decision any longer. "I'll talk to Lord Ravenstone today."

"Good. Now eat your breakfast." He turned to leave. "Oh, and Polly?"

"Yes, Papa?"

"When you talk to the earl, make sure you give him back his coat."

Her stepfather left the room, closing the door just as her bewildered gaze bounced to Lucas's coat lying in a crumpled heap of blue by the side of her bed. The same coat he'd taken off last night when they'd been … She groaned and buried her face on her pillow. She had run out of time. Her "affair" was now over, before it even had a chance to fully begin.

Oh, she was going to give Lucas his coat, all right. And then she was going to kill him.

• • •

What the hell did she want from him?

Lucas hurled the book he'd been trying to read across the room in disgust. The blasted woman wouldn't even let him read! And he'd thought this whole damned thing would be easy.

He had to get out of here. This courtship nonsense of his own fiancée was just that. Nonsense. He was done playing her games.

He had never been much for courtship anyway—he preferred women who were content with the promise of jewels and gowns and who were as uninterested in messy, emotional complications as he was.

But *this* woman! This woman made him jump through hoops, and still she wouldn't give him the answer he sought. He was running out of time.

What more did she want from him? He'd come to this remote town to make her his countess, he'd ingratiated himself with her family, he'd played the perfect gentleman, he'd pleasured her … Lucas groaned and reached for his cravat, turned to the mirror and proceeded to tie it into intricate knots as he got ready to tutor the woman's little brother.

I can't take much more of this.

It had taken all of his control to leave her bed last night. If that weren't enough, he'd spent the rest of the evening reliving each moment she'd spent in his arms, remembering the arousing sounds she'd made, the scent of her, how wet and warm she'd become for him, the way she'd looked as she found fulfillment. He felt himself harden and cursed roundly.

He would not allow any woman to lead him around by his bollocks. That's how it began … if he were wise, he'd leave now and find some other bride before he ended up like Father. Or worse, he might end up like his mother.

He finished tying his cravat and turned away from the mirror. *I am nothing like Mother!* And he certainly wouldn't allow himself to care for any woman and give her the power to destroy him. That was the most important lesson he'd learned from Leonard Drake.

Lucas raked his hand through his hair in frustration. He ought to strip the woman bare, have his way with her and go straight to her stepfather. He'd fantasized about bedding her so many times it was amazing he hadn't gone blind. He'd never had a problem with controlling his urges before.

What was it about this woman, who most people would consider to be plain, that fascinated him to the point of obsession? Her beauty lay in the details one had to notice to appreciate. The delicate, graceful hands that healed with a gentle touch, the smooth complexion despite hours spent under the sun, those haunting hazel eyes and the floral and sunshine scent of her. He was a man who'd been trained from an early age to look at details, and the details in this woman were driving him insane. If his actions last night did not produce the results he wanted, he was likely to have his first temper tantrum in his adult life.

He took a deep, calming breath. "I need a drink!"

"I agree. Which type?"

He whirled to find Penelope watching him from the doorway. "We use alcohol for mixing medicines, so I'm certain we'll be able to find whatever drink you need," she added.

"What the hell are you doing here?"

Her eyes widened at his tone. "Did you just *snarl* at me?" She shook her head in derision. "I should have known you'd be a bear in the morning. You look awful."

"Thank you," he replied through gritted teeth. "If you have nothing more to say, I suggest you get out of this room if you know what's good for you."

"Oh, I think you'd want me to stay."

"And why is that?"

"I've come to discuss terms. Of our marriage."

Just like that, his black mood lifted. He stared at her, unable to believe his ears. "You're marrying me?"

"If we can agree to terms."

Of course. He should have known she would want to bargain. The woman still had to learn how to give in graciously. "Very well." He crossed his arms over his chest. "State your terms." *This should be interesting.*

She strode to the fireplace and started stoking the fire with a poker. "Ummm … first of all—"

"Penelope?"

"Yes?" she squeaked.

"Let go of the poker, sweetheart, and sit down."

She stiffened. "I don't need to sit down. This shouldn't take long," she protested, but she put the poker down.

Lucas almost smiled. She was so transparent. "What are your terms?" he asked in the same tone he used to soothe a skittish mare.

She finally looked at him. "First, Nelson will have to come with me." She smiled apologetically. "He has become attached, and I will not break the dog's heart by leaving him here."

"Agreed."

Her eyes widened. "And ... and Gertie must have a retirement cottage of her own." Then, as if realizing the boldness of her demands, she hastily added, "It doesn't have to be grand, of course."

"Of course." He crossed the room and joined her where she stood by the fireplace. "Anything else?"

She took a deep breath. "Well, I did notice you like ordering people about. You shall not order me about."

"I don't think you would ever let anyone order you about."

"That's true," she agreed. "To be honest, I thought that was going to be our main problem."

He chuckled. "And are those all your terms?"

He wanted this over with quickly and finally have her saying her vows on the aisle, but from the look on her face, he knew they'd only just begun.

• • •

Penelope stared at him. He was agreeing to all her terms ... *and far too readily*. It made her want to find out exactly how far he'd go for duty and his dratted honor. "I want Colin to go back to school."

"Done."

"And for Sarah to have a London Season."

"Agreed."

She was beginning to enjoy this. Hmmm ... what else? "My family can visit us whenever they want."

His brows rose as he stepped closer to her. "Whenever they *need*."

"Yes, and … you will shelter any animal that needs a home."
When his brows knotted, she clarified, "I mean, if possible."

"If possible."

"And you shall not have a mistress!" Good grief, where did *that* come from?

"I will be faithful," he vowed.

That gave her pause. "*Really?*"

"Yes."

That was unexpected. She knew noblemen usually kept mistresses. It was common knowledge that even her own father had died with his. "I see. Then, I will be faithful, too."

"I expect nothing less. Is there anything else you want?"

She bit her lip. Did she dare? *Well, why not?* "And I want ten thousand pounds."

He cupped her face in his large hands and lowered his mouth to hers. "So would I," he murmured against her lips, calling her bluff.

She gasped. "You devil! You knew all along—"

Lucas cut off the rest of her words with his mouth as he gave her a deliciously thorough kiss. She sagged against him when he finally lifted his mouth from hers, her arms wrapped around the waist of the man she loved.

As Penelope stood there in his arms, she contemplated this momentous occasion. True, it lacked the flowery prose and grand speech that little girls dreamed of the moment when their future was sealed with the man who was to be their husband, but then, she'd never done anything the traditional way. She doubted many would-be-brides barged into their betrothed's chamber and bargained terms like a merchant.

And this was why she loved Lucas. Ever since they'd met, he'd accepted her for what she was, with all her faults and limitations. She wasn't blessed with looks, money or any sort of position in Society, and yet he'd come for her. After a lifetime of being ignored or merely thought of as useful, she was finally being seen and appreciated for nothing more than being herself. He'd been the man of her dreams all her life, and he was now hers.

He didn't love her, but he seemed to genuinely want her. With this man, she could be herself without fear of disappointing him. For now, that was enough.

It had to be.

She laid her cheek against his hard chest and savored the intimacy of the moment as they stood there, holding each other. After several minutes, Lucas pressed a kiss against her hair.

"Penelope?"

"Hmmm?"

"What made you finally decide to marry me?"

She glowered at him. "Papa found your coat. You left it in my room last night."

His eyes widened. Then he released great gusts of mirth, his massive shoulders shaking with laughter.

"It's not funny!" She pummeled his chest.

Lucas caught her wrists and held them together behind her, holding her against his large frame while his whole body continued to quake with laughter. "I suppose we'll have to talk to your stepfather. I've clearly overstayed my welcome here."

She pouted. "Yes. He's waiting in the study."

He gave her another fierce kiss. Then he held her hand and tugged her along with him as he strode out of the room. "I always knew I liked your stepfather."

• • •

The meeting had to wait until the afternoon because Penelope's stepfather was called out to attend to one of the villagers who'd had an accident on his farm. When Dr. Walker returned, Lucas was summoned to the library for the discussion of marriage settlements.

"Please sit down, Ravenstone," his future father-in-law said, gesturing to the rose-colored settee.

As soon as he had taken a seat, Dr. Walker launched into the many reasons Penelope did not have a dowry to speak of.

Lucas waved the explanations off, stating once again that he did not require his bride to have a dowry. He then explained the terms of the bargain he and Penelope made earlier in the day. With each word, Dr. Walker's eyes widened until Lucas feared they would pop out of the poor man's head.

"She told you not to have a mistress?"

"Yes," he confirmed. "Penelope can be quite forthright in her demands."

"She can be that," Dr. Walker averred. "I must say, my lord, you are very calm for someone who has been caught ravishing a young woman in her own house."

He felt himself redden. "I am engaged to your stepdaughter, Dr. Walker. She is a grown woman, and my intentions are honorable. What we do with our time is no one's business but our own."

"Of course." Penelope's stepfather gave him a speculative look. "But I want to know something."

"Ask away."

Dr. Walker hesitated. He sipped port from his glass, appearing to mull the situation over. "You, my lord, strike me as a person who is very meticulous and deliberate about what he does. So why did you leave your coat in my stepdaughter's bedchamber?"

He smiled ruefully and glanced at the suit of armor in the far corner of the room. "I thought it was the best way to get her to realize what she truly wanted out of this whole affair."

"I had just come to the same conclusion myself." Dr. Walker grinned. "Very well, my lord," he added, shaking Lucas's hand. "Welcome to the family."

"Thank you, sir."

A knock sounded at the door. "Lord Maitland is here, sir," Gertie announced. "Should I show him to the drawin' room?"

The baron burst into the library, waving Gertie aside. "I do not need to be shown to the drawing room. This is clearly where he is." Maitland first looked shocked to see Lucas, then the baron straightened and said stiffly, "Ravenstone."

"Maitland," he acknowledged, contemplating the old man through the rim of his glass of port. "I was beginning to think you didn't know where your niece has been staying all these years. What brings you to Highfield Manor?"

The baron strode to the nearest chair and sat without waiting for an invitation. "What game are you playing, Ravenstone? I demand to know what you think you are getting out of this."

"Lord Maitland," Dr. Walker said. "I respectfully remind you that you are in my home, and I do not tolerate such rudeness to my guests. Furthermore, his lordship is about to become part of our family."

The baron's palm slammed against the arm of the chair. "You fool! How could you believe this man," he pointed a crooked finger at Lucas, "would actually want to marry the plain little chit Edmund sired?" His eyes blazed at Lucas. "Do you really think you could convince anyone that a man of your station would want anything to do with someone like Penelope if you didn't have some hidden agenda?"

He smiled coldly. "You are one to talk about hidden agendas. What has prompted you to finally deign to visit your niece, Maitland?"

The baron frowned. "You are not going to turn this around on me. I demand to know—"

"Lord Maitland!" Dr. Walker interrupted. "I will say again that you are in my home, and we do not tolerate such lack of respect in this house. Moreover," he put a palm up to silence the baron's disagreement, "Penelope is of age. It is her decision who and why to marry someone. As her stepfather, I respect her decision. And so should you, don't you think?"

"You idiot!" the baron raged. "I do not believe this. Where is she? I demand to speak to my niece at once."

"And so you shall." Lucas stood up and walked over to the suit of armor in the corner of the room. He reached up and opened the helm. A pair of hazel eyes, opened wide in surprise, stared back at him.

"Butter the crumpets," Penelope muttered. "How did you know I was in here?"

He grinned. "I knew you wouldn't be able to resist being part of a bargaining situation."

"This is outrageous!" the baron fumed as he rounded on Dr. Walker. "You have utterly destroyed years of training in proper decorum and produced this … this shameless hoyden who is not worthy of the Maitland name."

"She is every bit a Maitland as you, Hugh." Eleanor Walker's usually soft voice filled the library.

Everyone turned to see Penelope's mother, who was standing in the doorway wearing an herb-stained apron over her white muslin gown. "You visit us for the first time in fifteen years, and you have the gall to talk of proper decorum."

Lucas watched in fascination as the soft-spoken woman sauntered into the room with the grace of the baroness she once was.

Dr. Walker spoke first in a cajoling voice. "Eleanor, my heart, this is not the time and place to bring up the past."

"The past has come to us, Robert, and it is time we face it." Eleanor's expression softened as she turned to Lucas. "Penelope told me your father killed himself after Edmund tried to get out of the betrothal contract, my lord, and I would like to clarify something once and for all." She pointed accusingly at the baron.

"Edmund, God rest his soul, never cared enough about the title to confront Leonard Drake."

Eleanor's eyes blazed as she shifted her attention to the baron. "It was *you* who ordered him to break the contract, wasn't it? You're responsible for Leonard Drake's death."

Lord Maitland looked as if he was about to suffer from an apoplectic fit. "How dare you! I merely reminded Edmund of his responsibility to the Maitland line, as I am now trying to remind Penelope."

"It was always about that with you, wasn't it, Hugh?" Eleanor asked in a quiet voice. "You couldn't tolerate the fact I married a common country physician, so you punished my daughter for it. But you have no hold over us anymore."

"We shall see about that."

"Please, will everyone calm down," Penelope burst out. The hinges of the armor creaked as she slowly made her way to the center of the room. She looked so out of place, so uncertain and strangely vulnerable, even in that damned armor, that Lucas had to restrain himself from going over to her, pulling her into his arms and banishing her heartless uncle. He understood she wanted to deal with this herself, and he was willing to let her as long as he could remain where he could watch over her.

Penelope looked at everyone in the room before finally addressing her uncle. "Apologies for my attire, Uncle, but I was not aware you were paying us a visit." She adjusted the visor before continuing, "I am sorry I did not turn out the way you expected."

"You can be whoever you want to be, Polly," Eleanor said encouragingly.

Penelope's laughter was muffled by the helmet. "Mama, please, can you stop being supportive for one minute and just listen to what I have to say?"

"Of course, Polly. We are listening."

Penelope rolled her eyes before turning her attention back to the baron. "Uncle, I have already given my word to marry his lordship. I know you will appreciate matters of duty." When her uncle did nothing but sneer, she continued, "I intend to marry Lord Ravenstone, and there is nothing anyone can do to stop me. I would, however, deem it a great honor to have your blessing."

Lord Maitland turned a nasty shade of red. "Of all the bloody nerve!" His hazel eyes raked Penelope from head to foot. "You are a disgrace to the Maitland line. Your father would have been appalled by this, and I am ashamed to call you my niece."

With that last statement, Lord Maitland picked up his hat from the chair and left the room. Moments later, the front door slammed shut.

"Apologies for that, Ravenstone," Dr. Walker muttered. "I honestly do not know what prompted Lord Maitland's visit. He has never done that in all these years."

"I must be getting popular," Penelope observed, staring at the door. "So many visitors this week. First, you, my lord, and now my uncle." She shook her head in dismissal of the entire event. "If everyone will excuse me, I will go upstairs and change."

Eleanor Walker looked skeptical. "I doubt you'll be able to get out of that armor without any help, Polly. I shall go with you."

Mother and daughter left the library, leaving Lucas alone with Penelope's stepfather once again. Uneasiness warred with his sense of victory. This was a decent family, and Maitland had been right to be suspicious of him. He *did* have his own agenda.

Dr. Walker strode to the fireplace and stoked the embers with a poker. "How odd that news of your impending nuptials would affect Lord Maitland so."

He shrugged. "It's not so unusual. Many families would not welcome an alliance with the tainted Ravenstone title."

"We know you, Ravenstone, and we are far removed from Society." Dr. Walker turned to face him. "I do not care what people say about you, I only care about my stepdaughter's welfare. I believe it is a sound match. Penelope is an assertive sort, and she needs someone who is strong enough to handle her."

She is a pain in the neck, Lucas thought. The woman was forever trying to jeopardize her health by going in headfirst into a situation without thinking all of the details through. Their impending marriage was a testament to that fact. Lucas had taken advantage of her impetuous and passionate nature to get what he wanted.

He ignored his conscience's tiny protest. He had done what he needed to do to get her to the altar; it was his duty to do so. Lucas had honored his father's need for revenge, and the Ravenstone fortune was now secure. By all rights, he should have been happy with the results of his actions.

So why did it feel just a little wrong? When he found out that Penelope planned to have an affair with him, he set out to save her from herself. He'd wanted to teach her a lesson about playing games with men like him, and had delivered the lesson with the finality of a parson's trap.

Penelope seemed to trust him now so completely, she was actually willing to marry him despite his reputation and what her relatives were saying. He hoped she would never find out the Maitlands were correct in their estimation of his character. His fingers flexed against his glass of port and he forced himself to relax his hold.

He dismissed his uncharacteristic anxiousness as nothing more than wedding nerves. There was nothing to worry about. Penelope was about to be his, forever. He smiled at the thought.

Life with the nymph would sometimes be exasperating but never boring. And the nights would always be exciting. Intense desire flared through his body as last night flooded his thoughts. He could still hear the erotic little sounds she'd made, the way she'd writhed against his hand and gave of herself so freely. He was looking forward to teaching her more about desire and passion on their wedding night. His embarrassing eagerness made him feel like a randy youth with his first lady.

Then Lucas remembered the way Penelope had looked in that suit of armor mere moments ago, and he had to restrain the urge to laugh. He had never encountered a woman quite like her in his entire life. She didn't fear him or get excited about the danger he represented.

Dr. Walker refilled his glass, and he gave the older man a respectful nod.

"Thank you for taking care of Penelope," Lucas said with quiet gratitude.

Dr. Walker smiled. "Don't tell her you said that; Penelope likes to take care of herself."

"She will not have to do so any longer," he promised with a smile of his own.

Chapter Twelve

It was her wedding night.

Penelope let her new lady's maid, Bess, fuss over her hair. Her decadent bedchamber was a stark contrast to the wedding this morning.

She and Lucas were married in a simple ceremony in the little village church up on a hill that overlooked Bouth. Everyone had turned out to witness the wedding, contributing flowers to her bouquet and giving the newlyweds their well wishes.

She wore her mother's wedding gown, a magnificent creation of rose satin embellished with flowers made of lace, which had to have some last-minute alterations as Penelope was shorter and more buxom than her mother. Lucas had arranged everything, even down to the food and drinks, which The Mucky Duck had provided. The event was as perfect as a wedding could be for a bride who knew the groom was not in love with her.

She noticed the cool satisfaction Lucas had radiated throughout the ceremony. He may think he was so cunning by leaving his coat in her bedchamber the other night, but the truth was he had merely provided her with an excuse to claim what she had wanted all along. She only hoped he did not regret his decision. Strange how life turned out. She had dreamed of being with Lucas for almost her whole life, and now they were husband and wife.

At one point during the wedding banquet, she'd spied the earl across the field talking to some villagers, listening to their plans for the spring planting and giving advice on the best strains of crop and wheat to plant. He seemed to sense her looking at him because he raised his head to give her a reassuring smile.

Penelope smiled back, before turning her attention to Mari standing beside her.

"How does it feel to be a countess?" Mari asked.

"To be honest," she admitted, "I feel uncomfortable in this gown. It is too tight. I don't think I'll be able to eat any of the food you made for fear of ripping the fabric."

Mari giggled. "I doubt you'll have to suffer long. Your husband looks as if he can't wait to turn in for the night."

Though she had never seen a man naked, she knew what married couples did in the bedchamber. Nevertheless, it was disconcerting to think everyone knew what she would be doing that night.

Penelope changed the subject. "I am glad David was able to attend the wedding, even if my uncle did not want him to."

"Yes," Mari said lightly. "I am amazed he was able to do the decent thing."

"He's not so bad, you know. I mean, once you get to know him."

"I already know far too much about that man," Mari countered before dismissing the subject. "When are you leaving for London?"

"Tomorrow. Lucas's sister is having her first Season, and I thought we must be there to give our support. We will have a proper honeymoon after the Season."

"Excellent! I will be leaving for London soon, as well." Mari beamed. "I received a letter from a publisher, and he wants to meet me in person to discuss my book."

"That is wonderful news! You can stay with us."

Mari waved off the offer with her hand. "I am staying with my aunt and uncle. Nothing is certain yet, so I may not be there long."

"Well, make sure to visit us when you're in Town."

"I will," Mari promised. "The Nevilles are coming over here to congratulate you, so make sure you have a smile on your face." With that, Mari left her side to help herself to some pudding.

Penelope pasted a smile on her face as she watched the Nevilles approach. The plumes on Mrs. Neville's head threatened to fly away as they caught the slight breeze. Thankfully, her mother waylaid the couple before they reached her.

Releasing a sigh of relief, she turned to seek a moment alone. She closed her eyes as the wind cooled her face, and she breathed in the grass-scented breeze. She was thankful to find a moment of peace amid the raucous laughter and music swirling about her.

"You look like you're about to cast a spell on all of us, nymph," Lucas whispered behind her.

She turned and gave her husband a serene smile. "I saw you talking to the farmers. Did you find their conversation edifying?"

"I hope you do not mind if I sometimes wander off to discuss crop rotations and fertilizers. It is what saved the Ravenstone fortunes, after all."

"I do not mind at all, Lucas. I'm glad the villagers no longer act oddly around you."

His brow arched in sardonic amusement. "They seem to be willing to forgive my reputation now that I have made an honest woman out of you."

She laughed, feeling lighthearted for the first time since the reception had started. "I still haven't forgiven you for letting Papa find your coat in my bedchamber."

Lucas reached up to tuck a wayward curl behind her ear. "Let that be a warning to you, Penelope. I always get what I want in the end."

She had a feeling he was not merely teasing. Then he took hold of her hand and all thoughts of who tricked whom scattered to the winds.

"Shall we dance, my dear?" Lucas asked, pulling her to the makeshift dance floor. "We can start the dancing and leave soon after. What do you think?"

"So eager to leave, my lord?"

He pulled her into his arms as the musicians struck up a waltz. "You have no idea," he rasped against her ear.

They left the party shortly after, heading for one of Lucas's smaller estates in Kendal. Her mother hugged her goodbye, and Papa shook her husband's hand, telling them they would visit soon to discuss the several business ventures Lucas had advised him to invest in.

Colin and Sarah were eager to visit London, too. Even Gertie had given them a tearful goodbye. It was during the farewells that it hit Penelope how everything was about to change.

Her life was with Lucas now.

And as Bess finished fussing over her hair, she decided to make the best of the situation. She was married to the man she loved. It was already more than what most women could ask for.

Her logical side said she should be content. Lucas was taking her to London to share his life, which was certainly more than what Father had done for Mama in all the years they'd been married. But her heart yearned for things just beyond her reach, things that involved loving, loyalty and trust. Things she'd witnessed between her mother and stepfather.

Her heart was stupid. And impossible to ignore.

She didn't even know anymore why Lucas had been so determined to marry her. Resorting to blackmail in the form of a discarded coat spoke of something more than duty. It was the action of a man who would stop at nothing to get what he wanted. It sparked a tiny bit of hope in her soul.

"You look wonderful, m'lady," Bess gushed.

She surveyed herself in the mirror and had to smile in agreement. Bess had done wonders with Penelope's hair, making it shine with highlights of red in the candlelight, instead of just the plain brown she was used to. Would Lucas notice?

"Thank you, Bess. I don't think my hair has ever looked this nice."

Her maid glowed with the compliment then excused herself from the bedchamber with a mysterious smile, as if she knew something Penelope didn't.

But, of course, Penelope knew what was about to happen. What was taking Lucas so long to open the connecting door between their bedchambers? Was he giving her time to get used to the idea of having a husband at night? She didn't need time to get used to the idea. Lucas had made her wait for more than twenty years already, and she was waiting no longer. It was time to take what she wanted.

With a deep breath, she smoothed the wrinkles from the frilly lace nightgown, barely registering the golden velvet drapes hanging on the four-poster bed she passed as she walked to the connecting door.

This was it, Penelope thought. On the other side of the door was where her dreams lay, and all she had to do was reach out and take them.

Without another thought, she silently opened the door and walked into her husband's chamber.

• • •

Lucas saw Penelope as soon as she came in—a forest nymph who'd ventured out of the woods, swathed in near transparent lace that whispered across her voluptuous body, the candlelight simultaneously hinting at and hiding the delights she had to offer.

Lucas could not help feeling a little awe. He'd been prowling his bedchamber, not certain whether he had the right to go to hers. He'd been at sixes and sevens since the wedding, a ceremony he'd ensured had as many witnesses as possible, in case there was a cause to question its legality in the future. He'd done it. The Ravenstone fortune was safe.

But it was a hollow victory. He wanted more. He wanted this nymph who'd enchanted him from the very first, the woman he'd tricked into becoming his bride. Penelope had teased him about it at the wedding reception, but he wasn't sure if she meant it. Did she still want him now that he'd given her a glimpse of his true character? That he was not the noble, honorable man she thought he was?

Yet *she'd* come to him tonight. Looking lovely and seductive with her hair piled loosely on top of her head, the tendrils glinting with fire in the soft light. "You were taking too long to come to me," she said in a throaty whisper that floated across the room. "I didn't want to sit and wait for you again. I thought if I did, I could be waiting another twenty years."

His eyes widened at her jibe. Only Penelope would think of claiming her husband on her wedding night instead of waiting in her bedchamber like a good girl. She must have sensed his indecision and made the choice for both of them.

She bit her lip as she stopped by the foot of his huge bed, and she rubbed her palms on her skirts, unwittingly giving him a better view of her lush form as he stood there by the fire. She was nervous.

He walked over to her, not certain if he had any right to touch her. He took her into his arms anyway. She felt so good to him. Her arms wound around his neck, pulling him down to her.

"I didn't want to wait another twenty years to know what it's like to be yours," Penelope whispered against his lips.

He groaned in response to her sweet words. His hands roved up and down her body. She was rounded in all the right places, and he ached to touch and taste her. All of her.

"Are you certain this is what you want to do, nymph?"

The fire in the hearth shone in her hazel eyes, reflecting the flame coursing through him.

"I've been certain of it for years," she whispered.

He wasted no more time mentally debating whether or not this was the right thing to do. He wanted her. She wanted him. They were married. Tonight, they would have each other.

He'd taken advantage of her trust in him, but this evening she had made her decision, and Lucas was not fool enough to refuse something freely offered. Not when he wanted it so much.

More than anything, he wanted to make up to her for the way he'd used their desire for each other to force her into marriage. He wanted to make sure that by the end of this night, Penelope would want this marriage as much as he did. So even if it killed him, he was determined to go slow tonight. This would be the wedding night she deserved.

"Come here, Penelope," he said as he pulled her against his rigid planes, loving the feel of her body, so soft and so *right* against his.

Penelope kissed his neck, making him groan. "Lucas?"

"Yes, nymph?"

"I have never done this with anyone before."

He nearly choked on his laugh. "I know."

"But I have seen animals mate. At the farm."

He lifted his head to stare at her flushed face. She said the damnedest things.

"What I mean to say is, now that we are doing this to make babies, would you require me to be lying on my front or on all fours?"

His hands stopped their roving for a second as he considered how the hell he was supposed to reply to her question. And then he cupped her face between his hands. "We'll go with what feels right when the time comes."

"But I want to—"

He captured the rest of her words with his mouth. He kissed her gently, wanting to reassure her. But when she slid her tongue against his bottom lip, he let her have what she wanted as the desire that had been building between them since the moment they met exploded.

Growling deep in his throat, he lifted her up against him, wrapping her legs about his waist, then carried her over to the soft bed and gently laid her against the satin sheets.

Penelope watched as he took off his dark silk dressing gown, baring himself as he stood by the foot of the bed. She kneeled on the bed, getting closer to him, her eyes riveted on his fully aroused body.

Perhaps his size was scaring her. He decided to confront the problem head on.

"Would you like to touch me?" His voice sounded gravelly to his own ears.

"Like this?" she asked as she innocently gripped him in her tight little fist, torturing him.

"Christ, yes," he rasped out. He held her hand, showing her how to please him.

She put her lips to the flat planes of his belly, and he almost came right then. He forced himself to hold back, determined to let her have her way with him. Who would have guessed this sweet country girl would be so uninhibited in bed? And she was his. Entirely, exclusively his. Lucas exulted at the thought.

He couldn't take the torture long. "Enough," he said, shrugging off her hand. "This night is for you, nymph."

"But, I like—"

"I know," he ground out. "I like it, too. But if I let you go on any longer, the night will be over before it's even begun."

He captured her mouth again, drinking in the joy of her as his hands went beneath the flimsy lace that was her nightgown, touching her bare skin. She moaned and pressed herself against him.

"What do you want, love?"

Penelope's eyes filled with an emotion he did not entirely understand. "I want you to see me," she said softly. The statement was filled with longing and a wealth of meaning he could not grasp.

She slowly unhooked the front fastenings of her nightgown, letting it whisper down her body and lie in a pool of lace atop the bed sheets around her feet. He closed his eyes as his cock hardened to stone. She wasn't wearing anything underneath. No stockings, no chemise, no drawers ... nothing. Christ, this was going to be a long night.

Penelope stood on the bed, the fire from the hearth silhouetting her form. She was a vision from his dreams as she looked down on him.

"I want you to finally see me, the way no one else ever has," she said as she laid her hands on his shoulders, easing the tension in the muscles there with her fingers.

He buried his face in her soft belly, inhaling her scent. "I see you, sweetheart." His hands roved over her buttocks and thighs, marveling at the endless smoothness of her skin as he spread kisses down her navel.

"Lucas!" she gasped when his mouth found the damp, glistening curls between her legs. The scent of her arousal filled his head.

"I've been wanting to do this for so long." He cupped her in his hand, looking for her core and then finding it.

He stroked her gently, tracing every fold and curve until his fingers were slick with her moisture. She was perfect. She started to make faint, gasping sounds, and her hands bit into his back.

"So responsive," he whispered against her skin. "So eager."

With one last kiss to the curve of her waist, he pulled her to him and laid her in the middle of the bed, following her down, then he leaned up to take in her full, wonderful body. He needed her to relax. "Look at me, Penelope."

• • •

Penelope opened her eyes and touched her hand to his hard cheek as he hungrily gazed at her naked form. She could see his need, the barely restrained passion blazing in his midnight eyes, and she gloried in it. In this, at least, they were equal. Lucas may not care for her the way she did for him, but tonight he seemed as desperate.

"You have no idea how many times I've imagined seeing you like this," he whispered hoarsely, his hands claiming her. "You are even more beautiful than I imagined."

There was no chance to reply as his mouth claimed hers again in a fierce, devouring kiss that she met with enthusiasm. He was making her feel so wanted and needed, and he spread pleasure with every touch of his hand down her body.

One of his hands cupped her breast, and another rested on the curls between her legs. His tongue stroked inside her mouth in tandem with his hand kneading her breast and his finger moving on the incredibly sensitive nub he'd found at her core. She jerked against him, overwhelmed with the sensations rioting through her as his hand plumped her breast, circling the nipple, and his finger relentlessly caressed her center in ever-quickening circles.

She kissed him back with all the desperation she felt. She was riding a wave of tension, she felt herself tightening, raining moisture as his finger stroked faster, firmer. She sighed against his mouth and she sucked his tongue, his bottom lip, needing something she did not know if she could have.

"Lucas!" she gasped as he released her mouth to bury kisses down the length of her neck.

"I'm here, sweetheart," he said as he nibbled on her collarbone.

His finger was driving her mad; her legs started to quiver as she opened herself wider, arching her hips to get more of his amazing caresses. And then she felt a broad finger slide deep inside her. She moaned then, unable to stop herself from thrusting her hips to meet him.

She clung to his shoulders, kissed any part of him she could reach, wanting to reciprocate the incredible feelings he ignited with his skillful hand as he slid another finger inside her and stroked her core more firmly. She moved with his hand, her chest heaving with each shallow breath, reaching for the peak she knew was just beyond her reach. And with one last push, she went past it, crying out as she climaxed, and streaks of the purest pleasure washed over her.

His fingers gentled, guiding her as she drifted back to earth slowly, feeling his lips nuzzling her breasts. She cupped his head to drag it back up to hers, and blazing onyx eyes met her dazed ones. She pressed against his hand and he groaned, gripping her hip to still her movements. "You will be the death of me, Penelope."

She smiled and leaned up to whisper in his ear. "I want more."

He lifted his head. There was a primitive look in his eyes as he stared at her. She pulled him back to her, angling his head for her kiss as she said softly, "Make me yours tonight, Lucas."

A deep groan tore from his chest as he leaned over her, his big frame shuddering at the contact of their skin, and then his kiss was blatant and carnal, his tongue driving deep, making her open her mouth wider as heat built inside her again. His hands slid down every curve of her body, his touch almost rough with his urgency.

He tore his mouth from hers to follow the path of his hands, and then his lips were at her breasts, making them ache as he sucked first one straining nipple and then the other. She clutched his head against her breast, offering herself to him as her body arched to meet his seeking mouth.

"I love the way you respond to me," he said, his voice harsh as he slid between her thighs, parting them wide. She felt his hardness against the damp curls at her center and she moaned as he rubbed himself against her most sensitive part. "I love the sounds you make, the way you get so wet … "

Suddenly, he slid down and his face was just above the place he was rubbing with his body. She could feel his harsh breathing against her. Dear God, what was he doing? She swallowed her embarrassment when she felt his fingers opening her, exposing her most private part to his eager gaze.

"Do you like it when I touch you here, Penelope?"

He slid a finger down her middle. His mouth was so close to her core, she felt his words against it.

She was barely able to answer. "Yes."

She looked down at him and had to close her eyes against the erotic sight of his dark head hovering there between her legs.

"God, Lucas … "

He muffled a laugh against the inside of her thigh. "I want to taste you, Penelope. Please, let me taste you." He put his head back where it was, so close against her moist flesh.

She lifted her hips to meet his mouth, giving herself to him. It was all the permission he required. His fingers opened her and his mouth swooped down, kissing her in the most intimate way imaginable. She could do no more than grip the sheets and enjoy as his tongue tasted her damp folds, finding every secret crevice. She sighed, loving the feel of his lips against her. It was like when he caressed her with his fingers, except better. More intense. And then his tongue found the swollen peak of her sex, and she was lost.

Her fingers clenched in his hair, and she felt his growl of approval as he continued to lash at her in quickening circles and his fingers teased at her wet entrance. She felt the wave ride her again as he worshipped her with his mouth and fingers until she was writhing against him, pressing herself against his wicked mouth, which had become the center of her world. He sucked at a particularly sensitive spot and suddenly she was climaxing again, riding the violent wave as it crashed onto shore.

Her body was still racked with tremors when Lucas kissed his way up her body and she felt him press his heavy, aroused length against the place where his mouth and hands had just been.

He surged into her tight entrance in smooth, short strokes, his passage eased by the damp wetness she rained down on him. When he reached the shield of her virginity, he stopped. "Penelope?"

She opened eyes and shifted her hips, making him groan as he kept himself still. "Do you know what's going to happen now, sweetheart?"

She smiled. "I'm going to be yours."

Another groan tore from his chest, and he kissed her, swallowing her cry of pain as he gave one fierce thrust, burying himself to the hilt.

"I'm sorry," he rasped, kissing her cheeks, her closed eyes, her temples. "I had to do it, sweetheart. I am so sorry. God, you are so tight."

"It wasn't so bad."

He lifted his head to stare at her. She cupped his cheek in her palm and he turned to kiss it, moving a little as he did so.

"Do that again."

He grinned. "This?" he swiveled his hips once more.

She cried out. "Yes!"

He growled his answer. "With pleasure." And he started moving against her, retreating almost all the way out and slowly thrusting back in, giving her body time to adjust to his size.

He kissed her again, his mouth gentle as he rocked against her.

Sliding a hand between them, he started stoking the fire in her until she relaxed, and she pressed against him, her body matching his movements.

"Like that, Lucas. Harder."

Lucas groaned and gave her what they both wanted. She felt his body throb as he thrust deeper, harder into her. She sighed her pleasure against his ear. She pressed herself against him and his thrusts became more urgent as he drove into her in hard, demanding strokes.

They moved in unison as heat flared between them and they were both gasping for breath. He tugged her knees up higher to pound against the very heart of her. She gasped his name as they moved faster and harder, racing for the edge together.

"You're mine now, nymph," he said hoarsely as sweat dampened his forehead.

"Yes, I'm yours, Lucas … I've always been yours."

"Mine … mine … " He said again and again as he thrust powerfully into her, filling her completely.

Suddenly she tightened around him, crying out his name as she convulsed beneath him. He thrust deeply one last time and followed her into oblivion, pouring himself into her. When he finally collapsed against her, she cupped his face in her hands.

"You are mine now, too," she whispered.

She felt him shudder, then he rolled onto his back and held her tight. She laid in his arms, and waited for his reply, but the silence between them remained unbroken.

Chapter Thirteen

"It's impolite to ignore your sister-in-law, Olivia," Lucinda Milthorpe, who insisted on being called Aunt Lucy, advised.

Olivia was reading a book, sitting across Penelope in the luxurious Ravenstone town coach as it made its swaying journey toward Oxford Street.

Penelope sighed. It had been her idea to take Olivia on a shopping expedition, hoping they could get to know each other better.

"Lady Olivia isn't ignoring me, Aunt Lucy," she retorted. "She is ignoring *both* of us."

Olivia started. She closed her book with an audible snap. "Forgive me. I didn't intend to be so rude."

She met Olivia's familiar midnight gaze. "I would like to say how welcome you have made me feel during the two days we've known each other, Lady Olivia."

Olivia gave her an uncertain look. "Thank you, Lady Ravenstone."

"However," she continued, "as we both know, it would be a complete and utter lie."

Aunt Lucy released a horrified gasp.

"I … I'm not certain how to behave," Olivia admitted, following Penelope's example of bluntness. "I've never had a sister before, my lady."

She smiled. "First of all," she said gently, so the younger woman would realize she meant no offense, "sisters don't call each other 'my lady.' May I simply call you Olivia?"

Olivia nodded.

"Good. And you should refer to me as Lady Ravenstone."

"If it pleases you, Lady Ravenstone."

"I'm joking! Call me Penelope," she said with a laugh.

Olivia gave a tentative smile. "All right. Penelope."

"Well!" Aunt Lucy remarked, "That wasn't so difficult, was it? It's depressing how polite Society insists on being so formal with their own families. It must have something to do with being in Town."

The elderly woman shook her head in a severe manner. "I feel I must warn you, Penelope, the London air is not healthy for people. Why, I've noticed since Olivia and I returned from Ravenstone—that's your husband's principal estate, by the way; it is located in Surrey. Such a grand and marvelous place, so much quieter than my nephew's townhouse. You remember I told you about my nephew, Lord Westville? Well, there's always some sort of debauched, manly amusement going on in his house. It will give you the ague—well, since returning from Ravenstone … what was I talking about, dear?"

Penelope gave Olivia a conspiratorial grin. "You were telling us about London."

Aunt Lucy brightened. "Ah, yes. London. It will give you the ague."

Olivia smiled apologetically. "Aunt Lucy often suffers from illness."

"I wouldn't be plagued with so many illnesses if it weren't for the unhealthy London air! I believe it's the thick, impenetrable fog that kills. It will give you—"

"The ague!" they chorused.

Aunt Lucy blinked. "We've stopped. We must have arrived. Let me handle my modiste, dear. She is very exclusive, but a more annoying woman I have never met. She talks incessantly … "

Aunt Lucy kept up her chatter while a footman helped the ladies alight. She led the way through Oxford Street, complaining about the London air.

"Good Lord," Penelope whispered to Olivia. "Is she always like this?"

"I'm afraid so." Olivia shot her another apologetic look. "I'm very glad to have someone else to talk to now."

"I don't blame you," she replied.

"Can we visit a bookshop after the modiste's? I'm almost finished with my book, and I'd like to purchase another."

"That sounds divine," she agreed. "I should like to buy books for my stepfamily. My siblings love to read, too."

"We shall go to Hatchard's," Olivia decided. "They have a little of everything in there."

Penelope noticed how the elegant London shoppers were giving them a wide berth.

"What is wrong with everyone?" she asked Olivia.

Olivia looked around them with a solemn expression. "They recognize Aunt Lucy. Everyone knows she is playing chaperon to Raving Ravenstone's sister."

"Don't ever call yourself that again."

"Everyone else does," Olivia sadly pointed out.

"Not everyone," she insisted when she noticed a familiar face. "I see my friend, Mari, exiting the milliner's. Let me introduce you to her."

"But, Aunt Lucy—"

"Won't notice if we're gone for a few seconds," she assured her sister-in-law. "She is too busy yammering about the dangers of the London air."

She dragged Olivia with her as they hurried to Mari's side. After the introductions were made, it was decided that Mari would join them at the modiste's, as Penelope was not an expert when it came to fashion and she trusted Mari's opinion.

Once inside, Penelope was thankful for Mari's presence, for Aunt Lucy had complained of a headache and ensconced herself on a sofa in the shop's corner. There were fabrics of every imaginable make, colorfully laid out on every available space of the shop, fashion plates suggesting ensembles were artfully arranged in strategic spots, and a very haughty modiste, Madame Claude, suggested styles of which Penelope had never heard. The only thing she couldn't find in the shop was the sign indicating how much the services were.

"How do I know which ones are costly?" she mumbled.

Mari laughed. "All of them are costly. Don't look so concerned. Ravenstone will expect his wife to be dressed in the height of fashion."

"We can probably make these clothes ourselves," she said, feeling uneasy.

"Don't even think of it," Mari warned. "You're a countess now, Polly. You have to look the part. Enjoy yourself. Here," Mari pointed at a fashion plate, "this mint evening dress will look lovely on you. I adore the paisley pattern trim. It's like the one we saw in that magazine."

"Ah, *mademoiselle* appreciates exquisite design," Madame Claude approved while she openly scrutinized Penelope's features. "Lady Ravenstone, you are to make your debut tonight?"

She nodded. "Lady Olivia, too. She is to attend her first ball at the Uffingtons'."

"If it pleases, I should like to present to you a gown I have designed." Madame Claude proceeded to whisper, "Your ladyship shall be the only one allowed to see it, for I have been waiting for the right person to wear my creation. The gown has a ... *comment dites-vous*—otherworldly quality. If you will follow me?"

She glanced at Mari, who nodded. "I would be honored, Madame Claude."

"*Non,* the honor is mine, my lady. Please," Madame Claude gestured to a room hidden from view of the main shop floor by a pair of ruby-colored, velvet drapes. "Come with me to my workshop."

After the private consultation, Penelope felt prepared for the evening's festivities. She also insisted that Mari order a gown for herself, an invitation her friend gleefully accepted.

By the end of their shopping expedition, even Olivia was joining them in teasing Aunt Lucy, who enjoyed having an audience and seized the opportunity to complain about the thickening London fog.

. . .

Lucas looked up from documents piled up on his desk when he heard the big commotion out in the hall. Penelope, Olivia and Anthony's Aunt Lucy must have finally returned from their shopping expedition. Lucas was more than a little curious about the result of Penelope's idea to spend time with his little sister.

Olivia was a quiet sort, the kind of person who took a while to get comfortable around new people. It would take some time for her to get used to having an older sister like Penelope, who took things in stride and assumed the same unaffected, casual air with everyone, whether they were a footman or an earl.

In the two short days since she first stepped foot in his townhouse, his bride had managed to learn all the servants' names, and they were bending over backward to do her every bidding. Even Finchley, his very proper butler, could not resist her charming ways.

The minute Penelope learned Finchley used to be a furniture maker's apprentice, she'd asked if he could make a writing desk for her instead of hiring one of the well-known furniture makers who enjoyed the patronage of the *ton*. She said she planned to put it in the drawing room, where everyone could admire it.

Her thoughtful action had endeared Penelope to his elderly butler, who understood the business opportunity the new mistress had offered and was spending every minute of his free time working on the new Countess of Ravenstone's *escritoire*.

Lucas opened the study door and smiled in amusement at the sight that greeted him. Penelope, dressed in one of the new pale muslin gowns Aunt Lucy's modiste had hastily put together, was directing the footmen, who were carrying armloads of parcels upstairs.

His wife scowled at one. "Sammy, you should not be carrying anything until your burned hand has healed. Let me take that from you."

Finchley stepped in before she could climb up the stairs to the footman. "I'll take care of it, my lady."

Penelope gifted the butler with a grateful smile before turning to his sister. "You are going to look beautiful in these, Olivia!" she said with ill-concealed excitement. "I don't know much about fashion, so we were very lucky we ran into Mari while we were in Oxford Street."

"The gowns you chose complement your figure, Penelope," Aunt Lucy stated. "Even through my pounding headache, I could tell they made you look like a fairy princess."

"Why, thank you, Aunt Lucy. I shall make you some chamomile tea to relieve your headache," his wife promised. "Then, perhaps, you'll say I appeared more like a nymph than a fairy princess."

Aunt Lucy looked thoughtful. "Now that you mention it, Madame Claude's creations make you look quite ethereal."

"Lucas says I look like a nymph," Penelope said proudly. "I never thought I'd say this, but I so enjoyed picking out fabrics, being poked and prodded … "

Lucas's wide shoulders shook with laughter as he listened to the rest of the conversation.

" … and that gentleman we met at the bookshop—I will not be surprised if he pays us a visit soon."

"He was very nice," Olivia murmured.

He frowned. "What is this I hear about a gentleman?"

Penelope whirled at the sound of his voice. "Lucas! Olivia and I met this young man at Hatchard's. I think he said he was Lord Blakewood, and he was kind enough to help Olivia find this book she wanted to read."

Lucas stilled. "Was he?"

Viscount Blakewood was the son of one of the men whose business practices had led his father into dun territory. Lucas had repaid the old man in kind, and the scandal that ensued had contributed to Society's labeling him Raving Ravenstone. It didn't take a genius to figure out what Blakewood's son was planning by seeking out Lucas's sister.

He gave Olivia a stern glance. "You are not to talk to Blakewood again, do you hear me?"

Olivia picked at her skirts. "Yes, Lucas."

He felt Penelope's disapproving stare. He ignored it. "It looks as if you have many things to do to prepare for the Uffingtons' party tonight, sister. Why don't you run along upstairs?"

"Yes, Lucas." Olivia ran upstairs with Aunt Lucy at her heels.

His wife waited until the girl was out of earshot before giving him her opinion. "What was that all about?"

"I do not know what you are referring to." He strode back into his study.

She followed him and shut the door with a resounding crash.

"What the devil was that for?"

"I thought it would be more dramatic," she quipped. "What is your problem with Blakewood?"

"His father and I have an unpleasant history, which resulted in the man's financial ruin. He ran off to France and spent his last years there, leaving his son to pick up the pieces. It would be best if Olivia stayed away from Blakewood."

"I see." She cleared her throat. "I believe your worries are premature. It was nothing more than a friendly chat at a bookshop."

He sat down behind his desk and picked up the documents he'd been reading before the ladies arrived. "I intend to make sure they have no further interactions."

She hesitated, casting a cursory glance at the burgundy leather furniture that stood in stark contrast to the green and gold floor-length curtains of his study.

He watched her as she touched a bouillotte lamp before looking around for something else to occupy her hands. His body tightened as he thought about suggesting something he very much wanted her to do with those hands.

Lucas shifted uncomfortably in his seat. It wouldn't do to spend too much time with his little nymph. He'd done his duty to marry her. He had other responsibilities to think of now. He enjoyed her company, and she was delightful in bed, but he refused to let his desire for her take over his entire life. Already she had gotten under his skin. If he weren't careful, he'd end up becoming as pathetic as his father.

The ghosts from the past screamed a warning in his mind.

His hand tightened to a fist. "Is there something else you wanted to say, madam? I am very busy."

Penelope jumped at the sound of his voice—maybe he'd been too curt. He cursed, dismissing the ridiculous worry. It would be better if they didn't spend so much time together. He didn't want her to get too attached to him—attachment led to expectations, and expectations inevitably led to disappointment. He didn't want Penelope to be disappointed in him.

She moistened her lips with her tongue, and for a moment he was riveted by the action.

"Well, Penelope?"

Penelope looked at him speculatively, as if trying to gauge the color of his soul. "It's only … I don't think Blakewood means any harm. He was exceedingly nice to Olivia. It was the first time I'd seen her really smile in the time I've known her."

"Olivia is not the smiling sort. And it is my duty to protect her until the time comes for her to marry."

Penelope took a seat on one of the burgundy leather chairs across his desk. "She is also your sister, and I think you intimidate her. You were rude to her just now."

"I merely told her to prepare for the Uffingtons' party tonight."

"That's just it," she muttered. "Did you even ask her how our shopping expedition went?"

"I already heard how it went from your edifying commentary out in the hall." He didn't want to talk about his sister any longer. He'd been craving another taste of Penelope all morning, and she was here in his study with the door firmly shut. "I look forward to seeing you in the new gowns you have bought, nymph."

"Really?"

At the naked hope in her eyes, he found his first smile. "Yes, really."

He held a beckoning hand out to her. "Now, come over here and show me how grateful you are for those gowns."

Penelope took his proffered hand, and he tugged her onto his lap. He crushed his mouth to hers, savoring her sweet lips, growling his pleasure when she opened her mouth to welcome the invasion of his seeking tongue.

"I've missed you," she said in a breathy sigh when he finally managed to lift his mouth from hers.

His hand slid beneath her skirts and petticoats to find her bare thigh. She squirmed in reaction. Her rounded bottom came into contact with his erection, and he groaned. She was a natural temptress.

"Show me where you missed me," he whispered against her ear.

In answer, Penelope took hold of his hand, which had been caressing her thigh, and inched it upward, urging him to cup her heat, showing him exactly. Her uninhibited action tore another groan from Lucas's chest as he explored her moist, welcoming folds. She was already very hot, very wet for him. He trailed kisses across her collarbone and mentally consigned his worries about spending too much time with his wife to the devil.

He lifted her off his lap and set her on his desk, sweeping the surface clear with his arm. Documents, missives and ledgers went flying across the room.

Penelope looked up at him in confusion. "Lucas?"

He slid her legs apart and stepped in between them. "Just hold on, sweetheart. I'll take care of everything."

He quickly worked the fastenings of her gown, loosening the bodice, her stays and chemise to expose her naked breasts to his devouring gaze. Hungry for her, he proceeded to kiss every inch of her exposed flesh, fondling her until her breath came in ragged gasps, mingling with his own labored breathing.

He knelt before her, tasting her womanly core with an urgency and desperation he'd never known, losing himself in the scent of her desire. As soon as she cried out with her climax, Lucas was on his feet, opening the falls of his trousers, unable to wait any longer.

Failing to be gentle, he pinned her back on the desk and joined his body to hers with one fierce, demanding thrust. *God, she felt so good.* His large shaft stretched her out, filling her. She cried out, wrapping her legs and arms around him, and he groaned as the change in angle allowed her to take in even more of him.

Their mouths fused together, tongues mating as their bodies moved in a hard, wild rhythm. He pumped into her in powerful strokes, neither of them noticing the desk drawers rattling as she clung to him for the ride, and he felt the pleasure take over her again. Her body convulsed around him, milking him. Lucas groaned her name as he thrust himself to the hilt inside her one last time and claimed his own release.

He collapsed on top of her. He buried his face in her neck as he gasped in deep, panting breaths. The scent of sexual satisfaction surrounded them, and his eyes remained closed as he savored the way his wife enveloped his body in every way imaginable, clinging to the blissful place she'd taken him.

But awareness was already returning, and with it, a dawning realization crashed over him. He'd completely lost control with this woman. He opened his eyes, registered the surface of the desk and remorse burned in his gut. He'd taken her right here in his study, for God's sake.

What was wrong with him?

He levered himself off her and righted his trousers, then he lifted her off the desk, steadying her when she stumbled on her feet. Wordlessly, he started straightening her gown, unable to meet her gaze.

What was it about this woman that made him lose his mind whenever he touched her? Never had he known such overwhelming passion, this overpowering need to possess her and bind her to him completely that took precedence over everything else. If he hadn't known better, he'd think that some otherworldly force was behind this insanity. That she really was a mischievous nymph who had decided to play with him.

He stared at her face, noting the lovely tint of her cheeks, her pretty lips that were swollen from his kisses. He felt himself harden, and his mind reeled as he realized that he wanted her again. Immediately. He stepped back in awe.

"Lucas?" Penelope called out, her uncertainty clear. Her chin trembled as she reached for him.

He shook his head in an attempt to clear it, thankful when Finchley discreetly knocked on the door. "What is it?"

Finchley opened the door and gave a discreet cough. "Begging your pardon, my lord, but Lord Westville has arrived. He said you were expecting him."

He sighed and raked a hand through his hair. "Yes. Show him in, Finchley."

A moment later, Anthony walked in. Amusement lurked in Anthony's eyes as he looked at the heap of documents on the floor, then at Penelope, before finally resting his gaze on Lucas.

"Am I interrupting something?" Anthony's gaze shifted back to Penelope, and he bowed respectfully. "Forgive my forwardness, my lady, but I haven't seen Ravenstone in weeks."

Anthony cast Lucas a sidelong glance. "The last time we saw each other, you were on your way out of Town to pick up some baggage."

Lucas scowled at his friend. "If you can stop grinning like an imbecile, Anthony, I'll introduce you to my wife."

Penelope excused herself from the study soon after the introductions were made, mumbling something about changing her attire and made for the door to leave the men to their business.

He watched his friend follow Penelope with his gaze as she exited the room. Lucas cleared his throat, and Anthony turned to face him.

"Your new countess is enchanting," his friend remarked.

Enchanting was the perfect term to describe the nymph. She had cast a spell on him from the moment he'd met her in that coaching inn. Even now, it was all he could do to concentrate on what Anthony was telling him.

"News of your sudden marriage has swept the Town. Everyone is curious to see the new Countess of Ravenstone."

He sighed and sank in the chair behind his desk. "They will see her soon enough," he grumbled. "We are going to the Uffingtons' ball tonight." He gave Anthony a direct stare. "I trust my sister has not caused you any trouble while I was away?"

"No," Anthony assured him, taking a seat on one of the burgundy leather chairs on the other side of the desk. "Little Olivia was well behaved as always. I've no doubt she will get an offer before the Season ends."

With the small talk out of the way, they started talking business. Now that the Ravenstone fortune was safely in his hands, Lucas could go back to investing without worrying if his inheritance would be snatched out from under him.

It had only been three weeks since he was last in Town, and not much had changed in that time. Anthony filled him in on the latest news, but his thoughts kept wandering back to his wife. He had the uneasy feeling he'd hurt her with his silence after their last encounter.

He'd lost himself completely and had probably been too rough with her. He stared at his desk surface in contemplation. He didn't doubt Penelope's enjoyment of their lovemaking. He knew she found fulfillment. And yet, he couldn't shake off the haunting image of her looking at him with that vulnerable, lost expression so soon after their interlude.

He grimaced. He probably owed her an apology. He didn't know how wives expected to be treated after performing their marital obligation, but he suspected they expected more than mere silence. *Damnation. Marriage is hard work.*

The problem with Penelope was that she was unlike any other woman he'd known. She probably wouldn't be soothed by flowers or trinkets. Hell, he was probably going to have to adopt a few abused donkeys to soothe her ruffled feathers. And then a thought hit him. "Anthony, is Colonel Martin in Town?"

"He is, as a matter of fact. Why do you ask?"

One side of Lucas's mouth kicked up. Penelope would love to meet the colonel. It was the perfect way to atone for what had taken place in his study.

Chapter Fourteen

Penelope went up the winding grand marble staircase and headed for Olivia's bedchamber.

She needed to put her encounter with Lucas behind her. She thought she had finally reached him today, but she saw the panic in his eyes after they'd made love and the relief in his features when Lord Westville had interrupted their discussion. It was obvious her husband regretted the entire interlude.

That hurt, but she tried to focus on the positive. She knew Lucas had been trying to avoid spending time with her since their wedding night. Oh, he joined her in bed every evening, but during the day, he kept their discussion light and impersonal. There had been none of the teasing banter she had shared with him at Highfield Manor. They'd spent the long journey to London discussing travel arrangements, and since arriving in Town there had been so much to do, they'd hardly talked at all.

At least they had finally spent some time alone together during the day, even if he'd regretted it afterward. She angrily cast thoughts of her confusing husband and marriage aside. For the moment, she would focus her efforts on Olivia. Penelope wasn't the only one who'd been hurt today by Lucas's callousness.

She reached Olivia's bedchamber and knocked on the door once before letting herself in. Olivia was sitting on the frilly bed, her yellow muslin dress arranged carefully about her.

"Have you chosen which gown you're wearing for the ball?" Penelope asked.

Olivia looked up, and it occurred to Penelope once more how very much the girl resembled Lucas. Her eyes were the same shade of midnight, and her raven hair tended to curl at the ends like her brother's. Her coloring wasn't the only thing she had in common with her brother either. There was something about Olivia that seemed too somber for a girl of eighteen.

Penelope rummaged through the young woman's closet. "I think you should wear that pale pink gown. You would look beautiful in it."

"Did Lucas send you up here?"

She whirled. "Of course not! Your brother is downstairs in the study with his friend, Lord Westville."

Olivia's fingers trailed over the cover of the book they'd bought at Hatchard's. It was a tome on architecture, written by a man named Gibbs. Penelope didn't care a whit about the subject. In her opinion, merely thinking about architecture was already such an arduous process that *reading* about it would be sheer, unmitigated torture. So she decided to discuss their visit to the bookshop instead.

"It was very kind of Lord Blakewood to recommend that book. I must admit, I don't know anything about architecture myself."

Olivia's features softened with a dreamy smile. "I've met him before, you know."

"Who?" She sat on the bed beside Olivia. "Lord Blakewood?"

"Yes. We talked before Lucas sent me home to Ravenstone while he claimed you."

Her eyes narrowed. "Your brother thinks it's a bad idea for you to associate with him."

"Lucas doesn't even know him! Lord Blakewood is a gentleman right down to the tips of his toes."

"His toes, really?" she teased. "I didn't realize a man's toes could be an indicator of whether or not he was a gentleman. I usually rely on things such as clothes and manner of speech."

Olivia giggled. "You say the oddest things, you know."

"I know."

"I am nervous about tonight," Olivia confessed.

She nodded. "Me, too."

"You are?"

"Of course. You're not the only one who's having a 'come-out.' And I am not nearly as statuesque as you are, so it will be difficult for me to stare down the gossipers."

Olivia giggled again. "I shall be right by your side to do the staring down for you."

"I would appreciate that. The important thing," she advised, "is that you have fun. If you are not enjoying yourself, then all of this would be no different from sewing with a broken needle."

"A broken needle?"

"Pointless."

"Thank you," Olivia said simply.

The statement surprised her. "For what?"

"For making me laugh."

She smiled and got off the bed. "You're very welcome."

* * *

The laughter was back in Penelope's face when Lucas spied her from the balcony that evening at the Uffington manor. His eyes were drawn to her like a magnet as he debated how best to approach her. He'd spent part of the evening at his club, as Anthony had advised, to confront the gossip about his sudden marriage. He'd endured surreptitious stares in the club, but no one had actually dared to ask him about his married state until David Maitland came in and joined him for a glass of brandy.

"Ravenstone," Maitland said, seating himself across from Lucas. "I thought I'd find you here."

He inclined his head in acknowledgment. "Maitland."

The air of anticipation that swept across the roomful of aristocrats was palpable. He didn't have to wait long before one of the gossiping fools approached the table.

"By Jove, so it is true then?" asked Lord Haynes, an aging fop with a balding head, as he moved toward Maitland. "Ravenstone has married your cousin?"

"Yes, it is," Maitland confirmed. "I attended the wedding myself."

Lord Haynes's bushy brows shot up. "By Jove. So you have married her, then?" he demanded of Lucas.

"Maitland has just told you that I have done so."

"Well, by Jove! Rumor has it you did get married. Odd, that."

He turned his head very slowly, pinning Haynes with his gaze. "You find it odd that I have married?"

Lord Haynes's moustache twitched. "By Jove," he croaked before walking away.

Maitland chuckled and lifted his glass to Lucas in a mocking toast. "If only I could do that to annoying little gossips."

He crossed his arms over his chest. "What are you doing here, Maitland?"

"I arrived this morning," Maitland explained. He took a sip of his brandy before continuing, "I thought Penelope might need my help in confirming her identity, seeing as my father couldn't even be bothered to go to your wedding."

Lucas arched one brow in a sardonic gesture. "Why are you suddenly so interested in Penelope's welfare? I understand you have not deigned to visit her in years."

"I understand you had not deigned to visit her at all," Maitland shot back before he continued his explanation. "I have recently found out some truths about my father, and I think it's time I make up for the mistakes he made."

That sentiment was something Lucas understood very well. So it was without hesitation that he informed Maitland of Penelope's itinerary for the evening.

"The Uffingtons?" Maitland paused, gathering his thoughts. "I shall have to change my attire, but I will be there to show my support."

"I appreciate that," he said quietly. If Maitland attended the ball, there would be no further questions about Penelope's identity.

His wife had been so concerned about his reputation and Olivia's debut, it hadn't occurred to her that she would also be under scrutiny. In typical Penelope fashion, she had been worrying about everyone but herself. Even during their bargaining over marriage terms, the things she had asked for concerned her stepfamily, her servant and even her dog, instead of herself. Except for her demand for him not to order her about or to take a mistress. He smiled at the memory.

Now that he was her husband, it was his privilege and duty to make certain she remained safe. Protecting her reputation had been foremost in his mind on the way to the Uffington ball. The minute he arrived, however, he realized his concerns had been unnecessary. The nymph seemed to have found a way to captivate London's elite with her unique combination of humor and warmth, the way she did with everyone she encountered.

Dressed in a decadently graceful puce-colored, velvet gown with ruched sleeves and a pleated skirt with gold and silver stripes at the hem, Penelope looked like a sorceress from an Arthurian legend, a complete antidote to the jaded occupants of the ballroom.

His jaw tightened as he noticed the man she was dancing with. Ethan Banks, a simpering fop who had entered Society a couple years ago, was twirling his wife around the dance floor and, in his opinion, holding Penelope much too close.

Lucas told himself it was not jealousy that made him hurry down the stairs and cut through the endless sea of people. It was natural for any man to be annoyed at the thought of having to cut through another man to claim his wife for a waltz.

• • •

It amazed Penelope that Ethan Banks had the nerve to approach her now after he had told her a couple years ago that her lack of dowry made marrying her an impossibility, and then started courting Mari barely a week after dropping his suit.

She'd never had any deep feelings for Ethan, but for those few months she had believed at least there was someone who seemed to appreciate her and not how useful she could be. How wrong Penelope had been about this man. Her lips curved with amusement as he twirled her about the dance floor in a waltz—how inferior this experience was to the waltz she had shared with Lucas at their wedding.

What did Ethan think he was going to get out of this?

She didn't have to wait long for an answer.

"Please accept my felicitations on your marriage, Penelope."

"Thank you."

Ethan looked uncomfortable. "I noticed you were friendly with the Duke of Granderly's daughter."

"Lady Beatrice appreciated my advice about her cat's flea problem. She said she would try my recipe for peppermint soap as soon as she gets home."

Her dance partner's brows furrowed. "Indeed? Well, I was wondering if you could introduce me to Lady Beatrice. You and I are old friends after all, are we not?"

Her smile froze. "Of course. I will introduce you to Lady Beatrice if time permits." *Right after I warn the young woman about you, you money-grabbing weasel.*

He looked relieved. "I appreciate your help, Penelope. Have I complemented you on your gown, by the way? You look radiant tonight."

Lucas's bored drawl made both Penelope and Ethan stop in mid-step. "She does look beautiful, does she not?"

She whirled around to see her husband's forbidding features, his eyes glittering with an unsubtle threat as they rested on her dancing partner.

"Banks," Lucas clipped out, "you don't mind if I cut in, do you? I have been looking forward to dancing with my wife all evening."

Ethan paled as Lucas advanced on him. "Not at all, my lord." He bowed to Penelope before stepping back as if he couldn't wait to get out of reach.

Lucas's arm snaked around her waist, and he expertly maneuvered her into the waltz. "You seem to be enjoying yourself, my dear."

He sounded like he'd just swallowed ash. She tried to hide her smile. "I am."

"How do you know Banks?"

Her smile widened. "He offered to marry me once, a long time ago."

"While you were engaged to me?"

"Yes."

"I shall have his head on a platter."

Laughter spilled from her lips, which garnered curious stares from the other couples on the floor, who visibly strained to hear the conversation between Raving Ravenstone and his new countess.

"You are not putting anyone's head anywhere," she whispered. "I did not accept his suit, Lucas. So there is no need to be jealous."

"I am not jealous."

"I'm glad."

A grunt was all the reply she got.

She rolled her eyes. "What took you so long to get here?"

"I was delayed by your cousin."

She gaped at him. "David is here?" She looked around her. "Where is he?"

"He will be here soon." Lucas whirled her to a halt near the French doors that led to the gardens. "Come, I have a need to discuss things with you." He was about to tug her out the door when David appeared at their side.

"Penelope! How wonderful to see you here, cousin!" he said in a voice loud enough to be heard by the people milling around them in the crowded ballroom. "I hope you're not missing the Lakes too much. London can be quite confining."

She hugged her cousin with enthusiasm. "David! My goodness, you look impressive tonight." She looked over his shoulder, as if trying to locate someone. "I wish Mari was here, but you should dance with Olivia, if you can find her. She's been dancing all night."

She noticed the coolness in David's eyes at the mention of Mari's name. She had no opportunity to comment, however, because David suddenly launched into a discussion of politics with Lucas. Lucas's friend, Lord Westville, soon found them and joined as well. They were talking about the merits of reform when she felt her stocking slide down her leg.

"Excuse me, I have need of the retiring room," she mumbled before striding carefully to the far end of the ballroom, smiling at people who wanted to greet the new Countess of Ravenstone along the way.

Several people seemed disappointed that she was not stopping to chat. She already knew what they wanted to know. They would ask first if she was well, and then they would express their concern about her fate. The less tactful ones would warn her about Raving Ravenstone and assure her they would be there to assist her if needed.

Assist her with what, she wondered.

It was only her first ball, yet she was already tired of people's assumptions. And it was not even her character being scrutinized. She wondered how Lucas could have borne it all these years.

She strode through the empty, darkened corridor. She had no idea which door led to the ladies' retiring room. She tried the first door on her left and promptly tripped over a small furry creature, which yelped in astonishment.

"I am so sorry, little dog," Penelope whispered, as she reached out to light one of the small wall sconces. The faint light from the sconce revealed a library.

"Wrong room," she muttered.

Still, Penelope realized she was quite alone in here. Acting quickly, she adjusted her garters and was about to leave the room when she heard a muffled noise.

Slowly, she turned back, noticing as the little dog scurried out of the room that it had a rope around its neck. Who would take it out for a walk at this time of night?

She cautiously stepped deeper into the large, dark library, following the strange, scuffling sounds. Soon, she heard voices. A man and a woman were talking in hushed tones. Penelope knew she blushed as she thought of what she might have interrupted, but the voices sounded angry, not amorous.

"I told you to leave the dog," she heard the man hiss.

"The boy wouldn't leave without it."

"Well, we have tied the boy up, so there is no need for the dog."

"But it knows what we are doing now!" The woman's voice was frantic.

"Shut up! Everyone is busy with the ball. No one will pay heed to a yappy dog. Now get the boy; we have wasted too much time as it is."

She jumped into action as soon as she heard them struggling to get the window open. She searched for "the boy" and found him in a narrow aisle slumped against one of the bookshelves with his mouth gagged and his hands bound behind him. This was an abomination! He could not have been older than nine. His eyes widened when he saw her and she put a finger to her lips, warning him to be silent.

This was clearly a kidnapping. She didn't know who the child was, but at that moment, all that mattered was he needed her help. She wished she'd worn something less cumbersome, for her gown made it very difficult to move quickly. She knelt in front of him and started fumbling with the ropes at his back when she heard the man's incredulous voice behind her.

"Who the hell are you?"

She whirled and faced the barrel of a pistol pointed straight at her. She grabbed the boy and backed deeper into the aisle. She could see only the man's silhouette as he confronted her.

She swallowed a lump of what tasted like panic. Though she knew she would excel at panicking if she indulged in the emotion, at that moment she thought it best to try to remain calm.

"What are you doing to this boy?" she asked, backing deeper into the row of shelves.

The man blocked the only exit, but she knew pistols became less accurate the farther away the target was, so she tried to place as much distance as possible between her and the weapon.

"Stay right where you are, lady. We are taking him away, and if you stay out of our business, we will let you live."

The kidnapper's female accomplice appeared behind him. "Ned? What is going on here?"

"Some Society chit wandered into the wrong room. But she is going to stay put and let us leave, ain't that right, m'lady?"

"Ned, I don't feel good about this—"

Penelope wasted no more time. The boy stumbled and she grabbed a fistful of books, hurling it straight at the kidnappers. A deafening shot rang out just as she ducked to tug the boy up on his feet while a searing pain numbed her right shoulder.

"You're not going anywhere, lady!" the man hissed.

At that moment, she knew she was going to die. It seemed an apt end to her life as well, she thought deprecatingly. Even to her last breath, she would prove to be useful, for there was no way she was going to let these villains take the little boy.

"You're not going anywhere either," she vowed with only a slight tremor in her voice.

Penelope lifted a heavy book threateningly.

Lucas's voice filled the room. "Penelope? Are you in here?"

She clutched the boy in her arms. "Lucas! Help!"

The kidnapper swore and whirled to face Lucas, who greeted him with a large, bunched fist. The accomplice wailed as Lucas hauled the man up by his collar and shook him.

"Teddy!" Lady Uffington shrieked from the doorway. The accomplice used the commotion to make her escape through the open window. "Stop!" Penelope screamed, but she was too late. The woman had already escaped.

Several people poured into the library, probably drawn by the pistol going off, only to see Lucas holding a barely conscious man in the air by his collar while she clutched a small, bound and gagged boy.

A few men ran to help Lucas apprehend the kidnapper, binding his hands and feet while the constable was summoned. She never let go of the child.

Lady Uffington seemed to finally shake out of her stupor. "Teddy!" she screamed again.

Penelope let go of the boy, who ran straight into Lady Uffington's arms. "Oh, Teddy, thank God you are safe," she cried as she freed her son's hands and held him close.

Penelope watched it all happening as if in a dream—her right shoulder ached, and her feet remained rooted to the floor until Lucas stepped into the aisle and pried the heavy book she'd forgotten she was holding from her hand.

"You have a lot of explaining to do, madam."

Penelope registered the worry in his gaze and she forced herself to speak. "I—" she cleared her throat and tried again. "I hit him with the book—"

"I know."

"He was going to take the boy—"

"I know."

She glared at him. "Then why are you asking me for explanations?"

"Are you all right, Penelope? He didn't hurt you?"

"No," she said, and then she remembered something. "Lucas, the pistol—"

"Has been taken out of his hands," he reassured her. "He was the boy's nurse's lover. They were going to take the Uffington child away and demand a ransom for him."

She suddenly felt light-headed. "Then it's fortunate I went into the wrong room."

She cried out when Lucas grabbed her shoulder.

"Good God, you've been shot!"

"What?" She saw the blood on Lucas's hand at the same time she felt warm liquid trickle down her arm. "Oh. You're right."

After that she had a vague awareness of Lucas sweeping her up into his arms as the world spun, coinciding with the severe pain in her shoulder. Everything seemed to slow down, and she realized she was going to faint mere seconds before darkness claimed her.

Chapter Fifteen

The news of Penelope's attempt to save the Uffington heir had spread all over Town, and people who would not normally step into Lucas's townhouse poured in to visit and express their concern. Penelope's brave rescue of the little boy had made her an instant heroine among the females of the *ton*.

It was a damned nuisance.

But as the days of Penelope's recuperation went by, Lucas realized she was not the only one who was being treated differently. People who had made it a point to avoid him, such as the Duke of Granderly, came to visit with his daughter, Lady Beatrice, in tow, not only to check up on Penelope but also to commend Lucas for the way he had saved his wife from the kidnapper.

He rarely left Penelope's bedside. She hadn't sustained a fatal injury, but the sight of her bleeding was something he would never forget. What had struck him most as he sat there by her bed was how small and vulnerable she appeared, engulfed in bed sheets with her shoulder swathed in bandages. He alternated between berating himself for failing to protect her at the Uffingtons' and restraining the urge to shake her still form for once again plunging headfirst into a situation without thinking about the repercussions.

Trust Penelope to think of defending herself with a handful of books. The villain had probably been too far away to hit with her reticule. Once she was well enough, he would have a long talk with her about her impetuous nature. He did not want to go through the scare she'd given him ever again.

She could have died. Did she not consider what losing her would do to him? He couldn't understand why the thought troubled him so, but there was one thing he could no longer deny: he cared about Penelope. In a way that surpassed duty.

He had never met anyone like her. She always put everyone else's concerns above her own. Only Penelope would have dared to try to rescue a strange child from danger without thinking of her own safety. Most people would have run for help. Her utter disregard for herself made him feel quite selfish. And guilty. Because he, too, had taken advantage of Penelope's selflessness.

"Butter the crumpets," he muttered.

He was not going to be like his father. He would not allow his wife to matter so much to him that he forgot his duty and everyone else. Lucas was so engrossed in his internal turmoil, he didn't realize Olivia had walked into the room until she spoke.

"How is she?" his sister asked.

He stretched his long legs out in front of him. The small chair he sat on was damned uncomfortable. It was a miracle the thing was able to hold his weight. "She's still sleeping. The doctor said she will be fine in a few days."

Olivia nodded. "Does this mean we will not be attending any more balls?"

He heard the disappointment in his sister's voice. "I don't see a reason for you to stop going to a few soirees while Penelope recuperates. At any rate, it shouldn't take long for her to get back on her feet again."

"Lucas, do you like being married?"

The question gave him pause. He hadn't really given much thought to whether or not he *liked* being married. It was his duty, and as far as he was concerned, his feelings had nothing to do with it. But it was damned difficult trying to stay aloof from someone like Penelope. It was also, he was learning, quite pointless.

"It is not so bad," he allowed.

Olivia sighed. "I am glad to know you will not be alone after I get married."

"Have you set your cap on a particular gentleman?"

She blushed. "Why would you think that? I only meant I would marry someday, and I have been worried about leaving you alone."

It had never occurred to him Olivia might be concerned about him. "Bloody hell. I am not an invalid, sister."

Olivia made a helpless gesture. "I know, but you have devoted many years of your life to raising me, Lucas. Now that I'm grown, I was concerned you might get lonely after I marry. But now you have Penelope."

He gazed at his sleeping wife and smiled. "Now I have Penelope."

And he was going to make certain he never lost her.

• • •

A week later, Penelope looked down at the raucous crowd from the Ravenstone box at the Theatre Royal, watching the fascinating antics of the theatre patrons.

The dandies gathered below were putting on quite a show before the performance even began. Everyone who was anyone turned out to see Edmund Kean perform *Othello*. Moreover, she knew that Lucas suggested they attend tonight so the entire *ton* would see she was healthy and well.

"Everyone is expecting Kean to be at his best tonight," Olivia remarked. "But I'd wager the actor is foxed again, as per usual."

Penelope laughed. "I wonder which of his inner demons will come out to take a bow at the end of the performance." She was in good spirits tonight, and her jovial mood had nothing to do with the anticipation of tonight's play.

No, her happiness was due to the fact that she and Lucas had been getting along very well the past few days. He'd rarely left her side during her recovery; he'd read to her and made sure she ate enough and slept well. He took Nelson out on walks and even allowed the dog to sleep in the library.

He was proving to be a most devoted husband, and she suspected he was beginning to care for her. A part of her knew she shouldn't be hoping too much, but she couldn't help it. If people saw this tender side of Lucas, they would never believe him capable of the ruthless things they said he'd done. If he was merely doing his duty, then he was certainly enjoying it.

She heard a commotion behind her and knew it was another Society member who had entered their box to convey their relief that she'd recovered from her ordeal. It had been going on all night, and she was starting to feel like a restored historical artifact on display before the entire *ton*.

So her eyes widened in shock when she heard Lord Blakewood's voice as he approached them.

"Good evening, ladies," Blakewood said, though his eyes were on Olivia's face. "I trust you have recovered from your recent ordeal, Lady Ravenstone?"

She looked pointedly first at Blakewood, and then at a blushing Olivia, then back at Blakewood. "How very kind of you, my lord. I am doing very well."

"And you, Lady Olivia? Did you enjoy the book I recommended?"

Olivia batted her eyelashes. "I found it to be quite entertaining, my lord."

Blakewood grinned in a boyish manner. "I knew you would be entertained."

"It was very entertaining, my lord."

Penelope unfurled her fan and waved it about quite vigorously while Blakewood and Olivia stretched a conversation about being entertained to the point of awkwardness. Olivia clearly had developed a *tendre* for the young man, and Blakewood seemed to return her affections.

In truth, she didn't think Blakewood had any evil intentions toward Olivia. The young man seemed to be genuinely enamored of her sister-in-law.

Lucas would not be pleased.

She was proven correct when her husband entered the Ravenstone box. He ignored her warning glance and went straight for the young lord.

"Blakewood," Lucas said in a challenging voice. "I am certain you will understand if I requested you not to linger. It is getting damned crowded in this box."

Lord Blakewood reddened. "Not at all, my lord," he muttered before bowing to the ladies and taking his leave.

Olivia glared at Lucas. "You didn't have to be mean to him. He was behaving like a gentleman."

"I told you to stay away from Blakewood."

"But why? He has been nothing but kind to me since I met him."

"I have my reasons," Lucas muttered as he sat beside Penelope. "Now quit harping on about this subject. The performance is about to begin."

The curtains went up, and silence went over the crowd. Penelope hardly noticed. She knew Lucas meant well, but as someone who had teenage siblings herself, she knew he was going about this all wrong.

"She likes him," she whispered.

"Bloody hell, don't you think I know that?" Lucas hissed back.

She waited another moment before continuing. "I think he is being genuine."

Lucas snorted. "Ah. Apparently, you have become an expert on human psychology, and would now proceed to share your perceptive insights to your poor, beleaguered husband. What makes you think he is being genuine?"

"Because my teeth didn't leave a dent on his words," she quipped, resisting the urge to hit him with her fan. Really, did he have to be so condescending?

Lucas apparently didn't find her remark so amusing, and he was quiet throughout the performance and on the way home. She let him wallow in his bad mood until later that evening, when she heard him prowling his bedchamber. She waited until he dismissed his valet, then she let herself in through the connecting door between their suites without knocking.

"We need to talk," she said firmly, watching him pour a hefty measure of brandy into a glass.

Lucas turned to her, glass in hand. Even in his black silk dressing gown, he looked very male, powerful and intimidating. "I am not in the mood to talk, nymph."

She gathered her courage and walked deeper into the big chamber, which was kept from being chilly by the enormous fireplace that blazed with flames.

"I know you do not approve of Blakewood," she began, "but I must warn you nothing will be achieved by bullying your sister."

The blaze in Lucas's eyes put the flames in the hearth to shame. "You think I'm a bully?"

"What would you call yourself then, after that display in the theatre?"

His jaw clenched. "I would call myself a man who is doing his duty by his sister. Now, enough of this nonsense and get into bed."

"Heavens above!" She almost stomped her foot in frustration. "I cannot believe a man who can casually quote Wordsworth would be concerned only with duty."

"You'd better believe it because I am not going to change. Not for you or anyone."

This wasn't getting her anywhere. She had to find another way to reach him. "What about your sister? Is it not your duty to make sure she's happy?"

Lucas tossed back healthy measure of brandy. "She will be happy if she stays away from Blakewood."

"You are the most stubborn man I have ever known," Penelope muttered. "Would it be so bad if Blakewood courted her? That man is not out for revenge. You, of all people, should understand that."

He slammed his glass on the small table beside him. "I do not know what you mean."

She threw her hands up in the air. "Blakewood must surely hate his father as much as you do your own."

His jaw tightened. "Bloody hell! I don't hate my father."

"Do you not? He left you to deal with the duties he was too weak to face, the one person who should have taken care of you." She walked to him and caressed his rigid cheek, her voice softened. "I know how you feel. I, too, had a father who never faced up to his responsibilities. I kept wondering why he was never home, why I wasn't good enough for him to want to watch me grow up."

"Penelope—"

"I wasn't born a boy, but I was useful in my own way. I could be traded for an opportunity to merge with the Ravenstone fortune."

"Sweetheart, stop."

"When he did come home, he never asked about me. He didn't want to see how I was doing with my studies. He just went straight to my nurse and cheated on my mother. I wasn't anything but useful to him until the day he died."

Lucas pulled her to him. "Oh, sweetheart … "

The tears she'd been holding inside her for so long started to fall in big, fat drops. "I loved him so much, but I was never enough for him. I wasn't enough to make him want to behave decently. I wasn't enough … "

• • •

Lucas roved his hands over her back in a helpless gesture of comfort. "Hush, sweetheart. No more."

He kissed her fragrant hair, hating himself. In all the time he'd known her, he'd never seen her cry. Not when her stepfather's creditors had insulted her or when her uncle had rejected her or even when she'd been shot. She was crying in earnest now, and his heart ached for the heartbroken little girl she had been.

It was the first time she'd confided in him. Furthermore, it occurred to him as he held her that he felt closer to Penelope in that moment than he ever had with anyone in his life. It made him want to tell her things he'd never told anyone.

"Sometimes, Penelope, it is not us who are lacking. It is the people around us."

She lifted her head and raised wet, hazel eyes to his. "What do you mean?"

"I was the one who found my father right after he shot himself in our hunting lodge."

Her pink lips parted, but she remained silent.

"Up until that moment, I thought he was everything I wanted to be—loving, dependable and caring toward his tenants."

He shook his head. "But he took the easy way out and left a boy of sixteen to deal with the mess he left behind. He didn't even think to leave a note to tell me where to begin."

He cupped her soft cheeks in his large hands, his thumbs rubbing away the tears. "If I seem like a bully, it is only because I want Olivia to be able to depend on me to do my duty. I do not want to let her down as our father did."

"Your sister loves you very much, Lucas."

He emitted a laughing groan. "I don't think she loves me very much at the moment."

"Nonsense," she said. "How could you ever doubt Olivia's devotion? Any woman who spends any amount of time with you knows how easy it is to love you. I, myself, had forgotten over the years. Yet all you had to do was show up in that country inn, and I fell in love with you all over again."

It seemed to Lucas that the night suddenly became more vibrant, more vivid. The burgundy silk coverlet on his enormous bed looked more inviting, the fire in the hearth blazed just a little higher, and the stars outside shone a little brighter.

Penelope loved him.

Her declaration affected him so fiercely, he couldn't breathe for an instant.

"You love me?"

She gave him a teary smile. "Of course. Why do you think I married you?"

"Your stepfather found my coat in your bedchamber—"

"Please." She waved a dismissing hand. "If I told Papa I didn't want to marry you, he wouldn't have pushed the issue."

He stared at her in wonderment. "You love me."

"Why do you look so surprised? Goodness, what do you think was the reason I let you kiss me that first day at the inn, or touch me during our picnic, or—"

He never let her finish. His mouth claimed hers in a kiss of tender possession, drinking in her sweetness while his large hands memorized her luscious form, molding her soft, delectable body to his hard length.

Chapter Sixteen

Judging from his kiss, Lucas liked hearing she loved him. Relieved, Penelope kissed him back, reveling in the groan that tore from his chest as she slid her tongue between his lips to taste the contours of his mouth. There was something different about Lucas's lovemaking tonight. She felt it in the almost reverent way he touched her.

She lifted her head to give him better access to her neck, sighing her pleasure when she felt him nibbling on her collarbone and then soothing her sensitive skin with his tongue.

"Say it again," he whispered against her ear.

"I love you," she moaned.

Lucas revealed her body slowly, lifting her nightgown and kissing every inch of skin he uncovered before moving on to remove the next piece of clothing. By the time he'd fully unveiled her and his gaze raked her form, she was a mass of quivering limbs, desperate to feel the exquisite sensations she knew only he could give her.

She slowly untied his dressing gown, revealing the muscles of his chest. Her hands whispered against his flat stomach, making his hard flesh leap in reaction. She loved this man. And as she let his silk dressing gown fall to the floor, she tumbled him down to the enormous bed to prove it.

She climbed on top of him, kissing his hard cheeks and the column of his throat, and she smiled when she felt his hands clench in response.

Lucas rolled her onto her back and hovered above her. His eyes shone like onyx when he growled out a command. "Say it again."

"I love you."

His hand went to her breast, making her gasp. "Again."

"I love you."

His mouth fastened on her breast, and she buried her fingers in the soft hair at his nape as streaks of pleasure pooled inside her. His hand went to the mound of curls between her legs. "Again."

"Lucas … "

He opened her folds, drawing a thumb down her middle, and she cried out at the intense sensation as his fingers played at her opening. He was driving her crazy.

"Say it again, nymph."

"I love you!"

His finger delved deep inside her wet heat, and she arched her hips to meet him, her arms going around his shoulders as he caressed her relentlessly with his wonderful fingers. His other hand gripped her waist, leaving her no place to hide as his knowledgeable male hand found all her secrets.

"Christ, nymph, you feel wonderful here."

And then his mouth was on her as well. Her head thrashed on the pillow and her breath started coming in short gasps. She was all his for the taking, and she ground herself against his mouth, opening her legs wider, moistening his fingers even more while she let him feel all of her.

Moments later, she was coming apart in his arms, lifting her legs in blissful surrender as waves of ecstasy crashed down on her and a cry tore from her throat.

His caresses lightened as she surfaced back to the world, but it was a long time before she could open her eyes. When she did, she saw him hovering above her, his face a hard mask while his eyes glinted with triumph.

"I love you," she whispered.

A strange, unholy light came over his features. And he smiled.

Penelope rolled back on top of him, taking him by surprise. "I love you," she said as she rained kisses down his chest. She licked his flat nipples and smiled when she heard him groan in response.

Her hands traced the hard muscles of his stomach, and then went lower.

• • •

Lucas stopped breathing. His body throbbed as her hand hovered above the place he most wanted it to be. Hell, he didn't know how he'd survive if Penelope didn't touch him soon.

She did something even better. She slid down his body while her tight little hand gripped him. He felt her moist lips against his swollen shaft as she whispered, "Can you feel how much I love you yet, Lucas?"

He groaned. "Penelope … "

His eyes shut in surrender when her mouth closed over him. Moments later, a choked gasp escaped him and his eyes snapped open as her sweet tongue licked him, her elegant fingers gripping him. She was every man's dream, and she was all his. She loved him. The thought drove him mad with wanting until he could take no more.

He dragged her back up and gripped her waist, positioning her until she was poised against his fully aroused body. He saw her eyes light up with curiosity.

"We can make love this way?"

He gritted his teeth as her essence rained down on his swollen manhood. "Why don't you take me inside you, and we'll find out?"

He lowered her to him, showing her what he meant until she caught on and took over. She rode him, taking him higher and higher inside her until he was buried to the hilt.

He summoned the last vestiges of his control and held back, torturing himself as he gazed up at her beautiful face during this amazingly intimate moment. Each erotic little moan she made drove him nearer to the brink, and he kissed her breasts, desperately wanting to taste and savor her as she found her rhythm and rode him harder. He sucked hard on her nipple, making her scream.

"I love you!" she cried again and again as her tight sheath convulsed around him.

He surged into her, her vow of love ringing in his ears as he spilled himself inside her in a long, long release that left him awed, spent.

A long time later, Lucas gazed at the dying flames in the hearth while he held his sleeping wife in his arms. As he stroked her sleeping form, a strange feeling of peace, absent from his life since his father had died, washed over him.

He kissed her hair, inhaling the feminine, intoxicating fragrance that was Penelope. He recalled her sweet avowal of love and felt his body tighten. He could lose himself in her again.

He shook his head in amazement. He wondered if he would ever get his fill of this lovely woman. The soft contours of her body fitted his perfectly, and she slept in his arms as if she belonged nowhere else. He cuddled her closer.

She loved him.

The knowledge sent a shaft of light in the dark recesses of his soul, illuminating places he'd thought buried and gone long ago. And in the midst of his profound contentment, fear started to take root.

Would Penelope still love him if she found out the truth, the reason behind his reappearance in her life? Would she still let him touch her if she found out he was not the noble, honorable man she deemed him to be? That he'd married her to secure his inheritance?

He didn't realize his grip on her had tightened until she stirred in his arms.

"Lucas?"

"Go back to sleep," he whispered, nuzzling her neck.

Penelope turned in his arms until she was facing him. The firelight turned her skin to gold, and her hazel eyes were glowing, more green than brown in this light.

"You are so beautiful," he said truthfully. "The most beautiful woman I have ever known."

Her eyes widened. "No, I am not. But thank you."

"You are," he insisted.

She grinned. "Then the world must be full of blind men, for I vow not one of them would agree with you."

Overwhelmed by the sweet wonder that was his wife, he replied, "It must be, or else they'd see the amazing way your eyes turn from green to brown, depending on your mood. How their depths hint at the mysteries of the forest." He touched his lips to hers. "And how generous your lips are, lips that seem to be made for kissing."

She blushed.

"And how you make a man think of strawberries when a blush tints your creamy skin."

She laughed. "Strawberries?"

"Mmmm." His hand roved down her body, sending a blissful sigh to her lips.

"Go on," she said. "What about the other parts of me, my lord?"

He grinned, feeling lighthearted for the first time in years. Of all the women in the world, only Penelope would be brazen enough to fish for compliments so blatantly.

He kissed her neck and dipped his head lower, smiling against her skin when she shivered in response. "I need to be reminded. Let me take a closer look at the rest of you."

His wife's hands wandered the planes of his back, pulling him to her. "I would hate for you to claim things without seeing the evidence first," she teased.

He emitted a laughing groan as he proceeded with his investigation.

Chapter Seventeen

It would take some time to get used to being sought after. People surrounded her. Everywhere Penelope went, people wanted to talk to her, and her every move was noted by London's gossips. She was the Town heroine, and everyone seemed to want a piece of her.

"Since I went through a lot of trouble to reach you, madam, I think I deserve a dance," Lucas said when he finally reached her side.

Without further preamble, Lucas took her hand and led her to the dance floor. It all happened so quickly, she didn't have time to do anything but tread along in his wake and whirl about the dance floor with him in a sweeping waltz.

She was about to ask him which friend her uncle had talked to when she saw a black scowl sharpen his features as he looked at something over her shoulder.

"I see Olivia is still not heeding my advice to stay away from Blakewood," Lucas muttered.

"Oh. Is he dancing with her again?"

"Again?" He looked fit to be tied.

She nodded. "He was her partner in a quadrille earlier in the evening."

Her husband's eyes narrowed. "Apparently, I need to have a talk with Blakewood."

"Yes, you do," She agreed. "Shall I invite him over for tea?"

His gaze snapped back to her. "I'll take care of Blakewood."

"No, you will not."

"I won't?"

"No. Lucas, I told you I believe his intentions are honorable, and if you give him a chance—"

"Over my dead body."

"Don't say that! I wouldn't be able to bear it if something bad happened to you."

"Because you're in love with me," he stated with a smile.

She almost groaned out her frustration. "This is hardly the time to discuss such things, but yes, I'm in love with you. Are you happy now?"

"Very. I would like to take you out to the gardens, so I can show you how happy I am."

Penelope resisted when he tried to whirl her to the sidelines, near the French doors leading to the grounds. "Hmmm. I think you are trying to change the subject. We were discussing your sister and Blakewood."

"And I told you that I was going to take care of it."

She gritted her teeth. Lucas could be so intractable. "How will you take care of the matter? By frightening young Blakewood?"

"I can be very convincing when I want to be."

Well, so could she. "You are going about this the wrong way, Lucas."

His grip on her waist tightened. "Olivia has never disobeyed me before. I will not tolerate it."

"She is a grown woman now. Don't you think you should show her you respect her choices? You have raised an intelligent young woman, Lucas."

"Her wisdom seems to have left her," he muttered. "I can sense that you are dying to suggest a plan of action. Out with it, nymph."

"I think you should welcome his suit. That way, they wouldn't be sneaking about behind your back, and we can get to know him better."

"No."

"You already know they're going to continue seeing each other regardless of what you say. Wouldn't it be better to have them do it in the open, so we can supervise?"

"He will ruin her to get back at me."

"You sound like my uncle."

Lucas was clearly outraged. "Bloody hell, woman, I am nothing like your uncle!"

She gave him a pointed look. "He, too, is very stubborn and convinced you married me only to get back at him."

Lucas seemed content to remain silent.

"Well?" she prodded.

He gave her an impatient look. "Well, what?"

"Did you marry me only to get back at my uncle?" She didn't know why she was pursuing the issue. She really should stop before Lucas gave her an answer she did not want to hear.

The last strains of the waltz were dwindling, and Lucas whirled her to a halt before whispering his reply. "I do not give a damn about your uncle."

Do you give a damn about me? Penelope had to bite her tongue to stop herself from asking him the question as they took a turn about the ballroom. She was about to continue pressing her point on the subject of Olivia and Blakewood when an elderly gentleman of average height and a distinctive Irish accent approached them.

"Ravenstone, you should introduce me to the lovely young lass on your arm," the elderly gentleman suggested.

Lucas grinned. "Good evening, Colonel Martin. I am glad you were able to make it tonight. My wife has been looking forward to meeting you."

She stood there like an idiot as her hero, Colonel Martin, bowed low in front of her. For the first time in her life, she had absolutely no idea what to do. Should she hug him? She wanted to hug him.

"Speak up, lass," Colonel Martin demanded, straightening. "I didn't come all this way just to be stared at."

Penelope could feel her blush at the reprimand. "I am a big admirer of your work, colonel."

"So I heard." Colonel Martin grinned. "Your husband told me about the way you defended a donkey from a violent, drunken carter."

"Lucas helped, too," she admitted.

"Did he?" Colonel Martin gave him a speculative glance. "It would be good if your husband supported my efforts in Parliament."

"I doubt my wife will ever speak to me again if I don't," Lucas joked.

When Colonel Martin turned back to her, his voice was serious. "Lady Ravenstone, I came not only to meet you but to ask for your help."

"I'll do anything I can," she assured him.

"Your husband told me you are aware of the *Cruel Treatment of Cattle Act*."

Penelope smiled. "And I know you are responsible for that law, colonel."

The elder gentleman nodded. "A few friends of mine want to form a society to make sure the law is upheld when it comes to the treatment of animals such as cattle."

"I see."

"It's still in the early stages," the colonel said. "But we would appreciate any help you can give us. People listen to you, and rumor has it you are gifted with talents for treating sick animals."

"I do my best," she confirmed.

The colonel grinned. "Well, if you would honor me with a dance, we can talk about the particulars."

It was not a request, but she didn't mind in the least, and with Lucas's approval she joined the colonel in a lively country reel.

Colonel Martin danced with a level of energy that was unexpected for a man of seventy odd years, and Penelope had trouble keeping up with him let alone concentrating on the conversation.

He moved like a man possessed. If this was how he danced, she could only imagine the vigor with which he policed the streets of London to apprehend those who disobeyed the law and abused the beasts in their care.

"Your husband was right to suggest I meet you," he admitted right before the leaders of the dance called another step.

"Is that so?" she asked breathlessly as they danced down the line.

"Ravenstone said you would be willing to help us organize the society we are planning to create. There are always animals in need of tending."

She nearly collided with another couple as she and the colonel moved down the line. Talking to one's partner while dancing a country reel was tricky, especially for someone like her, who had not had many opportunities to participate in any sort of dancing in her life.

"I would be delighted to help," she promised.

The lively dance offered no more opportunities to talk and by the end of it, she was out of breath.

"Are you tired already, lass?"

She could only nod.

"You would probably be more suited to supporting the cause rather than implementing it." Colonel Martin stared at her, as though reaching a decision. "Would you like to meet my friends?"

When she nodded her assent, he led her straight to a group of people who were involved in a discussion near the edge of the dance floor. She was introduced to a bespectacled man called Sir Thomas Fowell Buxton and another named Sir James Mackintosh, who were gracious enough to include her in the discussion of founding a formal society that would aim to put measures in place so that Martin's Act was implemented.

A few minutes later, Lady Uffington joined the group. "I am not an active participant," she said, "but I agree there's a need to uphold the law for the vulnerable so they are not abused."

She was glad to have another woman on board, and she was about to say so when Lady Uffington softly said, "Thank you for saving my son."

"It was nothing, my lady. I only did what anyone would have done in that situation."

Lady Uffington studied her for several minutes before stating, "I disagree. I can't imagine what would have become of my Teddy had it not been for you and your husband."

She didn't know what to say to that, so she commented on the plight of the kidnappers instead. "I heard the boy's nurse has been apprehended."

Lady Uffington discreetly cleared her throat. "Yes. And you will be glad to know I have taken your advice and given the girl's family some money. I cannot forgive what she did, but I thought you would approve."

"That's, er, very magnanimous of you."

"Thank you. Since Teddy's rescue, I have been thinking a lot about what it means to be of 'noble' class." Lady Uffington smiled. "Now then, where is that handsome husband of yours so I can thank him as well?"

Penelope scanned the room. "I do not see him anywhere."

Her hostess shrugged. "Perhaps he went out into the gardens for a breath of fresh air." She gave her an approving look. "You have changed Ravenstone, you know. He used to shun soirees such as this."

"His sister is enjoying her first Season," she reminded the older woman.

Lady Uffington's brows rose. "There was no need for him to re-enter Society's ranks to launch his sister. He is doing it for you, my dear. I never thought Ravenstone would be so devoted a husband."

She almost smiled. Lucas might not love her yet, but he had certainly dedicated himself to his husbandly duties. Then again, performing duties was a big part of who Lucas was. His devotion might not have anything to do with her at all.

The group was discussing the best ways to disseminate information when Olivia appeared at her side, accompanied by Lord Westville.

"Olivia, is anything wrong?" Penelope looked questioningly at Lucas's friend, but he avoided her gaze by flicking an imaginary piece of lint from his superbly tailored evening coat.

Olivia's clenched fist crushed her lacy handkerchief. "I cannot find Lord Blakewood, and Lucas is also nowhere in sight."

Westville hesitated before speaking. "We are not certain what is happening. I am sure Ravenstone knows what he is doing."

"He is going to kill Lord Blakewood!" Olivia wailed.

"Calm yourself, Olivia," she said quietly, "Lord Westville is correct. This is no time to go into hysterics. Lucas knows what he is doing."

Olivia shook her head. "He is going to murder Lord Blakewood, and everyone will say Lucas was acting just like our mother."

Penelope turned to Westville. "My lord, would you mind taking Olivia home while I try to find where my husband has gone? I don't think she can take any more of this, uh, excitement."

"Of course," he said. "My aunt and I will take care of her."

"Lady Wortley will not mind your absence?" Olivia asked.

Westville looked uncomfortable at the mention of his current mistress. "Lady Wortley will find someone else to entertain her tonight." His discomfiture was obvious as he faced Penelope. "How do you plan to get away from here if you fail to find Ravenstone?"

"Lucas will not leave me here without a means to go home. Even if I fail to find him, I am sure he has made some arrangements."

Westville seemed doubtful. After a moment's hesitation, however, he accepted her explanation. "Very well, but send word if you need me to come back."

She swallowed past the lump in her throat as she watched Westville take Olivia away, stopping only to collect Aunt Lucy before they were swallowed by a rainbow of ball gowns.

She waited a few minutes more before excusing herself from Colonel Martin's group, stopping every once in a while to talk to people while surreptitiously scanning the ballroom.

There was no sign of Lucas at all.

Where was he? She couldn't believe he would actually ignore everything she'd said while the two of them were dancing. She refused to believe it.

Lucas loved his sister. She knew he was capable of seeing past his duty of obligation and relent for the simple reason it would make Olivia happy. She had to convince him of it, because if she couldn't convince Lucas to bend enough to consider his Olivia's happiness, what chance did Penelope have of ever convincing him to love her?

She pasted a smile on her face as another group of people crowded around her, and she danced when someone asked her to dance. But every second that ticked by, Penelope was aware of Lucas's absence. She reminded herself to have a little faith every time she scanned the room and failed to see his face.

But as the minutes turned to an hour, she felt the tiny hope that had flared in her heart since their wedding burn out.

Chapter Eighteen

Lucas finally tracked Blakewood in the Uffington library. He'd been searching for the young man for the better part of the last half hour.

The hesitation he felt when he strode into the large, dimly lit room thoroughly annoyed him. There was no reason to feel like he was betraying Penelope by pursuing a goal she did not approve of. This had nothing to do with her. Bloody hell, he was only doing his duty by protecting Olivia.

This was not the time to weaken in his resolve. Just because Penelope gave him endless pleasure in bed did not mean he would let her control his actions out of it. He'd been far too indulgent with her as it was.

"Blakewood," he called out to the young man standing in the middle of the room. "A word, if you please."

The other man slowly turned around to face him.

"Well, if it isn't the heroic Earl of Ravenstone," Blakewood said in a voice dripping with sarcasm. The dim light from the wall sconces threw shadows across his face. "Why am I not surprised to find you here?"

"I came here to warn you," Lucas intoned. "Stay away from my sister. If you have a problem with me, then come to me, and we will deal with it as men."

Blakewood emitted a harsh laugh. "What makes you think I have a problem with you?"

"Come, now, we both know you blame me for what happened to your father."

"You have no right to talk about my father!" Blakewood's hands clenched into fists. "You gave him no choice but to flee to France, leaving my mother and I to deal with the mess he left behind."

He cocked one eyebrow in response to the young man's heated display of emotion. "Your father got exactly what he deserved for his unethical financial strategy. Do not delude yourself that I was the only one who would have sought justice for what he'd done. He was lucky he was not hanged for his crimes."

"You're lying!"

"If you do not believe me," he said derisively, "ask his man of affairs."

"Hah! I will do no such thing."

Lucas turned to inspect a painting that hung on the far side of the room. "That's up to you of course. Frankly, I do not care what you do with your time as long as you spend it far away from Olivia."

"How touching. I didn't realize you were such an affectionate brother."

He kept his tone light. "If you harm my sister in any way, I will make sure you end up just like your father."

"Bastard!" Blakewood's fists clenched once more. "I would never harm Lady Olivia."

"Then why aren't you courting her properly, as a lady of her station deserves?"

Blakewood gave him an incredulous look. "Are you telling me I may call upon her at your home?"

He was appalled by his own suggestion, but he wasn't backing down now. He had to find out if Blakewood's intentions were honorable.

"I am telling you," he clarified in a dispassionate tone, "to grow a spine and make an attempt to behave honorably, instead of cowardly scurrying under a lady's bonnet."

With that last goading statement, Lucas made for the library door.

He didn't know what made him taunt Blakewood into courting Olivia properly, as Penelope had suggested. There was simply no explanation for his actions. *Damn! Now I have to deal with Blakewood calling upon Olivia!*

Since he'd known Penelope, she'd made him do things he would never have normally done. And he wasn't only thinking of the things he'd had to do during their courtship, such as tutoring her half brother or advising her stepfather on investments.

She'd made him care about her to the point where Lucas was doing things against his better judgment to please her. His actions tonight were uncomfortably reminiscent of his own father's weakness when it came to catering to his mother's whims.

Bloody hell! I am not *turning into my father!*

He strode through the ballroom, looking for the person who was responsible for this disaster. He found her almost immediately, talking to a group of people who fawned over her. He approached her and gained a bit of satisfaction when she looked up and turned to him at once.

"Lucas!" Penelope said his name as if she had been clinging to it for dear life. "I have been looking everywhere for you."

He glanced at the people milling around her. "So I gather. Are you ready to go home?"

She looked at him searchingly. Whatever it was she saw in his expression made her acquiesce to his politely worded command.

"Yes, I am a little tired."

He led her out of the ballroom and into the foyer, then lifted her up into their waiting coach. He stared at her as the coach swayed and moved away from the Uffington house, wondering yet again why this one tiny woman had such a volatile effect on him.

"Lucas?" she asked. "Are you well? Is everything fine?"

"I am all right, nymph. But I do not know if everything is, indeed, fine."

"What do you mean?"

He hesitated before replying. "I have told Blakewood to stop sneaking around behind my back and court Olivia properly if his intentions are honorable."

"You have?"

"Yes," he confirmed. "I am not happy about it, but—"

He grunted as she landed with a soft thud against him. His arms closed around her. "I gather you're pleased?"

"Oh, yes, Lucas. Very pleased. You do love your sister, after all."

He had to turn away from the hope shining in her eyes. "God, Penelope, do you always have to look at me that way?"

"What way?"

"As if you think I'm the answer to all your dreams. Let me tell you right now that I am not."

"I disagree."

"Then you will be in for a disappointment. Don't assume I agreed to let Blakewood court my sister because you suggested it. I did it because I thought it was the right thing to do."

"Of course."

He shifted her on his lap. "You will not wrap me around your little finger. I am not a lapdog who will do your every bidding."

"I never said you were a lapdog."

"Dammit, Penelope, why do you love me?" He regretted the question as soon as the words left his mouth. What the devil was he doing? Why was he forcing her to see the error in her judgment when it came to his character?

His own answer hit him with a force that took the breath out of him. He wanted to know if she could love him for what he really was—a man who was far different from the paragon she assumed he was. And he wanted her to think that, despite everything, he was still noble and honorable and admirable. Christ, he wanted stupid, impossible things.

"I love you because you are brave, kind and generous," Penelope answered.

Each word was like a stake that stabbed into him. "I am not kind, nymph."

"And you accept me for who I am," she added.

"What choice do I have? You are my wife," he grumbled.

Penelope slid off his lap. "Butter the crumpets! This is turning into a daft argument. What is the matter with you tonight?"

He was grateful to be saved from forming a reply when the coach stopped in front of their townhouse and a footman opened the door.

"Please help my wife out, Harris. I have just remembered that I have to meet someone at my club."

Though Penelope gave him a strange look, she apparently decided not to question him further. Thankful for being given a reprieve, he made sure Penelope was safely inside the house before giving the order to his coachman to drive on. He was in a peculiar mood, and he didn't know if he could risk being with her tonight. He needed time to think and compose himself.

• • •

"His lordship must have had a very important meeting if he is staying away from home this evening."

Penelope met her maid's inquiring gaze in the mirror. "He must have, Bess, because he left as if the hounds of hell were after him."

Her voice probably sounded too sharp, because Bess looked almost ill at the possibility that she'd offended her new mistress.

"I'm certain his lordship had good reason," Bess said meekly before resuming her endless task of brushing Penelope's hair.

He did have a good reason, Penelope thought. She'd sensed his inner turmoil the minute they were alone in the coach. However, she failed to realize exactly what had been bothering him so until she heard the sound of the horses' hooves thunder away from the house in a much quicker rhythm than usual. Lucas was fighting her, and tonight he'd performed a strategic retreat.

Until that moment, she had been too afraid to actually believe Lucas could ever begin to care for her. Until tonight, she'd been trying to be content to love him and not to expect him to return those feelings. He'd been kind and generous, and he seemed to want her very much. What else could an unwanted bride ask for? After all, their wedding had been only a matter of honor to him—it wasn't as if she was particularly useful to a man like Lucas, what with her lack of dowry and social connections. She'd been too scared to fight for his love.

But perhaps she wasn't so unwanted anymore. Lucas's actions after he'd talked to Blakewood spoke too loudly to be ignored.

He was a man who had witnessed his father broken by love, and he was scared. Lucas was battling what he was feeling for her with everything he had at his disposal, and she didn't like it. His actions affected both their lives, and she had the right to mutiny if she didn't agree with his motives.

She gave her maid a bright smile. "In future, perhaps we can give Lucas a better reason to stay in than to go out."

Bess's hands stilled. "What do you mean, my lady?"

Her smile widened to a grin. She was going to give him exactly what he wanted. She was going to engage him in a battle of wills he could not win. It was time Penelope became the wicked nymph Lucas claimed her to be and weave a spell around her target. If he'd felt the need for a strategic retreat when she hadn't even been trying, he would stand no chance after she was done with him.

"Tomorrow, we are going shopping," she declared.

If a woman was going to wage a battle of epic proportions to bring a man to his knees, she was going to need the right clothes.

Chapter Nineteen

A week later, she was no longer so certain of victory. She stared at the overturned phaeton in mute misery as Blakewood and Olivia ran over to her side. The afternoon sun glinted on the sleek equipage, making it look both splendid and tragic.

The phaeton was the latest victim in the series of failures she had endured since taking on the challenge of winning Lucas's heart.

"Penelope! Are you all right?" Olivia asked.

Her co-conspirator was clearly worried. Since she had a limited experience with men, Penelope had sought Mari's advice during tea one afternoon. Olivia had overheard the conversation and agreed to help. The drive in Hyde Park was Olivia's idea. She was beginning to think her sister-in-law had suggested it only to spend time with Blakewood.

She looked down at her muddied carriage gown, one she had selected particularly to impress her husband. And it did look impressive—a magnificent creation in a shade of deep emerald trimmed with silver that glistened in the sun and silhouetted her form. Her beautiful gown was ruined, and so were her plans of spending the day with Lucas as chaperones.

"I am fine," she grumbled as she walked over to a copse of trees where Lucas was soothing the pair of Friesian horses who'd been spooked by the accident.

How was she to win this battle of wills when nothing went according to plan? She approached him with as much dignity as she could muster.

"How are they?" she asked, referring to the horses.

Lucas flicked her an amused glance. "It will take some time for them to calm down enough to be safe to ride again."

"The phaeton is drawing a crowd, but I don't think there's any major damage because of the accident."

Lucas smiled. "Thank God for that. I think you've had enough driving lessons for the day, though."

"You're not angry?"

He finally gave her his full attention. "No, I am not. Why would you think I would be angry?"

"Because I was the one who convinced you to let me handle the reins."

Lucas chuckled. "It was your first time handling a team, and a phaeton is trickier to drive than a curricle." One of the horses jumped and he tugged at its reins, whispering soothing words that the nervous Friesian showed no sign of believing.

"You were doing very well until you decided to make the team gallop—they were going too fast to be able to make that last turn safely," he proclaimed.

She had also been doing just fine until she decided to take on Lucas. At least he wasn't angry with her. In fact, he'd been treating her with nothing more than amused indulgence the whole week.

On Monday, he only laughed when the cake she baked for him came out burned to a crisp. On Tuesday, he smiled before calmly beating her at chess. Lucas's smile was in evidence again on Wednesday, when it rained during the romantic picnic she had arranged for them, and his laughter echoed in the gardens when Nelson stole the scones from her plate. By Thursday, she was in deep despair. She had the disturbing suspicion Lucas knew exactly what she was trying to do, and his amusement was rattling her already frayed nerves.

In fact, he only stopped laughing at her in the evening, when he took her to bed. Their lovemaking had become a sort of challenge, where neither of them backed down as they kissed and caressed each other until they were both mad with wanting and declaring their need in a shattering cadence of groans and sighs. The only time she saw a glimpse of what Lucas felt for her was when they were between the sheets.

She finally noticed his lack of progress with soothing the horses and decided to offer assistance. Lucas moved away from the team to meet her halfway as she walked up to the nervous pair.

"You should probably stay away from them, Penelope. It's not safe to deal with a frightened horse, and these two have only been in my stables for a couple of days. I do not know them that well," he warned.

She was not daunted. She might not be capable of driving a phaeton, or making her husband fall in love, but she knew how to deal with horses.

● ● ●

Lucas hesitated, debating the wisdom of letting Penelope near his team, wondering if this was another one of her tricks. He'd known what she was about with her sweet attempts to "woo" him this week, for she had been anything but subtle about it.

He'd wanted to lecture her regarding the folly of her plan, but truth be told, after she'd burned the cake on Monday, he had been more than curious to see what she would try next, and he'd looked forward to their encounters more than he cared to admit.

He frowned. If Penelope knew how effective she has been so far, she wouldn't stop until she had him begging her not to leave him if she ever found out his reason for marrying her. Already she was driving him to unparalleled heights of desire as he tried every night to please her until she shuddered beneath him and swore her love for him.

He stiffened. His wife was trying to break him. He knew he was playing a dangerous game, but he couldn't help himself. Even so, this was different. Penelope could easily get hurt if she went near the nervous animals.

Before he could refuse her request, however, she reached the horses, touching first one and then the other—at one point she reached up and pinched the horses' upper lips. She never grabbed the reins to steady the pair.

He could only watch, enthralled, while his wife soothed the Friesians with her touch, never uttering a single word. For no words seemed necessary between her and his animals. She was in her element here.

"How did she do that?" Olivia asked from behind him as they watched the horses follow Penelope as if in a trance to the phaeton, which Blakewood and some onlookers had righted.

He shook his head. "I don't know," he admitted. "Penelope has been working with animals her whole life, so she must have learned a thing or two about charming horses." Not only horses, judging by several of the *ton*'s open admiration of the spectacle that was his wife as she sauntered back toward him.

"Penelope, that was amazing!" Olivia said. "You must teach me how you did that."

"Of course," she readily promised. "But all I did was reassure them everything was under control."

"That was amazing," Olivia repeated to herself as she watched Penelope return to the phaeton to make sure the horses were still fine.

"You approve of your new sister-in-law, then?" he asked quietly.

His sister turned to him before replying, "I really do." She gave him a cheeky grin before adding, "She must truly love you, because I actually still have trouble believing she agreed to have you."

"You impertinent chit," he chided good naturedly. "Am I such a bad catch, then?

Olivia rolled her eyes. "Let me put it this way, if you'd come to *me* and said you had to marry me to save the Ravenstone estates because you couldn't circumvent Father's will, I'd have told you to go to the devil."

His gaze shot back to his wife and his heart stopped when he realized she'd made her way back to them, close enough to hear the remark. Penelope's face paled, and her lips parted. If he needed any more indication of the disaster that was about to occur, Penelope's look of betrayal more than sufficed. Damn it, why hadn't he warned Olivia that Penelope knew nothing of their father's will? The words that tumbled so casually from his sister's lips had the decimating effect of a violent explosion, and the victim stood frozen in shock for several minutes.

He couldn't believe this was happening. The stupid words pounded in his ears, and a lump formed in his throat as he helplessly watched Penelope's eyes narrow with accusation, then she seemed to recover her composure and she gave an overly bright smile before turning to his young, foolish sister and said in a hollow voice, "I'm glad I was able to help."

"You're always helpful to others, Penelope," Olivia declared, blithely unaware of the tense undercurrents flowing between the other people in the conversation. "I must go and see if Lord Blakewood needs any help." Olivia gave Penelope an impulsive hug, apparently not caring that Penelope's gown was spattered with mud. "Thank you for convincing my big ox of a brother to give Lord Blakewood a chance. I would never have been able to talk him into doing that." She gave a conspiratorial grin. "We girls must stick together, right?"

"Right," Penelope answered in a barely audible whisper, her gaze never leaving Lucas's face as Olivia walked away.

The lump in his throat choked any reply he could have made. He returned Penelope's pained gaze steadily, willing her to let him explain. And just as silently, her gaze told him that no explanation was necessary.

God dammit! Never in his worst imaginings did he consider that his own sister would cause his downfall. He wanted to hold Penelope and tell her he was sorry, that he had never meant to hurt her. He wanted to tell her it wasn't his fault she had seen something in him that simply wasn't there, hadn't been there for a very long time.

Most of all, he wanted to hear her say she still loved him—the real him—despite her disillusionment. And when Lucas realized the implausibility of his wish, the dark specters from the past took over what remained of his soul.

• • •

Reality is what we make of it.

The words she'd uttered the night Lucas had conspired to make her marry him revolved in her head as she stared at herself in the mirror, perched on the same chair she had sat on a week ago, conspiring to fight for her husband's affections.

"Reality is what we make of it," she whispered to the woman in the mirror.

Her own reflection stared back as she considered how words that had once seemed so intelligent and philosophical mocked her now. She'd made an entire reality out of her foolish assumptions and vanity, believing despite all the evidence to the contrary that one day she could make Lucas acknowledge his love for her.

In the silence of the evening, Penelope was forced to face the folly of her actions. It was no wonder it had been so easy for Lucas to refuse to admit he loved her. No wonder he'd never claimed to feel anything for her but physical desire. There had been nothing else for him to admit to. And the worst part of it was she couldn't even blame him for it, no matter how much she wanted to. Because even though his duty to the Ravenstone estates compelled him to withhold the reason for his reappearance into her life, he'd been honest about everything else.

There had been no reason for Lucas to lie, for she had been more than willing to lie to herself.

He never ran away from the dictates of honor and responsibility. He always did what needed to be done, even if fulfilling his duties came with an overfilled piece of baggage like her. She had just been too caught up in her fantasy to notice what should have been obvious. She understood his reasons perfectly. Unfortunately, understanding something did not make it any less painful or humiliating. A choked, hysterical laugh escaped her as she considered the mess she'd made of their lives because of her foolish dreams.

"You just had to do it, didn't you?" she accused the lady in the mirror. "You just couldn't help yourself."

She'd thought because she had nothing that was of use to him, there must have been some deeper reason that made him decide to make her his wife. And she had been right—Penelope had been more useful to him than she could have ever imagined, for her dowry had been nothing less than almost the entirety of the Ravenstone estates.

The flickering flame from the beeswax candle on the vanity wavered before her eyes as she fought back tears.

"Idiot," she whispered. She'd lived through the lonely years of her childhood clinging to the fantasy of him, and she'd proceeded to trap both of them in the fantasy by marrying him. She cringed at the thought of how uncomfortable she must have made him every time she blurted out how much she loved him. She couldn't blame him for that either, because even then, he had been nothing but a gentleman about it. God help her, she almost felt sorry for him.

And the sad fact was she couldn't leave this marriage any more than she could change his feelings for her.

She watched a small, pain-filled smile twist her too plump mouth as she finally accepted the truth, all the things she was, and all the things she would never be. She was no nymph. She was just plain, old Penelope, destined to wait for a man who, laden with duties, may or may not ever come. Because she was not enough for him. Had he ever really desired her or had he only done his duty to sire an heir?

Bile rose up in her throat. No, she shouldn't dwell on that. She simply would not be able to bear it if she went down that path. Instead, she grabbed her hairbrush and tossed it at the mirror, releasing the anguish starting to twist her insides mercilessly now. Anger rushed in to take its place. She was through waiting for him. Her foolish fantasy had done enough damage to their lives. It had to stop now. She could not do anything about the validity of their marriage, but she would do something about another aspect of it.

She started when she heard Lucas dismiss his valet in his own bedchamber. She strode to the door that connected their rooms and leaned her head against it, praying for courage. Then she drew a deep breath and opened the door.

Chapter Twenty

Lucas prowled his bedchamber like a caged, predatory beast, alternately hoping Penelope would show up as she had done every night since their wedding, and berating himself for the weakness that made him yearn to yank the connecting door and demand she come to him.

He'd been unable to tear his gaze from her during their uncomfortable drive back from Hyde Park with Olivia and the damnable Blakewood, who'd been utterly oblivious to the havoc that had been wrought that afternoon. He watched the last sparkle languish in Penelope's eyes as she stared out of the window of Blakewood's coach, and he didn't appreciate the stab of guilt that pierced through him at the sight of her looking quietly dignified and still, despite the mud-splattered emerald gown she'd been wearing.

He'd spent most of the evening in his club, trying to drown the memory of her heartbroken gaze with the finest brandy Brooks's had to offer. He was on his second bottle when the unpleasant feeling of indignation settled in his chest.

Why was he feeling so guilty about doing his duty? It was not his fault Penelope nurtured illusions of love where there was none. She had no right to feel betrayed, for she had brought it all on herself. He'd never lied to her about his feelings. And yet here he was, pacing a track on the Oriental rug in his bedchamber, waiting for her.

He whirled around when he heard her approach, unable to squelch the surge of relief that coursed through him at the sight of her.

Penelope strode deeper into the darkened room. With her almost transparent nightgown and bare feet, she looked exactly like a nymph who should have been tramping about in the woods. And despite the severity of the moment, his body tightened in response to her nearness. She stopped in front of him, just out of his reach.

"You win," Penelope said in a small, tired voice.

Her words confused him. What did she mean, he'd *won?*

She must have seen the question in his face, for she lifted her hand in a helpless gesture and then let it drop to her side before clarifying her statement. "I never should have fought for your affections. I should have realized there was nothing there to fight for." She let out a deep sigh. "You win."

He closed the space between them, searching her face for signs of what she was feeling, but for the first time since he'd known her, he couldn't find any emotion in her expression. "I never meant to hurt you," he stated, keeping the guilt slashing through him from his voice.

"Because you didn't think you could," she finished the statement for him in a resigned tone. She shook her head. "But you did hurt me, and the most galling thing about it is I understand why you did it." Her voice broke. "You had to keep what was rightfully yours, and you did what you had to do. You've always been willing to sacrifice your own needs to fulfill your duty."

He couldn't argue with her logic, so he admitted something else. "It was not such a great sacrifice," he rasped out.

His words spurned her into action. "Oh my God, Lucas, would you please stop with the lies!" She stepped back as if she couldn't bear to be near him any longer. "I am tired of being thought of as nothing more than useful, and I am bone-weary of lying to myself so I can be used." Without looking at him, she raised her arm to point accusingly in his direction. "I waited a *lifetime* for you, and you never would have come if it weren't for your father's will. So don't stand there and tell me you didn't think you were sacrificing yourself when you wed me to do your duty."

He was saying one wrong thing after another. He took a step toward her but stopped when she recoiled from him. "Listen to me. Stop moving away and just listen to me, nymph."

"Don't call me that!"

"Fine!" he shot back. He raked a hand through his hair as he tried to think of a way to reach her. "I wasn't lying when I said it wasn't a sacrifice. Dammit, Penelope, just because I can't love you back doesn't mean I don't want to be married to you." He drew a deep breath before confessing something he'd never told anyone. "It has nothing to do with you. I just can't love anyone, sweetheart. Whatever part of me that could have died with my father."

"Your father didn't love anyone either," she burst out.

He uttered a harsh laugh. "You're wrong, nymph. He loved my mother so much that when she died, his entire being went with her. You've only ever seen the good side of love, but I know how it can destroy a person and everyone around him. I swore long ago I would never let that happen to me."

Her head lifted and she finally turned to face him. "It seems to me your father loved only himself. If he truly loved your mother, he would have stayed to take care of his children, because you were the part of Vivian that was still with him." She gave him a look of pity. "Love makes a person endure, Lucas. It's the absence of it that destroys."

The words were so absurd they staggered him. "If you are expecting me to spout ridiculous promises of love, then you are more naive than I thought." He hadn't meant to be so blunt, but he couldn't bring himself to lie to her anymore either. "I desire you, Penelope. I have always desired you, more than anyone I have ever known and more than I have ever thought possible. But don't think I can offer you more than physical satisfaction, because that is all I have left in me to give."

She gave him an incredulous look. "Rubbish! Don't try to make me feel better by telling me you can't love anyone." She walked over to him. "I've seen the way you care for your sister, and the love you have for your servants. The only one you can't seem to love is me."

Her gaze slid to the crackling flames in the fireplace. "So I release you from our bargain," she said quietly. "You are free to find a mistress, Lucas."

He felt as if he'd been kicked in the stomach. "You no longer love me now that you know I can't return your feelings?" The words tasted like acid on his tongue.

A short laugh that was both bitter and hysterical escaped her. "I will always love you, Lucas. But I deserve more than a husband who stays with me only out of duty, and you deserve more than a wife whom you married because you had no other choice."

The finality that rang in her voice chilled him. She was breaking ties with him, and he didn't know what to say to convince her to not. "I don't want a mistress," he insisted. "Look, Penelope, I'm sorry I hurt you." He held her hand against his chest. "I never meant to hurt you, but don't do this, sweetheart. This isn't what I want."

She snatched her hand away. "Lucas, did you or did you not come to fetch me from Bouth only because of your father's will?"

"Dammit, Penelope—"

"And did you or did you not marry me to secure your inheritance?"

Christ. "Yes!"

"Then 'this' is where we are, my lord." She gave him scathing glance. "I let you make me feel like an unwanted fiancée for more than two decades." She poked him in the chest. "And I let you manipulate me into becoming your wife." She poked him again. "But I will be damned if I let you talk me into becoming your *whore!*"

And then she left his bedchamber, slamming the connecting door and leaving him to sleep alone for the first time since their wedding.

His jaw clenched as he watched her leave, fighting the urge to follow her into her bedchamber and show her just how badly he wanted her, to prove to her how badly she wanted him. He closed his eyes shut and balled his hands into fists at his sides as he forced himself to remain still. Frustration welled in him. If he went to her now, she would probably make him beg to spend the night with her. He gritted his teeth. He was not going to beg her to let him bed her. Bloody hell, he was not going to beg *anyone* for *anything*!

He shucked his dark silk dressing gown and flung himself onto the huge, empty bed, determined to make his fully aroused body submit to his will. He forced his mind to think of mundane matters such as the state of the crops in his estates and the profits to be made in the latest shipping venture he'd invested in. But as the dawn broke and the rising sun's rays flitted in through the gap in the silk curtains that hung by the window, Lucas finally accepted the fact that profits no longer gave him the satisfaction they once did. His last thought as exhaustion finally claimed him was a disturbing one.

He missed her.

His hand reached out to feel her side of the bed, and a surge of deep disappointment filled him when he found nothing but cold sheets waiting for his touch.

Chapter Twenty-One

"Of all the damnable, annoying, bloody nerve!"

Lucas threw the documents he'd been trying to read for the fifth time on top of the disorganized pile on his desk in disgust as he muttered aloud to himself in his study. "'This is where we are,'" he mocked. "I have a good mind to remind her precisely where the hell we bloody are!"

He threw his arm in an angry, sweeping gesture that encompassed the cluttered room where he'd ensconced himself for the past couple of weeks since his confrontation with Penelope. There were ledgers from his various estates piled on the chairs, and an overturned glass of brandy threatened to fall off the sideboard. The floor was littered with heaps of missives and bills. "We are in *my* house!"

Nelson emitted a loud yawn from the far corner of the room.

Lucas glared at the insolent dog. "That goes for you as well. If you don't like the way I do things, then you can bloody well sleep somewhere else!"

In answer, Nelson got up, turned around three times and curled back into sleep. He felt more than a tiny amount of satisfaction that the dog apparently wanted to be where Lucas was, which was more than he could say for the dog's equally exasperating owner.

Since their confrontation, Penelope had proceeded not only to banish him from her bed, but her entire life. She made no more amusingly sweet attempts to woo him or boss him around. Her laughter no longer rang out in the hall. There were no more of the teasing comments, moments of silent companionship, or the shattering declarations of love he'd become used to hearing.

He rubbed his face with his hands to wipe out the memories, the regret. His wife never did anything by halves. Penelope was now as determined to shut him out as she'd been steadfast in her devotion before that fateful day two weeks ago.

Two of the longest, most miserable weeks of his life.

Penelope immersed herself in meetings with Colonel Martin and his group, danced at balls as if she had no care in the world, and had reduced him to alternately hovering in his study or lurking in the halls, hoping to catch a glimpse of her. Not that she was home all that much these days. He'd tried twice more to talk to her to no avail.

Whenever he found an opportunity to get her alone, Olivia or his increasingly impertinent butler, Finchley, interrupted them with news of some terrible household emergency.

Everyone was conspiring to keep Penelope from him.

As of this morning, he was done trying to talk to her. He would do something better with his time by burying himself with work, instead of torturing himself with memories of Penelope splayed enticingly across his desk.

I will be damned if I let you talk me into becoming your whore.

Bloody hell, if she ever talked about herself like that again, he would gleefully wash her pretty mouth with vinegar.

Lucas picked up the documents on his desk, intending to attempt to finish reading at least two lines this time. Work would remind him of his duty. This was what he'd wanted—a wife who didn't bother him with expectations of any promises of spurious emotions so he could get on with his work and with his life.

He'd better get to it, then.

Many of his peers found work to be tedious and beneath them, but the truth was he loved this part of his responsibilities. He loved checking the details and knowing how his estates were doing. He loved knowing what his tenants needed and making plans of what to do next. Besides, contracts like the one he held in his hands in that very moment did not sign themselves.

The only one you can't seem to love is me.

His gaze jerked to the space next to the silver inkpot at the corner of his desk. First, he would need a pen. There must be at least a dozen of the bloody things in the cluttered room, yet not a single one was to hand. The last thing he wanted was to waste precious time searching out the damned pens.

I let you make me feel like an unwanted fiancée for more than two decades.

With grim determination, he strode to the door and yanked it open to find Olivia, Westville and Finchley in the hall huddled together in what appeared to be a riveting conversation conducted entirely in whispers.

"I find myself in need of a pen," he announced.

The three jumped guiltily at the sound of his voice, then proceeded to gawk openly at the sight of his nightclothes. They wore matching looks of confusion, as if Lucas had spoken in a language they failed to comprehend.

He leveled each of them a quelling glance, daring them to comment, before speaking once more. "A pen. To write with. There is none to be found in my study. I need one." His gaze swerved to his butler. "Now."

Finchley snapped out of his daze. "I shall fetch you a pen immediately, my lord." He paused to give Lucas a sidelong glance. "Er, to write with."

"Thank you." He watched Finchley scurry to the end of the hall, turn his head first in one direction and then the other, before heading straight into the kitchens. He sighed in frustration and turned on his heels to return to his desk, vaguely aware of Westville and Olivia following him into the study.

"Good heavens," Olivia said as she swept a crumpled piece of paper gingerly with her toe. "This is worse than we imagined."

He shuffled some documents and tapped them on the desk surface. "I'm working."

"On what?" Westville asked. "The revolution?"

Lucas dropped the documents, creating another jumbled pile on his desk, before glowering at his friend. "What the bloody hell are you doing here, Anthony?"

Westville grinned, undaunted. "I wondered if you would be interested in accompanying me and some friends to Tattersall's for the auction." His gaze lingered on the overturned brandy glass on the sideboard. "But it appears you are busy."

He decided to ignore his friend's mocking stare. "I have no need for new horses at the moment. There are other things that need my attention."

"Like your beard," Olivia said. "Honestly, Lucas, when was the last time you had a shave?"

His sister was becoming as brazen as his wife. At the moment, he didn't need more reminders of the nymph who'd cast a spell in his house and turned everyone against him.

"In the very unlikely event the two of you failed to notice," he said in a tone that made Olivia blanch and Westville raise his brows, "I am very busy."

"Obviously or you would have had time to change clothes before venturing downstairs," she pointed out.

Lucas tightened the belt of his dressing gown. He didn't bother to admit he'd been sleeping in the study instead of enduring the cavernous emptiness of the bedchamber he'd shared with Penelope.

Olivia gave him a worried glance. "Would you like to talk about it?"

"There is nothing to talk about except that I am very busy and the two of you are wasting my time."

Westville held his hands up in surrender. "Suit yourself." His blue eyes gleamed with speculation. "Perhaps I should ask your wife for advice on which horse to buy, since I will be stopping to attend a meeting with her group before going to Tattersall's."

Immediately after imparting the information on Penelope's whereabouts, Westville turned to leave. He took a single step before halting with a grunt. "I think," he croaked, "I have found your pens."

Westville used his foot to sweep away the discarded soiree invitation he'd stepped on, and three pens emerged from under his boot.

"He's right!" Olivia said with good cheer. "Pens do tend to stay inside rooms like the study." She clasped her hands together in front of her and turned to Lucas. "Well, brother, it looks like you shan't be disturbed any longer. I bid you good day."

Lucas returned Westville's challenging gaze steadily and indulged in a fantasy that involved thrashing the other man to a bloody pulp. "I shall join you shortly."

"I'll be waiting," his friend replied before adding, "Of course, if you take too long I might decide to go on my own." Westville's grin widened. "Meetings tend to adhere to very strict schedules, and Penelope would never forgive me if I arrive late. Charming woman, your countess. We've been spending quite a lot of time together recently—"

Fine. Lucas marched out of the study, noting that both Westville and Olivia turned to watch him as he passed them. He silently wished both of them to perdition. As soon as he reached his bedchamber, he rang for his valet.

What would he say to Penelope when he ambushed her in a meeting where she couldn't dance out of his reach?

He rubbed his beard. First, he needed a shave.

• • •

"I am getting published!"

Penelope glanced up to watch a bright smile light up Mari's beautiful face as they waited for the rest of the group to arrive for the meeting. Mari put down a tray of freshly baked teacakes on the table with a flourish.

"That's wonderful news!" She reached for a teacake. "Congratulations."

Mari sat on the cream settee opposite Penelope. "I've decided to stay with my aunt and uncle while I see if I can earn enough money to live on my own when my recipe book gets published." She released a blissful sigh. "Isn't it amazing? I might not have to go back to Bouth after all." She leaned forward, and the sun glinted on her hair, creating a halo around her. "Do you remember how we used to daydream about living in a cottage together if Ravenstone never showed?"

Penelope chewed on her teacake, ignoring the protest of her suddenly dry throat. "Yes."

"I'm hoping to earn enough to buy a little cottage somewhere, maybe open a shop with a big kitchen where I can bake and cook …"

Penelope reached for her cup of tea and gulped down a healthy amount, managing to suppress a coughing fit as the scalding liquid burned its way down her throat while Mari continued to itemize her plans regarding the mythical cottage. Penelope listened attentively, grateful her recent tea problems had gone unnoticed.

She was happy for her friend. Really, she was. Mari was on the verge of living her dreams. And Penelope would be so much happier if only it hadn't happened so soon after her own girlhood dreams had awakened her with the equivalent of a slap in the face. Maybe Mari would agree to let her live in the dream cottage, too.

She suppressed a grimace. Yes, she could live in a cottage, perhaps acquire the name "Mad Polly" and adopt thirteen cats before proceeding to spend her years making every situation uncomfortable for those around her by lauding about how much better things were in the good old days, before the whole world had turned against her.

Of course, she couldn't live in a cottage with her friend. Because she was married to Lucas.

Lucas.

Why couldn't he love her? He'd been so kind, generous and tender with her. Even now, after all the things she'd found out about their marriage, she could almost fool herself into believing there was something in the way he looked at her whenever they passed in the hall, something that made her think perhaps …

She sighed. She was doing it again, making castles out of hay. What was the use of distancing herself from Lucas if she constantly sought for him in her mind? It was bad enough she had to keep a frenetic social schedule so that she could do nothing more at night than sleep. Even then, she indulged in fantasies about the way her confrontation with Lucas ended, alternative dialogues she absolutely knew would one day drive her mad. Her fantasies varied from one day to the next, but they all ended the same way:

She'd confronted Lucas with the truth Olivia had unwittingly revealed and listened as he explained the only reason he kept quiet was he'd fallen madly in love with her and was afraid to lose her. Afterward, he would drop on bended knee, begging her forgiveness.

Then there was the one where Lucas denied everything and told her Olivia must have been mistaken, for he would never use Penelope in such a manner. Also, he had proof of his claim. Lucas would drop on bended knee and beg her to believe him, because he loved her and couldn't bear to be without her.

Those fantasies helped to ease the ache in her heart, but neither of them solved the fact that her husband had not even attempted to stop her from leaving his bedchamber after their confrontation. She had a fantasy that rectified this problem, as well:

Lucas already loved her, but he'd been so ashamed of his own actions that he couldn't bring himself to ask for her forgiveness, until he finally accepted he couldn't live without her. Lucas would promise never to deceive her again before dropping on bended knee to swear his love for her.

The last fantasy was the sweetest, because it was the only one that still had any realistic chance of happening, and she held it close to her heart as she slept.

In the harsh light of day, however, reality returned. The fact was, during their confrontation, Lucas said he couldn't love anyone. She had rejected his claim, but in the two weeks since their confrontation, she realized there were different kinds of love.

For example, she loved teacakes. She loved them, but she would not marry a teacake even if it magically jumped out of the tray and begged her on bended knee. The notion was so ridiculous she had to fight down a surge of hysterical mirth.

Good Lord, it's happening. I am losing my mind.

She had dared to fight for a love that had never been hers, and she was being punished for it to set an example for future generations.

"Polly, are you all right?"

Only then did she realize she'd been staring morosely at the teacake for what must have been at least ten minutes. "I'm fine," she lied.

Her frayed nerves were taking their toll. She didn't know how long she could live in the same house with Lucas, wondering if he'd taken a mistress every time she encountered him in the hall. Wondering if she'd been a fool to reject him. Weren't they happy together before that fateful day when everything had changed? *She* certainly had been. The thought of Lucas doing all the intimate things he did to her to someone else made her literally ill.

"I'm just so happy for you," she whispered, hoping her friend would not question her claim.

No such luck.

Mari frowned. "That's very sweet of you, but also hardly convincing. Do you want to talk about it?"

What was there to talk about? The simple truth was she had been very stupid. Was still very stupid, because she couldn't stop loving a man who was not for her.

"Is it your uncle?" Mari asked. "Has he done something to cause trouble?"

Penelope shook her head. "No."

"Is it your family? I thought their financial problems were solved," Mari probed.

She shook her head again. "Papa wrote recently to tell me everything was fine, and Colin is going back to school for the Michaelmas term."

"Is it Ravenstone then?"

"I wish," she muttered.

She wished Lucas had never fetched her from Bouth. She wished she could stop loving a man who had so little regard for her. She also wished she could think of something to say, so Mari wouldn't guess her marriage was in shambles.

"I wish I wasn't me," she finally said, half-jokingly.

Mari gaped at her. "What an awful thing to say." She cocked her head thoughtfully to the side, openly speculative. "If you don't want to talk about it, all you have to do is say so."

Now she had offended her best friend. They had always been able to talk about everything, so why was she hesitating?

Because it was *mortifying*. Because it was unfair. It wasn't fair that Mari was going to be living the life she'd always dreamed of, while Penelope couldn't think of a way to get out of the nightmare she'd put herself in.

"It's nothing, really. Nothing that good old Shakespeare couldn't use in a play," she grumbled, annoyed with her ungenerous thoughts. It was too early in the day to wallow in self-pity.

Penelope gave her a determined smile. "I daresay if my life were to be turned into a play, I would only approve it for staging if the actress who plays me is prettier than the one who'll be playing you."

Mari paused in the act of taking a sip of tea. "Oh Polly, I'm glad to see marriage hasn't changed you at all!"

They burst into great gales of laughter until they were both slumped on the settees they sat on.

• • •

Twenty minutes later, Penelope chewed on the last of the teacakes while she tried with all her being to ignore the fact that Lucas was standing in the corner of the room with Lord Westville, watching her eat while Colonel Martin regaled the group with news of events from the House of Commons.

"Your suggestion to add 'all other animals' to the proposed amendment to the *Cruel Treatment of Cattle Act* was a great success, Lady Ravenstone," Colonel Martin announced. "Of course, we thought adding the phrase would make the other MPs settle for adding only dogs, cats and monkeys to the Act, but the House passed the amendment!"

The group welcomed the good news with applause, but she sensed the colonel was not finished. She paused in the act of taking another bite of teacake. "What happens now?"

Colonel Martin shifted in his seat, his unease obvious. "Now, we wait for the Bill to pass in the House of Lords." He shook his head with regret. "Alas, my friend, Lord Erskine, is no longer around, and I'm afraid we don't have much influence with the aristocracy. But," he continued with his usual optimism, "there is always hope. Especially since your husband is here."

An uncomfortable silence passed during which she refused to yield to the temptation to look in Lucas's direction. He'd been staring at her long enough for her to realize that he was only waiting for her to make the mistake of glancing his way.

As if it wasn't bad enough, he looked unbearably handsome today. Even from the corner of her eye, she could tell his ebony velvet coat hugged his tall, muscular form perfectly, and the features revealed by his fresh shave proved he hadn't been missing any of the sleep she herself had been deprived of since their confrontation.

She was already weakening in her resolve to stay away from him. Letting him near her again would crumble it, and if that happened she would be back where she'd started—pathetically begging for any scrap of affection he deigned to throw her way.

Thankfully, she was able to gather enough strength to resist the pull of Lucas's gaze and keep a part of her mind focused on the discussion.

"'All other animals'?" Ethan Banks scoffed. "Does this mean every creature, including flies and ferrets, will be protected?"

"And what do you have against ferrets, Banks?" Fowell Buxton asked. He adjusted his spectacles before giving Banks the benefit of his full attention. "Do you think they don't deserve to be protected by the law, the way people deserve to be protected?"

Penelope stepped in to prevent an argument and to keep her mind on the meeting. "I'm glad the amendment was approved by the House of Commons, and I'm sure Mr. Banks didn't mean anything by his statement about ferrets."

Before she could even draw a breath, Lucas fired a question straight at her. "What are ferrets to be protected from?" His dark brow arched in arrogant challenge. "Without them, it would be very difficult to hunt rabbits, which provide meat for many families in need. They are very useful."

Useful. She didn't know if he said the word deliberately to rile her, but the hateful term snapped her control.

"I'm sure they are useful to people who hunt rabbits, which is why they need protection." She met Lucas's challenging gaze with a glare of her own. "The hunter is interested only in the rabbit, while the ferret faithfully serves by chasing the rabbit out of warrens for the hunter and doesn't even get anything out of it. The ferreter feeds them only occasionally with milk and bread, and they are usually kept in poor conditions."

"Hunting rabbits is what comes naturally to a ferret," he pointed out in an infuriating, calm voice. "And the ferrets get a place to sleep that is free from predators, which is more than what can be said for their natural environment."

"In their natural environment," she shot back, "ferrets get to eat the rabbits they hunt instead of having to settle for the paltry diet the ferreter imposes on them. It is a very one-sided relationship." She looked at him squarely in the eye before delivering a last statement. "Ferrets deserve better than to be misused by the ferreter, who is only ever interested in the rabbit the ferrets give him."

She felt Mari's reassuring squeeze on her shoulder and she glanced at her friend, who was watching Lucas with dawning comprehension.

"Perhaps," Mari said breezily, "the ferreter had better learn to give his ferrets more consideration, or he would find himself left with nothing but a dead rabbit in his hands."

Mari had always been perceptive and now she was giving her the support she needed. It gave Penelope the strength to issue a goading statement of her own.

"Oh, Mari, the ferreter would be ecstatic to have a dead rabbit," she said. "It was all he ever wanted in the first place."

The muscle in Lucas's jaw clenched. "Perhaps it was all he'd wanted *at first*," he bit out.

Suddenly she felt very weary. "I know lowly ferrets don't have much to offer other than their natural ability to catch rabbits." She drew a deep breath. "I just hope that for once, someone could give the ferrets some thought." Her gaze shifted to Colonel Martin. "People like you restore my faith in humanity."

"I must say, lass, that's a very interesting way of looking at ferreting," Colonel Martin mused. "What do you think, Ravenstone?"

Though Lucas's words were for the colonel, his intense gaze remained on her. "I think it's time for the ferreter to have a long discussion with his ferrets about how their relationship is to go on."

"How would he conduct a conversation with ferrets?" Ethan Banks asked in a bewildered tone.

"I think," Penelope retorted, "that as the ferreter has caught his rabbit, he should be decent enough to let his ferrets go, so they can be with some other ferreter who will treat them better."

She couldn't believe the audacity of her own words, and judging from his thunderous expression, neither could Lucas.

"I have done some ferreting in my day," Westville put in, turning everyone's attention to him. "And I assure you that my ferrets were fed and handled very well."

"*Shut up*, Anthony!" Lucas snapped.

The outburst had an immediate and varied effect on all the occupants of the room. Westville held his hands up in a mocking gesture of surrender, Mari gaped in amazement, and Penelope buried her face in her hands in mortification while the rest of the group endeavored to cover up the awkward moment by continuing the discussion about the amendment to the *Cruel Treatment of Cattle Act* with forced vigor.

She let the conversation swirl around her, hardly able to contribute any meaningful suggestions. She looked up only when she felt Mari nudge her side.

"He's still staring at you," Mari whispered.

She almost rolled her eyes. As if she needed anyone to point out that Lucas was at this moment boring holes through her body, raking her form with his very intimate, very inappropriate gaze, which was making her think very inappropriate thoughts. She resisted the urge to utter a sigh and wipe her damp palms on her skirts. She was feeling much too warm.

"I wouldn't give up on him just yet, if I were you," Mari advised. "I'm rarely wrong, you know."

She choked down an incredulous laugh. "That's true, but on the rare occasions when you are, it's usually about major things."

"What do you mean?"

She gave an indelicate snort. "Remember when we were learning the pianoforte, and you were absolutely convinced you'd personally discovered Mozart?"

"I was nine!" Mari protested in an outraged whisper. Then her gaze turned inquisitive. "What are you planning to do now?"

She wished she knew. Oh, she knew what she *wanted* to do, which was to march over to her husband and clobber him with the tray of teacakes. But that would surely shock the other people in the room.

She felt a flush heat her cheeks as she sensed Lucas's gaze linger on the column of her neck and focus on her breasts.

"I have to get out of here," she whispered to Mari. "But I don't want Lucas to know I'm leaving."

"Consider it done," Mari said.

Without further preamble, her friend stood up and loudly invited Penelope to view her newly finished painting. A few minutes later, Penelope was standing in the foyer with her friend, waiting for the coach to be brought round.

She was just about to thank Mari when Lucas called out to them, his deep voice filling the hall, making them both gasp in consternation.

"I'd also like to see this painting of yours, Miss Smythe," he said in a bored drawl as he stalked up to them. "Where is it?"

Her heart thundered in her ears. She looked helplessly at her friend and mouthed, *I'm sorry*, but Mari was apparently not done. Her friend peered up at Lucas, then she put her hand against her forehead and uttered a loud, choking sound before crumpling straight into the waiting footman's arms in the most graceful and thoroughly unconvincing imitation of a swoon Penelope had ever seen.

Chapter Twenty-Two

"That was very well done," Lucas muttered.

Penelope silently agreed. She watched with admiration as Mari was swept upstairs by the footman. Her lady's maid was tripping over herself and frantically waving a vinaigrette over her mistress's face. Penelope waited a few seconds before seizing on the excuse her friend had given her to get away.

She lifted her skirts an inch in preparation of running and affected a harried tone. "I have to go up there to make sure she's all right!"

Lucas grabbed her shoulders, and his firm grip bit into her skin just as she was about to bolt upstairs.

"Oh no, you don't," he warned. "You're not going to waltz out of my reach again, nymph."

His hold on her gentled, and she felt his thumbs tease the nape of her neck in an intimate caress. Her heart did a somersault as he turned her slowly to face him, and the look of blatant hunger on his handsome, aristocratic face when she gazed at him almost brought her to her knees. How many nights had she dreamed of him looking at her like this?

Too many, she thought. Much too many a night in her life she'd spent dreaming of him holding her, loving her. Many wasted, useless nights that could have been spent doing something more productive than waiting in vain for a man who wasn't interested. Who'd never been interested.

She opened her mouth to speak, but the butler's voice interrupted her thoughts.

"Your carriage has been brought round, milady."

Penelope's gaze snapped to the butler, who was looking at her expectantly. "Thank you, Jenkins." She shrugged free of Lucas's grasp and fumbled for something in her reticule, found it, and handed it to the butler.

"Here's the salve I promised. It's made from peony petals and roots. It should help soothe your muscle pains. I'm going upstairs to make sure Mari is all right," she announced, giving Lucas no choice in the matter.

"God bless you, milady!" Jenkins looked uneasily at Lucas. "Er, and you, too, milord," he added, handing Lucas's greatcoat and top hat to him.

Lucas took the garments from the butler without taking his eyes off her. "This isn't finished," he said in a voice only she could hear. "Go and sulk, if that's what you want. But when you're done, we are going to talk."

No, we won't. There was nothing left to say, and if she stayed, he would seduce her into bending to his will until she lost her humanity under his discipline.

He didn't love her.

A long time ago, someone had taken everything Lucas loved from him, and he'd survived by making sure he wouldn't love anything or anyone ever again. Nothing she could do would ever convince him to let go of the past, and until he was free of his burden, there was no place in his heart or life for her.

"I have to go," she whispered, unable to stand the sight of him any longer.

She had to think about what she would do now, and she needed to do it away from him.

• • •

Lucas slammed the carriage door closed after alighting in front of his townhouse. The action didn't appease the fury roiling in him one bit. "God dammit!"

His wife was twisting him from the inside out. He didn't like the look on her face when she said she had to go. She belonged with *him*. She wasn't going any damned where.

Before he could reach the front door, it burst open, and Olivia came flying through, hugging him and jumping in delight.

"Where's Penelope?" she asked. "I should wait until she gets home, but … Oh, Lucas, Bernard asked me to marry him!" She began jumping again, tugging on his hand. "You have to go and meet him in the study. He's waiting for you."

Fuck. "Who the hell is Bernard?"

Not waiting for an answer, he stalked straight into his study to find Blakewood dressed to the teeth, nervously tugging at his cravat. The man had a nasty sense of timing. Penelope was probably on her way home now, and Lucas wanted to discuss their marriage.

He wanted Penelope.

For one thing, she would know how to deal with Blakewood.

"Bernard, I assume?" he asked sarcastically as he seated himself behind his desk. He watched the young lord's face turn a dull red.

"I've asked Olivia to marry me," Blakewood said, as if he'd read Lucas's thoughts and needed to confirm them.

"So I've heard."

"She said she can't say yes until I've talked to you and you've given your consent," the young man added.

Of course she couldn't, she was only eighteen. He drummed his fingers on top of the desk as he sought a way to get rid of this suitor until he could get his own emotions under control.

"This isn't the most convenient time to have this discussion," he said. "Come back a few days hence, and we shall talk."

All traces of his earlier nervousness left Blakewood's person. He bolted out of his chair and slammed both palms on the desk. "I knew it! You said I would be welcome to court your sister, but you never had any intention of accepting my suit, did you? You only wanted to humiliate me."

Bloody hell. He was in no mood to deal with Blakewood's emotional display when he himself was having the devil of a time controlling his own temper.

"You humiliate *yourself* with this outburst," he pointed out.

Blakewood shook his head. "I thought I was wrong about you, but evidently Society was right to shun you all these years. You care only about seeking revenge against my father. You don't care if Olivia gets hurt."

"Sit down," he said in a voice that made the young man's face pale.

Blakewood hesitated before dropping his frame onto the seat he'd just vacated, tugging at his cravat once again.

"Now then," he began as soon as the younger man got hold of his emotions. "Suppose you tell me why I should accept your suit."

"I can take care of Olivia," Blakewood grumbled. "Admit it, the only reason you are hesitating is because it deprives you of the chance to humble me in front of Society the way you did with my father."

Olivia's outraged voice drifted from the doorway. "Is this true, Lucas? You're refusing Bernard's suit?"

"You will stay out of this, Olivia," he said through gritted teeth.

"He is," Blakewood confirmed. "He told me to come back in a few days, but I know he only means to embarrass me by giving me false hopes yet again."

Olivia stormed into the study. "You can't do this, you know. You can't play with people's lives. Haven't you learned your lesson from what you did to Penelope?"

"What did he do to his wife?" Blakewood asked, casting a contemptuous glance at Lucas. "You have not beaten her, have you?"

That was enough of Olivia's careless comments. He wouldn't even be in this untenable position if Olivia had kept her mouth shut about their father's will.

"I will not let you do this, Lucas!" she wailed. "If you don't give us your permission, we will run away to Gretna Green."

"Not if you are unable to leave your bedchamber," he warned.

He'd been too indulgent, both with his wife and his sister. All of it had to stop until they remembered who the head of this household was.

"Lucas, please be reasonable," his sister pleaded.

"I have been far too reasonable with you lately. You shouldn't even be here. This is between me and Blakewood."

"You're discussing my future. Don't I have the right to be here?"

"There is no convincing him," Blakewood said. "And I am not staying here to be insulted."

With that remark, Blakewood stomped out of the study. A few minutes later, the sound of horse hooves filled the hall as Blakewood's carriage rumbled away from the house.

A pained gasp escaped Olivia. "I hope you're happy!" she sobbed. "If you'll excuse me, I will go wait for Penelope. *She* cares about my happiness!"

His sister left the study without another word. He would no doubt end up looking the villain yet again when Penelope heard Olivia's complaints, but he didn't mind so much if it meant he could talk to his wife again.

Lucas straightened in his chair and tidied his desk so that it looked more presentable. She would probably be here in a few minutes, after Olivia talked to her. His wife always thought of others before herself, and Olivia's grievance would send her scurrying straight into his domain. Penelope wouldn't appreciate all this clutter.

Three hours later, he was still waiting in his study. He pulled a contract from one of the neat piles on his desk and tried to read, all the while aware of the clock ticking at the far end of the room.

When another hour passed without Penelope storming into his study, he decided to send for her. Surely he'd given her enough time to sulk and she was now ready to face him again. He tugged on the bell pull, and a footman named Sammy came in.

"You rang, milord?" Sammy asked.

How odd that a mere footman answered his summons. "Where is Finchley?"

Sammy stared at the wall above Lucas's head. "Well, as to that, milord, I'm afeard I don't know his exact whereabouts," he mumbled.

This was getting odder by the moment, but he knew Finchley would have a very valid reason for being missing in action. "Never mind," he said. "Would you please tell my wife I would like to speak to her?"

Sammy blanched. "I can't do that milord."

His patience was gone. "What the devil is the matter with you? Is your burned hand still paining you? You should tell her ladyship the balm she gave you isn't working. I'm sure she'll be able to make you a better one. She's good at that sort of thing, you know."

"I can't do that milord," Sammy repeated.

He tamped down the urge to shake the smaller man. "Why the hell not?"

"Because I don't know where her ladyship is."

The uneasiness in his chest drummed a throbbing beat in his temples. "She isn't upstairs?"

Sammy shook his head as words tumbled out of his mouth in a torrent of explanation and apology. "No, milord. Her maid doesn't know where she is either. That's why Finchley is gone. He's looking for her."

"And none of you thought to alert me of this fact?" he asked in a dangerously soft voice.

"Finchley said he'd be able to find her before you realized she was gone, milord," Sammy explained.

Before he realized she was *gone*? Did Sammy think Penelope had left him?

"Where's Nelson?" he demanded.

Sammy looked ill. "Her ladyship's dog is gone, too, milord."

Dear God, Penelope had left him.

She wouldn't have taken Nelson with her if she'd only intended to go for a jaunt in the park. She'd actually walked out of the house and *left* him. His uneasiness gave in to rage. How dare she leave him? She was his wife! They had a bargain. The thought propelled him from his chair and straight into the hall, where Olivia was pacing.

"Lucas!" Olivia exclaimed. "We hoped Finchley would find Penelope before you noticed she was gone, but he's been away for hours and there hasn't been any news."

He ran upstairs with Olivia on his heels and headed for Penelope's bedchamber. Her empty bedchamber. He prowled the room like a caged brute, searching for signs of where she might have gone, ignoring the sudden rawness in his throat that threatened to strangle him. Because he knew exactly why she'd left.

"She's not here, Lucas," Olivia whispered.

He whirled to face his sister. "Get out," he choked out.

Olivia backed away. "What are you going to do?"

Lucas raked a hand through his hair. "She couldn't have gone far, and she will have a lot of explaining to do when I find her. Tell Sammy to have my horse brought round."

Olivia flew downstairs to do as he'd bidden, and he sank onto Penelope's bed. Her floral scent lingered in the room, and he closed his eyes as rage roiled inside him once more.

He would find her, he promised himself in an attempt to calm the rioting flare of emotions in him. There were only a few places she could have gone. He would find her, he told himself again and again as he tried to hang on to his feeling of outrage at her abandonment. He would find her. The words became a chant, the only outcome he was willing to dwell on as he stormed out of the room and out of the house to ride into the suddenly bleak night.

Chapter Twenty-Three

The hired coach jerked sharply on a deep rut and Penelope winced, rubbing her aching bottom. To say the hackney didn't have comfortable seats was an understatement—it had nothing but two very thinly padded wooden boards with numerous holes in random places designed for a person's weight to roll into.

She glanced at Finchley, who was holding himself rigidly straight on the opposite seat. He'd given his glove for Nelson to chew so the dog would keep calm on the long road journey.

"I'm sorry you had to endure this, Finchley, but I couldn't let you go back to Lucas and tell him where I'm going," she said with a hint of contrition.

"It's of no import now, my lady," the butler replied with his usual hauteur despite the fact that she'd effectively kidnapped him when she noticed him following her on the way out of the livery stable. "'Tis my duty to keep you safe, and may I be so bold to say I arrived just in time. The coach driver back in the livery stable would have taken dreadful advantage of you."

"I was merely bargaining for price with him. I didn't think he might have another type of payment in mind. In any case," she added with a small smile, "I am exceedingly grateful to you for coming to my aid and finding us a better coach to hire."

Finchley gave a sigh and patted Nelson's satiny head. "Is there any hope of stopping at an inn somewhere, my lady? I'm certain Nelson needs to eat," he said hopefully.

Her eyes narrowed suspiciously. "I bought some food at the last coaching inn. There is no need to stop until we reach our destination."

"I assure you, my lady, I will not send a message to his lordship," Finchley said in a hurt tone. "It might not be my place to say, but the staff has been aware of the, ah, troubles between you and his lordship of the past weeks. His lordship will find you, my lady, and he will not be pleased."

She gave Nelson a piece of sausage. "I'm not interested in pleasing his lordship," she snapped.

She noticed both Finchley and Nelson looking at her despondently, and her heart filled with guilt. She probably should have left Nelson with Lucas. Lord knows the poor thing would've been more comfortable there, but if she'd left her dog, then she would have had a reason to go back. Both her pride and heart were wounded, but she knew through experience that all wounds, whether emotional or physical, healed with time and care. She couldn't risk giving herself an excuse to go back to Lucas, not when he'd been clear about his intentions at the meeting. Going back would only make her emotional wounds fester until they infected her soul.

Cowardly as it might have been to run away, it had been her only alternative.

"Forgive me, Nelson," she whispered, her heart wrenching at the sight of her loyal companion struggling to keep his balance in the rickety coach.

"How much longer are we to endure this equipage, my lady?" Finchley asked as another rut in the road sent all three of them jumping and wincing at the same time.

She hesitated, debating whether or not to tell the butler where they were going before they'd actually arrived at their destination. "Not much longer."

"You are not even going to tell me where we are headed?"

Penelope sighed. She might as well tell him, or he'd plague her for the rest of the journey. "We're going home," she announced.

Then she handed Finchley a plate of cold meats, forcing both of them to try to juggle their food and eat in silence.

• • •

Penelope's hometown hadn't changed at all since Lucas had first stepped foot in it.

The familiar sight of rolling, sun-kissed fields greeted him as he made his way up the valley to Highfield Manor. Two months ago, he'd journeyed here to fetch a long-forgotten fiancée. Now he was here to claim an errant wife.

A vision of Penelope opening the front door of the manor and flying into his arms lifted his weary spirit before he reminded himself that he was angry with her for her impulsive behavior. Because of her exaggerated fit of the sulks, he had been obliged to travel nearly the entire length of the country. He was dirty, tired and most annoyed. He had a good mind to make her beg him to take her back after this outrageous stunt.

Except it wasn't Penelope who opened the door as he approached the manor, but Gertie. His heart sank.

Gertie eagerly greeted him as he dismounted, and the entire Walker family stepped out of the manor.

"You're back!" Dr. Walker declared the obvious as he shook Lucas's hand before peering over his shoulder expectantly. "Where's Polly? Is she resting back at the inn? You shouldn't have gone to The Mucky Duck, you know. You're always welcome here."

Eleanor Walker motioned for everyone to go inside. "Please come in, we'll make sure your horse is cared for."

He struggled to contain his emotions as he followed the family to the library and tried to come up with a story of why she wasn't with him. "Penelope couldn't make the journey up, but she sent me here to claim any items she wasn't able to bring with her after the wedding."

Disappointment settled in his chest. He'd been so sure Penelope would be here. Before journeying north, he'd checked with Miss Smythe, who appeared to be embarrassed about their last encounter but unaware of Penelope's disappearance. He also paid Penelope's cousin a visit, but David Maitland seemed equally unaware that Penelope was missing. He had even attended another meeting with Colonel Martin and his friends, but none of them seemed to find Penelope's absence out of the ordinary.

Now that he knew Penelope wasn't with her family either, his annoyance with her drained out, replaced by something even worse: fear.

Penelope wasn't merely indulging in a fit of the sulks. She'd actually severed all connections with him and could be anywhere in the country. Anywhere in the world. With no one to protect her. Where thieves, highwaymen and all sorts of villains could get to her.

"I'm quite certain Polly has taken all of her things. How long will you be staying?" Dr. Walker's voice seemed to come from somewhere very far away, and he had to shake his head to clear it in order to hear the rest of the man's words. "Polly isn't pregnant, is she? Is that why she couldn't make the journey up?"

Good God, what if she's pregnant? Bile rose up in his throat at the thought of Penelope somewhere out there, cold and alone, pregnant with his child.

"No," he whispered, his throat raw. "At least, I don't think she is. She hasn't told me anything. I'm not sure—"

"All right," Dr. Walker interrupted. "So how long are you going to be staying?"

Lucas stared at the man who had raised Penelope, unable to admit he had misplaced Dr. Walker's stepdaughter.

"I'm only staying long enough for my horse to rest. There are things I must see to in London," he replied.

Dr. Walker inclined his head. "Ah, then at least have some tea with us and give us news of how London is treating our daughter. She said in her last letter that she's met Colonel Martin."

Needing to keep Penelope close to him in any way he could, he talked about Colonel Martin and the Season, going into details about things she'd said and the people she'd helped. He even told them about Nelson's state of health. He talked until his throat was dry, trying to delay the moment when he would have to leave the people closest to his wife's heart.

When he was certain his horse was fully rested, Lucas made his excuses to the Walkers and started on the weeklong journey back to London, where he immediately began making inquiries of the servants.

He drilled everyone from the gardeners to the housekeeper about the events of that day, but the only thing they could say was that Penelope must have used the servants' staircase to get out of the house, and so no one had noticed she was gone until too late. None of them knew where she might have gone.

He spent several days making discreet inquiries at the local coaching inns, but none of them had any recollection of seeing a woman matching Penelope's description. He'd been able to trace the livery stable where she'd rented a coach, but from there the trail had gone cold.

Three weeks after Penelope had left, exhausted and in need of sleep, Lucas went back to his townhouse and paced a track in the carpet in his study while a pain beyond anything he'd ever known gnawed at him. There wasn't much hope Penelope would ever come back to him. He was staring into the fire, contemplating what he was to do next when a commotion out in the hall drew his attention.

"I told you, his lordship isn't at home to visitors at present!" he heard Sammy yell.

"And I told you," a voice that could only belong to Lord Maitland replied, "I shall wait as long as it takes for him to see me. This nonsense has gone on long enough!"

He stalked to the door and yanked it open to find Lord Maitland and Ethan Banks swatting at Sammy while the footman tried to push them out of the house.

"It's all right, Sammy, let them in," he intoned.

The last thing he wanted was to deal with the baron, but the man might have some information as to where Penelope was.

"So," Lord Maitland began as he stalked past Lucas inside the study, "where have you hidden her? My man Banks over here," he gestured, "has not seen my niece for some time. I have had enough of your antics, Ravenstone. Where is my niece?"

The baron didn't know where Penelope was. Anger simmered as he gazed at the man who had caused both him and Penelope so much pain.

"Why should I tell you?" he demanded. "And why have you been spying on my wife? What do you want from her?"

Lord Maitland looked genuinely surprised. "I would've thought that of all people, you would understand. We are the same, after all."

"I am nothing like you!" Lucas hissed.

The baron smiled coldly. "Ah, there's no reason to deny it, dear boy, for I know the truth behind your reason for marrying my niece. You are like me, prepared to do anything for what is right, for our duty to our legacy. Your father never understood that, and neither did my brother. But you and I, we are the same."

He felt the blood leave his face as he stared at the baron, a man who had cast his own flesh and blood away to preserve the dignity of a title. *Dear God, am I just as bad?*

Penelope had waited for him all these years when he had all but forgotten her. Still, she'd restored his reputation, given him her trust, loyalty and love. In return, he'd used her to keep his fortune and deceived her about it. He'd never considered how his actions might have affected her life, he'd thought only of his duty to his earldom. All she'd ever wanted was for him to love her and he'd told her he was incapable of doing even that.

And in that moment, he knew.

He loved Penelope, had probably loved her all along. It certainly explained all his actions since he'd met her and accounted for the pain that slashed through him at the thought of never seeing her again. Self-loathing coursed in his veins. In his stubbornness and arrogant sense of entitlement, Lucas had driven away the most precious thing in his life.

Regret threatened to choke him as he returned Lord Maitland's gaze.

"I am nothing like you," he repeated. "I'm not going to let you use Penelope any longer. If you want to talk to her, you had better do it through your son."

"That's precisely why I want to talk to her. I want my son back!" the baron exclaimed. "All I ever did was try to ensure the Maitland name was not tarnished any more, and for that my son has rejected me. David is the next Baron Maitland, yet he won't answer my letters or agree to see me. He hasn't had anything to do with me since he found out what I did to Penelope and her stupid mother."

"It's nothing more than what you deserve. You aren't worthy to kiss the ground upon which Penelope walks. Get out," Lucas said, "I never want to see your face again."

The baron looked fit to be tied. "This is unacceptable!"

He hadn't been able to protect Penelope when this man hurt her as a child, but he was here now. He advanced on the baron.

"It is justice for what you've done to your brother's child. You will keep in mind that Penelope is now the Countess of Ravenstone. She is no longer your niece."

Without further preamble, he hauled the baron up to his feet and unceremoniously dragged him out of the study, through the hall and out onto the street. He turned to see Banks scurry past him to follow the baron out. Lucas strode back into the hall, filled with a sense of purpose. He'd taken the first step needed to put things to rights between him and his wife.

"Lucas? Is everything all right? I heard a commotion." Olivia's voice drifted from the stairs.

He smiled at his sister. It was time for step number two. "Send a message to Blakewood. He's going to escort you to the ball tonight, where you will announce your engagement."

• • •

A week later, Lucas stood on the sidelines playing chaperone to Blakewood and Olivia in yet another ball celebrating their engagement. The woman standing beside him tittered, and the sound grated on his nerves. Was this how it was to be for the rest of his life?

Penelope never tittered. She laughed the way she did everything else—with her whole heart. And at one time, her heart had belonged to him. He felt the familiar dull ache in his soul. In the weeks since his wife's disappearance, the words she'd said to him during the darkest night of his life had branded themselves into his memory:

Love makes a person endure. It's the absence of it that destroys.

He was now doomed to live her words, enduring endless days and nights of the relentless, unforgiving hell that would surely constitute the rest of his life, preserved only by the hope his wife would someday return to him so he could show her how wrong he'd been. About everything.

He took in the happiness in his sister's face as she danced with Blakewood. Olivia wore an expression of joy not unlike the one he wished to see on another face. He tossed back a healthy amount of champagne to wash away the bitterness.

If Penelope's intention had been to teach him a lesson, she'd pounded that lesson into him a hundred times over during her month-long absence from his life.

Among other things, he wanted to know if Penelope was safe. He had always been so sure of her, and now he was sure of nothing. He didn't know if she was well, or if she hated him. Well, she could not hate him any more than he hated himself. Where was she? If he could only find her, he would spend the rest of his life making it up to her. He didn't want to give up on their marriage without a fight.

"Thank you again for accepting my suit," Blakewood commented as he walked up to Lucas. "I promise I will be a good husband to Olivia."

"I know," he replied quietly.

"I find it odd your wife is not here. Surely you have told her about my engagement to your sister? I would have thought she would want to help Olivia with planning the wedding."

His gaze swerved to Blakewood. Why wouldn't this man leave him alone? "I'd hoped she would, too."

"I appreciate that she is busy at your country estate, but this is big news for the family, isn't it?"

Lucas's heart stilled. "She's busy at my country estate?"

"Isn't she?" Blakewood asked. "Colonel Martin said the carriage horses he rescued arrived at Ravenstone the other day, and your wife told him they are doing very well, all things considered."

"Yes," Lucas said, hardly hearing his own voice. "I'd forgotten about that. I intend to go home to give her the news about Olivia's impending nuptials myself." *Among other things*, he added silently as his heart pounded wildly in his chest.

Penelope was in Ravenstone! Thank God. Lucas gave Blakewood a distracted nod and walked out of the ballroom without another word. There was only one thing on his mind as he gave instructions to his coachman.

Lucas was going home.

• • •

"You look lovely, my lady, if I may say so."

Penelope finished rearranging her skirts and gave Finchley a distracted smile. She was going to an important meeting, and she was determined to make certain things went the way she wanted them to. She might have failed in her marriage, but she refused to fail in this.

"I don't understand why the man who is offering a home to the horses Colonel Martin sent wants to meet at the inn. Ravenstone is only a ten-minute drive, and he'd be able to see the horses then."

Finchley looked away and cleared his throat. "Perhaps he is exhausted after a long journey and would like to be able to retire immediately after the meeting."

"I would've been happy to offer him accommodation at Ravenstone."

"I believe he is hoping to receive your invitation," he sputtered.

She rolled her eyes. "Then why didn't he visit Ravenstone in the first place?"

Finchley's face took on the look of a trapped hare. "I don't know, my lady, I am not privy to the gentleman's thoughts … Oh, look, here we are!" he said with an air of desperation as the coach stopped in front of the Horse and Farrier Inn.

Finchley opened the door for her and helped her alight. "I will stay here, my lady, and keep the coachman company while you have your meeting."

She smoothed her skirts one last time. "Wish me luck."

Finchley beamed at her before he ushered her into the inn's private salon and promptly closed the door behind her with a precise click.

She walked further into the room, her heart kicking up like a wild horse when she saw Lucas emerge from behind the wingback chair that faced the hearth.

Dear God, he had found her. She fought the urge to yank the door open and flee.

"I see you're still in the habit of meeting strange men in private salons," he said quietly as he stalked up to her.

For a moment, she could only stare at him in confusion. What was he doing here? Was he angry? She was about to apologize for running away before she remembered she had told this man she loved him and he hadn't cared. *What do I have to apologize for!*

She recovered from her surprise and stood her ground with a verbal attack. "My God, but you are as persistent as a skin rash!"

Lucas's brows rose at her peevish tone, but he didn't comment on her unflattering analogy. "You gave me quite a scare, you know. You left without a word to anyone, and you took my butler with you."

"I apologize for the inconvenience, my lord," she said sarcastically. "As you have seen, Finchley is fine. Though I cannot vouch for his health after I'm through with him for conspiring against me."

"He's in my employ; his loyalty is to me."

"Ah," she said. "So you've come all this way from London to lecture me on household hierarchy?"

His sharp features were suddenly bleak with remorse. "I've come here to bargain with you."

She sucked in a deep breath. She was about to tell him she wasn't interested in any more of his bargains when she noticed the documents laid out on the low table next to the chair he'd just vacated.

"I've had weeks to think about how we are to go on from here. I didn't want to just barge back into your life, seduce you and take over, as I did before." Lucas gestured to the table. "Those papers give you complete control of the Ravenstone estates while they are under my name. It's all legal—you can keep as many unwanted horses or any other animals you want to keep, and you can use the profits from the estates to fund Colonel Martin's endeavors."

He was giving up control of his estates? The ones he'd tried to save by marrying her? She opened her mouth to speak but he silenced her with a raised palm.

"I would hand the estates to you if I could, but because we're married, this was the only way you could have control of them. You can speak to a solicitor and review the documents if you want to."

She shook her head. "No, that's fine. I trust you."

One side of his mouth kicked up in a faint, half smile. "I am giving you control of the estates because it's the only thing of value I have to give you."

She felt dazed. "Why?"

"Because I would rather live my life under your mercy than to be without you ever again," he rasped.

"Oh, Lucas—"

"You were right," he continued. "I've been living in the past for way too long, but I didn't realize it until you left me, until you showed me what a bleak future I had without you in it." Naked pain slashed his features. "If you would give me another chance, nymph, I'll spend the rest of my life making up for the way I've treated you."

She didn't know what to say. This was beyond anything she had ever expected from him. Lucas was giving up everything he thought was important. For her. It was an unbelievably amazing gesture. But it wasn't what she wanted at all.

"I love you, Penelope," he choked out, as if the words were being gouged from his chest. "It took me awhile to realize it, but I do now. I want you to have a choice, which is why I brought these documents. You don't have to share my bed if you don't want to, but please don't leave me like that again, sweetheart."

"Lucas—"

"The other documents on the table are divorce papers."

Her head snapped up. "You're going to divorce me?"

Lucas fixed his gaze just beyond her left shoulder as if he found it too painful to look at her. "The control of the estates is yours whether you stay married to me or not," he said hoarsely. "As far as I'm concerned, you deserve it after all you've suffered because of them. I'm not bribing you to stay married to me. If you don't want to be my wife any longer," he paused to clear his throat, "I can at least know I've done what I could to make you happy."

"*What?*" She didn't know whether to laugh or cry or hit him. She had a feeling she would end up doing all three.

"It's your choice, nymph. I want you to know that whatever you choose, you will be provided for."

Oh, her poor, tormented, fierce warrior. She wanted to throw herself into his arms and love him until all his hurt was healed. Instead, she chose to punish him a little bit for all the pain he'd caused her. "I don't need to share your bed ever again?"

Lucas hauled her against his shaking frame. "I want to share my life with you, sweetheart," he whispered. "Because without you, nothing in my life has meaning. Let me see you at dinner and breakfast and let me hold you at night. Let me be your home. Let me share my life with you, and I'll give you anything you want. Everything you want."

Happiness pierced her heart. How could any woman deny a man who was willing to give up everything to keep her? He was hers. After a lifetime of waiting, he was finally hers.

She walked over to the table and flung the papers in the fireplace—that's what she thought of his bargain. Then she faced him and raised her eyes to meet his.

"*You* are everything I've ever wanted," she whispered.

Lucas groaned as he reached for her and claimed her lips in a desperate kiss that was filled with yearning. She held him to her and kissed him back, a sweet kiss that spoke of a love that not only demanded, but forgave all.

"You're everything I'll ever want," she said against his lips.

Lucas held her tighter, giving her another fiercely tender kiss, and she gloried in it. For once in her life, she had a home. She pulled back and looked into his eyes.

"There's one thing I want to discuss before we get carried away," she said, only half joking.

Lucas tensed. "What is it?"

"Were you really serious about my not sharing your bed?"

His dark eyes searched hers intently. "Is that what you want?"

"No," she admitted. "I want to share myself with you, too. All of me."

Lucas hugged her tight. "Good."

"Besides, we'll make wonderful parents," she added.

"You've always been the soul of modesty," he teased before claiming her smiling lips again in a sweet kiss.

"I love you," she told him when he finally raised his head.

Joy was evident in his features, making him look much younger. "I was afraid I'd never hear you say that again."

Her lips twitched in amusement. "Me either," she admitted. "Lucas?"

"Yes, love?"

"How did you find me?"

Lucas laughed and kissed her again. "Someone reminded me that you like to hide in the most obvious places."

About the Author

Ivory was born in the Philippines and lives in Carlisle, United Kingdom, with her husband and their perpetually hungry canine. She'd love to hear from you. Contact her through *www.ivorythewriter.wordpress.com* or through her twitter handle @ivory_lei.

A Sneak Peek from Crimson Romance
(From *Shadow Beneath the Sea* by Joanna Lloyd)

Saturday, April 24, 1915

Lillian wrapped the cigar case in brown paper and, holding the string down with one finger, pulled it into a bow. "There you are, Mr. Reilly. This was the last box, but I kept them for you because I know they're your favorites."

The man gave a short tug at his pointed beard and reached for the parcel. "It's not just the cigars that are my favorite," he said with an exaggerated wink. "I don't walk two blocks out of my way just for these." At the sound of a loud cough from a far corner of the shop, Mr. Reilly shoved the parcel under his arm, tipped his hat to George, and left the shop.

Irritated at George's subtle displeasure over her banter with the customer, Lillian waited for him to speak. He completed the display of expensive cherry wood and maple pipes in a glass-fronted cabinet before giving her his attention.

"I don't like that man. I wish he would buy his cigars elsewhere."

Lillian picked up a duster and flicked at one of the shelves. "You don't like him or you don't like me talking to him?"

"Both. And if you would agree to my proposal, you could stay at home and not be subjected to the likes of him each day." George ran two fingers down his thick moustache, smoothing it over his top lip.

"I'm sorry, George, I can't give you an answer yet." She swallowed her guilt as the look of anticipation on his face changed to disappointment. Perhaps she should accept. Although he was more than ten years older and widowed, George would always treat her well, he made a decent living, and she liked him. And he was honest, a quality sadly lacking in her household. Thoughts of her father caused her to look up at the clock nailed above the shop door. If she left now, she would have time to enjoy the walk down to the wharves without hurrying.

With one hand reaching for her small, blue hat and the other gripping a large carpetbag, Lillian gave George a thin smile. "If you don't mind, George, I have an errand to run for Pa, and I must go."

"Is it something I should be aware of? He does work for me, after all."

She turned to face a small mirror and made a show of adjusting her hat. "I'm not sure exactly. An arrangement with a business contact for some merchandise for the shop." She gave a vague wave of her hand and stepped out into the street before George could question her further. It was better neither of them knew the full details of Pa's "errands." They usually involved something on the shady side of the law.

A loud yell caused her to jump back onto the curb as a motorcar coughed and sputtered around the corner, sending a spray of gravel and dust at her skirt. With the corner of her jacket held over her nose to mask the sharp exhaust smell, she ran across the street before she was assaulted by another of the dangerous vehicles.

There was still time before she had to be at the Hudson River Wharves to meet her father's contact, so she headed for Battery Park. Earlier in the week, she had seen a notice announcing an afternoon concert in the gazebo—a string quartet. Her lips spread in a slow smile, and she began to hum her favorite Mendelssohn piece. Her steps quickened and soon matched the tempo of the violin concerto playing in her head. The music flowed into the second movement, and she twirled with her arms spread outward, the carpetbag billowing from her right elbow. As the symphony reached a crescendo, she marched through the entrance to the park.

When she reached the gazebo, the members of the string quartet were already tuning their instruments, so she slipped into the midst of the gathering crowd. There must have been more than one hundred people, some sitting on rugs on the ground and others on small chairs. Children ran and played between the adults, and an air of expectancy rippled through the audience.

Finally, ensconced between a family with four children and an elderly couple, Lillian focused on the musicians releasing their first magical notes, like fairy dust, into the air. The hair on the back of her neck bristled as the violin and the clarinet brought to life Beethoven's stirring melody. Then the warm, mellow tones of the cello shimmied over her skin and curled her toes. With her eyes closed in rapture, she swayed, oblivious to those around her, lost in the symphony. The music leached the loneliness, guilt, and longing from her being, and for those few treasured moments, she wasn't Lillian Marshall; she didn't live in the Lower East Side; and she didn't have a scoundrel for a father.

Papa's love of music was the one good thing he had given her. Still clinging to the remnants of his privileged English upbringing, he would take her as a small child to Covent Garden to listen to the orchestras and bands. Once, after a big win at poker, he took her to the opera—an experience to cherish forever. She had continued to feed her obsession as she'd grown older, seeking out symphony recitals and band concerts, especially free events in the parks. George had even bought them tickets to see *Dancing Around* at the Winter Garden Theatre. Unfortunately, he had fidgeted with boredom throughout and shown no interest in discussing the performance afterward.

An elbow in her side as the crowd broke up jolted Lillian back to reality, and with a shock she realized she had missed the arranged time to meet her father's contact. Regardless, she hurried through the crowd, clinging to the possibility the man might have waited for her.

Focused on her predicament and not watching her step, she stumbled over a brown shoe. With a mumbled apology, Lillian tried to squeeze between the wearer of the shoe and his friend, both standing near the back of the crowd. But the friend jumped in front of her and clasped her arm.

"Whoa there, my beauty. Allow me to be of assistance. Plenty of room right here beside me if you'd like to stay."

Annoyed at the delay, Lillian shook his hand from her arm, dodged around him, and when he blocked her again, she stomped on his foot. At his yelp of pain, she frowned up at him. "As you can see, I don't need your assistance."

The other man laughed and bowed to Lillian. "Thank you, dear lady, for putting him firmly in his place. He needs that at least once every hour." She raised her eyes and was rewarded by a dimpled smile and fair, tousled hair. A twist of excitement looped through her as their eyes met. Embarrassed at her ridiculous response to a handsome face, she lowered her head and pushed through the crowd, away from the two men, toward the gate.

Over the rapid thumping of her heart and the murmur of the crowd, she heard the young man call out, "Wait! I don't even know your name!" *And that's how it would stay.* Such a gentleman would run a mile if he discovered her background. "A pity," she sighed. The burst of sensation that had her stomach jumping as if a swarm of locusts had been let loose was a small moment of pleasure, one she would hold onto and weave into her dreams.

Once through the gate, Lillian took off at a run, dodging pedestrians and horses, ignoring muttered protests as she weaved her way toward the wharves. She reached the fence at the Hudson River Wharves, breathless, clutching at a sharp pain in her side. First she rattled the fence to get attention, then called out to a group of men gathered near a small building. After ignoring her calls for some minutes, a large, swarthy man strolled over to the fence and lifted his eyebrows in question.

"Briggs. I'm looking for Gerry Briggs. Is he here?" she asked.

"Who wants to know?" The man's eyes ran up the length of her body, and he winked.

She shuddered at the insinuation. "I'm here on behalf of Walter Marshall. I have come to pick up a parcel."

The man's eyes narrowed. "This is starting to sound a bit suspicious. Perhaps I should fetch the foreman."

Fear, closely followed by a hot, rising anger at the demeaning situation in which her father had placed her, made it difficult to respond. A slow grin spread across his face, and he stepped through a gate in the fence, moving to her side. "It wouldn't have something to do with a shipment of silver snuffboxes, now would it?" At her sharp intake of breath, he nodded. "Unfortunately Mr. Briggs has finished for the day, but I may be able to help you. Of course I will require payment for my trouble."

"I'm sorry, but I have no money." She knew exactly the payment he wanted, and it had nothing to do with money.

As she spoke, he flexed his right arm and ran a hand down his bulging bicep as if to show her what was on offer. He then traced a dirty finger down her arm. "No money, what a shame. How else could you pay me, I wonder?"

With a deliberate movement, Lillian reached for his wrist, lifted it from her arm and dropped it as if it was a poisonous snake, at the same time taking a step backward. "There appears to be a mistake. It seems I don't need anything from you after all. In fact, I believe I would rather cut off my arm than accept your assistance."

His mocking laughter echoed in her ears as she bolted across the road, not looking back until she was hidden in the shadows of a small copse of sweet-smelling crabapple trees. Warily, she edged around a twisted trunk and breathed a sigh of relief that the dockworker had disappeared back into the untidy group of buildings decorating the wharf.

The empty carpetbag hung accusingly from her arm, and Lillian cringed at the thought of her father's wrath when he discovered she had botched the "errand." It would do her no good to explain the man's insulting behavior. Walter Marshall believed his daughter had been put on this earth to serve his needs and, until recently, she had not understood she had a choice. Even now, with the knowledge that she could accept George's proposal and be free of Walter forever, a sense of filial duty and an unfathomable desire to please her father kept her at his side. And how could she marry George when the truth was she didn't love him? He deserved someone who would return his love.

The hard, gnarly tree pressed into her back, and she let its living energy seep through her defeated body. At times like this, when self-pity bubbled inside her, Lillian had a strategy. She would open a door in her mind, throw all the unpleasant things through the door, and slam it shut before the black, slimy bits could slide back out. Then she would open another door, one that was filled with rainbow colors and happy laughter. But most of all, it was filled with music—music that filled her head and her heart with its cleansing sound.

She conjured up the last symphony from the concert at Battery Park, pushed away from the sympathetic tree, and let the beat of the music march her back toward the Bowery and home.

It was dusk, and the heavy aroma of beef stew wafted through the doors of the Bowery Mission. On Tuesday nights, Lillian volunteered at the soup kitchen, and any other night she would have stopped to greet Joseph, the hoary old man who ran the shelter. But two blokes, halfway down the shuffling line of eager clients, were jabbing their fists into the air, egging each other into a fight, and a rush of disgust washed through her at their show of male strength; one display of male muscle-flexing in a day was enough for her.

Further down the street, she spied the Bull's Head Tavern. Chewing on her bottom lip, she considered whether to brave the stink of hops and the suggestive leers of drunken workers. If she helped Pa home, it might put her in his good book. The tavern squatted belligerently, leaning on an awkward angle, like its patrons when they stumbled out at closing time, and dared her to enter. The last time she had tried to haul her pa out, the silly old bugger had set up such a ruckus that Lillian had left him sitting on his bum in the middle of the floor where he had fallen, somehow still balancing a tankard of ale. With an indelicate snort, she made her decision and turned away.

The sudden rattle of a street barrow startled her, and she sidestepped onto the pavement. The flower seller chuckled and threw her a limp violet phlox, then moved the barrow on, urging passersby to purchase her day-old, bedraggled flowers. Lillian turned into Claxton Lane and trudged up the concrete steps that led to the entrance door of the small townhouse. With a deep breath to gather her courage, she reached for the doorknob. Before she could turn it, the door flew open and her pa, his arms spread wide in greeting, urged her into the front room.

What was Pa doing home so early and looking almost pleased to see her? Perhaps she should go out and come back in again. Or maybe she had walked into someone else's home. She waited, trying to gauge her father's state of sobriety as she watched him drop into his armchair.

The smell of boiled cabbage and old grease drifted from the kitchen and briefly drew her attention to the small dining table, where plates and cups were strewn haphazardly, ready for the evening meal. Their daily helper, Marjy, had an extremely narrow repertoire of meals—most of them unpalatable—but she had outdone herself with this one.

"Ah, Lillian, my love. Come and talk to your old pa." Even the smell of Marjy's cooking seemed not to have spoiled his mood. She inched forward, licked her lips, and took one more step toward him. "Come on. Over here where I can see your pretty face."

She frowned at his kind words. He actually appeared sober, although his eyes were red-rimmed and the veins on his bulbous nose throbbed blue in the dim light. His gaze had not reached the empty carpetbag. Yet.

"You're going to be so excited when I tell you what we're about to do, my girl."

What scheme was he hatching now? It obviously included her, as usual. And, as usual, she had not been consulted. But his peculiar behavior indicated this was no ordinary scheme. A sense of foreboding seeped through her as a stream of possibilities churned her mind. She clenched her jaw, her heart a slow drum roll in her chest, while she waited for his next words.

"You and me, we're going on a grand adventure." He nodded and leaned forward as if the most exciting bit was still to come. "Back to England."

The breath caught in her throat as she reeled back at his words. Walter Marshall stood from his worn armchair, hooked his thumbs into his braces, and expanded his chest. "We are at last returning home." He paused for effect. "And we are going on one of the fastest, most magnificent ships ever built anywhere in the world." He brandished two tickets. "We sail to England in six days." He slammed the tickets down on the table and spread his arms in triumph. "On the *Lusitania*."

With a sharp gasp, Lillian slid limply into a chair, the carpetbag still dangling from her wrist. Every fiber of her being protested at the sickening thought of reliving the memory of her first rough, cold, and terrifying journey across the Atlantic. She had been eight years old when they'd left Liverpool to sail to New York. After the crossing, she had begun to have nightmares of the water sucking her into its inky depths. She had sworn it would be her last sea voyage. A hundred reasons not to go flashed through her mind. America was her home, England only a faint memory. And what about George? They both owed him so much. Pa was asking the impossible.

"I can't do it, Pa. I won't go on any ship. I'm not leaving New York; I can't," she said.

Walter was on his feet, his beefy fingers jabbing at her chest. "What do you mean, you can't go? I'm not giving you a choice."

She pushed his hand away. "My mind is made up. I'm staying here." Her head snapped back from the force of the blow, and the metallic taste of blood filled her mouth. Raw anger almost choked her as she pressed herself against the back of her chair. "Your family in England won't want you. And they've never wanted me."

"Ah, but that's where you're wrong. Your dear departed mother was the perfect daughter-in-law. Marrying her was the first thing I had done right in my family's eyes. After she died and they disinherited me—for a minor indiscretion—they wanted you to live with them. But I kept you away. If they didn't want me, then they weren't getting you, either."

Confusion at his words fogged her mind. "But why now?"

He moved toward her, his eyes narrowed. "Because this trip will net me a fortune. The ship will be teeming with rich nobs who will fall over themselves to play poker with me once word of my skills get out. I will be the prodigal son returning home, triumphant. And you will be the honey to sweeten the deal."

She blinked, unable to comprehend the extent of his mad self-deception. "Then you will be going on your own, Pa."

"You ungrateful, disobedient, useless piece of baggage. You'll do as I say! We're going, my girl, whether you bloody like it or not. It's time my family accepted me back and I was reinstated to my rightful place in society." He kicked out with his foot, tilting Lillian's chair precariously. As she leapt from the chair with her arms flailing to gain her balance, his gaze snagged on the empty carpetbag. "Where are the snuffboxes?" he shrieked. She threw the bag to the floor as if that would disassociate her from the fiasco. With one menacing step at a time, Walter approached until he was inches from her face. "Answer me, you stupid girl."

She took a step back, her arms in front of her for protection, his unstable temper turning her back into a trembling child. "I did my best, Pa, but the bloke you told me to ask for had gone home for the day." It was better to leave out the fact she'd arrived late.

Walter's neck flushed red with anger, and his bushy eyebrows folded over each other as he scowled at his daughter. For a moment he looked as if he would strike her again but then seemed to change his mind. Not daring to move, she watched him take two deep breaths, give his head a shake as if to rearrange his thoughts, and then lower himself back into the armchair. Lillian watched, unmoving, as Walter again pushed himself up from the armchair, straightened his waistcoat, and took measured steps to the front door. With his hand on the doorknob he called back to her. "I don't want to say something I will regret, so I am heading out for a quiet ale. I will eat dinner when I return." The door slammed as he left the house.

She stared at the back of the closed door, tears dripping onto her bodice. He had never mentioned her mother before. She always believed she'd been abandoned by everyone except her pa. Now it seemed he'd kept her isolated from his family for his own petty revenge.

Despite the shock of her pa's words, she knew she had to keep her wits about her, to keep ahead of his greedy schemes. Each new scheme was always going to be the last one—the big one that would make them rich. And each time, something went wrong. There had been a few occasions when he had won big at the gaming tables, but within days he had lost it all again.

Without a word, she climbed the narrow flight of stairs to her bedroom. Lord, it must have been a big win to buy tickets on this famous ship. She swallowed; even the thought of sailing to England made her nauseous.

But as much as she determined she would not go, she suspected Walter would find a way to convince her.

In the mood for more Crimson Romance?
Check out *Lord Monroe's Dark Tower*
by Elf Ahearn
at *CrimsonRomance.com*.

Printed in Great Britain
by Amazon.co.uk, Ltd.,
Marston Gate.